'Lord Francis Carey to see you, madam.'

And who the devil was Lord Francis Carey? thought Bel; but, before she could ask, Mrs Hatch was pushed, protesting, through the door and out of the room by a large gentleman, who turned to Bel, to say grimly, 'And now, madam, let us come to terms, and quickly. I know exactly what you are, and am not to be bought off by anything you can offer—either your person, or your promises!'

Dear Reader

A Christmas treat from Paula Marshall, THE CYPRIAN'S SISTER is another sparkling Regency. In Christine Franklin's HEART OF A ROSE, Patti is convinced she has to right a wrong. From America we have SWEET JUSTICE by Jan McKee, and a look at Pennsylvania coalmining in 1870 by Doreen Owens Malek. Quite a variety! Have a happy Christmas!

The Editor

Paula Marshall, retired with three children, has had a varied life. She began her career in a large library and ended it as a senior academic in charge of history in a polytechnic. She has travelled widely, has been a swimming coach, and has appeared on *University Challenge* and *Mastermind*. She has always wanted to write, and likes her novels to be full of adventure and humour.

Recent titles by the same author:

MY LADY LOVE
AN UNEXPECTED PASSION
AN AMERICAN PRINCESS
WILD JUSTICE

THE CYPRIAN'S SISTER

Paula Marshall

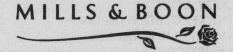

MILLS & BOON LIMITED
ETON HOUSE, 18–24 PARADISE ROAD
RICHMOND, SURREY, TW9 1SR

First published in Great Britain 1993
by Mills & Boon Limited

© Paula Marshall 1993

Australian copyright 1993
Philippine copyright 1993
This edition 1993

ISBN 0 263 78242 5

Set in 10½ on 12 pt Linotron Times
04-9312-78231

Typeset in Great Britain by Centracet, Cambridge
Made and printed in Great Britain

CHAPTER ONE

BEL PASSMORE was sorting papers in her late sister's
pretty study, a thoughtful expression on her face.
She had just read a letter written only three weeks
ago, dated May 21st 1818, a letter which bore out
what the great banker Mr Thomas Coutts had told
her yesterday afternoon. The letter was still in her
hand when there was a knock on the door, and she
lifted her head to call, 'A moment, Mrs Hatch, and
I will be with you.'

The house she was in, also her late sister's, was a
little jewel box, perfectly appointed, filled with
treasures. Above the hearth a portrait by Thomas
Phillips of that same sister, Mrs Marianne St
George, apparently known in London as Marina,
presided over the room. Marianne — no, Marina —
looked enchanting, a remote, cool goddess; Pallas
Athene, goddess of wisdom, rather than Venus,
goddess of love, which Bel had just discovered that
she had actually been.

Phillips had painted her at night in a grove of
trees, a sickle moon showing through them — perhaps, improbably, he had seen her as a chaste
Diana, because the Grecian robe she had worn, the
jewel in the shape of a half-moon in her hair, and
the tiny bow she was holding in one charming little
hand, reinforced the notion of a chaste huntress.

Chaste! Bel gave a sharp laugh, and returned to

her task, a task which she was determined to finish as soon as possible so that she might return to her own life, after deciding what she was to do with the remarkable fortune which Marianne's lawyers had told her that she had inherited, and which her visits to Thomas Coutts, of Coutts Bank, had confirmed in all its majestic details.

Three short weeks had been sufficient to change her life completely. Impossible to think that it was less than a month since she was living in the pretty village of Brangton in Lincolnshire, a parson's daughter, ignorant of anything but the banal round of pleasures and duties associated with a young and orphaned gentlewoman in the country.

Her life there with an elderly aunt in modest circumstances was made more easy because of the small income regularly sent to her by her widowed sister, living in London, who was happy to help out by remitting to Bel and Aunt Kaye a few modest pennies, as she had put it, when her husband had died, leaving her, she had said, everything.

Bel remembered Marianne's visits—she had to think of her as Marianne; Marina was someone whom Bel had never known. She had arrived, modestly dressed in her decent black, handkerchief to her eyes every time she had mentioned the late Henry St George's name; later, still modest, clothing good, but inexpensive, eyes downcast, visiting old friends, saying that she could not return to Brangton, all her social life was now centred in London.

Aunt Kaye had suggested to Marianne recently when Bel was reaching the age of eighteen that

Marianne might like to take Bel back to London with her, introduce her to Marianne's wide circle of friends, perhaps find her a husband with a modest if useful income, since there were few for Bel to marry in Brangton.

Marianne had looked at Bel, charming in a white muslin dress that was dated by London standards, wearing a straw hat with a wide brim, a sash of pale green silk wound round the crown, enhancing the combination of red-gold hair, ivory complexion and brilliant green eyes, with dark arching brows, which were beginning to make Bel a beauty after whom every eye would turn to look — especially as the face was matched with a figure of stunning perfection and grace.

But it was the look of perfect innocence, of candid, unaware charm which gave Bel her greatest distinction and which had made Marianne draw in her breath a little. 'Oh, no,' she had said vaguely, 'I think that Bel is formed for country living — her very name, the one we use, fits her so much more than a Londonised Anne Isabella would. She must marry some good little country gentleman, not some bored townee. Besides, town would ruin those delicate looks.'

Aunt Kaye, Bel thought, remembering this conversation, not many months old, was no fool, even if innocent of the great world.

'But you do not object to living among bored townees, Marianne,' she had said. 'Indeed, your own looks have improved since you left Brangton, not deteriorated.'

'Ah, but I am not Bel,' Marianne had replied

incontrovertibly, 'and I can best help Bel by providing her with a good dowry to take with her to her husband, and by your letting it be known that I intend to do so — *that* should serve to encourage gentlemen to come calling, who might be deterred by thinking that Bel is nothing but a poor parson's undowered daughter.'

'Oh,' Bel had said, 'do I really want to marry someone who might not offer for me if he thought that I had only a little to bring him?'

'You have virtually nothing to bring to him without my help, so we must use our common sense and my money,' Marianne had replied, she who usually behaved as though common sense were a virtue she might have heard of, but rarely practised, so airily unworldly had she seemed, 'when it comes to marriage and the setting up of establishments. Even the most virtuous and loving of men would expect his wife to bring something with her to their wedding-day; such a consideration would do him no discredit — quite the reverse. No, Bel must marry here, I insist.'

Well, Bel thought grimly, consigning yet another document to the fire, I now know why Marianne did not wish me to join her in London, and where all the money came from for the last ten years, to keep me in modest comfort, her in luxury, and enable her to leave me a fortune on her untimely death — and what am I to do about the fortune? For after all I am a parson's daughter, and a virtuous one.

But Marianne was a parson's daughter, too, said a tiny voice in her head, and that did not stop her from following the way of life which has enabled us all to live in luxury, instead of being little better than paupers since Papa died six years ago.

'I must think,' she said aloud, on her knees on the hearthrug, then thought, When Marianne visited us, she was so vague and gentle, almost otherwordly, so very much the parson's elder daughter that we assumed that she led a quiet life in London, full of good works and virtue; we were perhaps a little surprised that she did not remarry, to have someone to shelter her from the harsh realities of life.

The harsh realities of life! And what a joke that was. She remembered the letter arriving from the lawyers, to tell her that Marianne was dead, had died of a fulminating illness of the stomach, quite suddenly, after being in perfect health, and that Bel was her sole heir, and it was to be expected that she would visit London to settle 'your sister's considerable estate'.

That had been the first puzzle, 'considerable estate'. Marianne had always said that her fortune, which her husband had left her, was modest, had sighed that she could only dower Bel with a few thousands, and the papers for that, which had not been completed before her death, were waiting for her, Bel had learned when she reached London, her signature not now needed, since she had inherited all.

Bel had gone to London, leaving Aunt Kaye behind—that lady's rheumatics were troubling her more than usual—taking with her only her elderly maid, Lottie, as a dragon to repel boarders, as Marianne had said of her guardianship of Bel on her last visit — a piece of London slang, not too polite, she had added on Aunt Kaye raising her eyebrows a little.

The first surprise had been Marianne's home, in Stanhope Street, near the Park, now named after the Prince Regent. Bel had expected something small and modest, not the splendour of the house in a row which was obviously occupied by upper gentry, if not to say minor members of the nobility — a house near by, she discovered, had been occupied by Viscount Granville and his family.

The next surprise was the luxury of the furnishings, more splendid than anything Bel had ever seen before, paintings, tapestries, china, silver, bibelots, the three bedrooms also perfectly appointed, the small study so elegant, with its break-front bookcases, Buhl desk, cabinets of cameos and porcelains; the whole place reeked of wealth.

The two servants left — the rest had been discharged after Marianne's death — were a housekeeper and a maid of all work. The housekeeper was as close-mouthed as Lottie, and the little servant girl was the same — even Lottie complained that their conversation with her was limited to yes, no, and perhaps.

At first, nothing seemed untoward, except that, on seeing her immediate neighbours when leaving the house to visit the solicitors, Bel had bowed to them, a man and a woman, and they had both turned their backs on her. Perhaps, she thought, that was London manners, and then she remembered that when she had visited the church on the following Sunday, and those same neighbours had been there, the whole congregation had stared at her when she entered, and again when she left, and although the parson had greeted her his reception of her had been cool, and the whole thing had left an odd taste in her mouth.

And then the solicitors, Fancourt and Hirst. *That* had been most disturbing. On giving her name to a man in a kind of sentry box at a very grand office in Lincoln's Inn, he had stared at her in the most frank manner, almost insolent, waved her in with a quill, and, although she could not fault the grave gentlemen who had interviewed her and had informed her of the stunning size of her sister's bequest, there had been something distinctly odd about their manner.

Finally, all the papers signed and she having been given the address of Coutts Bank which she needed to visit to sign still further papers to take possession of her sister's account there, one of the two men, the younger one, had leaned forward and asked her, almost a grin on his face, 'I must enquire, madam, do you intend to keep on the business?'

'The business?' she had faltered, her wits, she thought afterwards, a little addled by the shock of her sister's sudden death, and the magnitude of what she had inherited. 'Pray, what business is that?' For she had not seen any evidence of a business in Stanhope Street, was only aware that Marianne had lived on what her wealthy husband had left her.

'Oh, come. . .' began Mr Hirst, to have a detaining hand put on his arm by the older man, Mr Fancourt, who said, very courteously,

'We must leave Miss Passmore to her grief, my dear Hirst. Time enough for her to think of other matters later,' and he bowed her out, both of them going through the polite rituals demanded in such circumstances.

Other matters? What could he mean? Bel thought. Happily her meeting with Mr Thomas Coutts was not so mysterious, that gentleman being a model of polite regret for her grief and congratulation on her great good fortune.

But even he looked at her keenly, enquired after her country circumstances, and then said, quietly, 'I expect that you will be going through your sister's papers when you return to Stanhope Street. It is of all things essential that you do so speedily. If. . .' and he hesitated '. . .if, after doing so, you feel that you require. . .assistance. . .pray do not hesitate to call on me.'

Bel took the puzzle home with her, for it to be resolved when she opened Marianne's desk, and began to look through her papers. Mr Coutts had given her a letter from Marianne, which she read before she did so. The letter was also baffling, and she read it twice, in some wonder.

Dear Bel

If you are reading this, I shall have died suddenly, without ever having told you my true circumstances which have enabled me to leave you what I hope is a more than modest competency. You will find some of the answers in the letters and papers in my desk, but the real meat of the matter is to be found in a secret cupboard behind the books on the second shelf in the right-hand hearth alcove in my study. It is for you to do what you wish with what you find. The cupboard is well hidden, but if you place a firm finger on the exact middle of the central panel, and push, it will open and you will find there—what you will find.

It was obvious to Bel that Marianne did not wish to put anything on paper, even in a letter reposing in Coutts Bank!

Having opened the desk, to find pigeon-holes stuffed with letters and papers, most of them apparently innocuous, if a little cryptic, she moved to the alcove, removed the books on the second shelf and did as her sister bid—to discover a cupboard, crammed with documents, two ledgers, plus a small cedarwood box.

Bel removed everything from the cupboard, and began to read through it, with mounting incredulity and a face which flushed hotter and hotter with every passing word.

Brutally and briefly she learned that her apparently modest sister had been a courtesan, a Cyprian, of the first stare. Far from having married the man whom she had met when a companion in London, Henry St George, she had been seduced by him, and then deserted, but left with a small apartment and a lump sum, both parting presents, his letter said, 'to one who has pleased me, but from whom my marriage now debars me.'

Bel read the first page of Marianne's ledger.

I was not deterred by this betrayal — seeing that it was the second which I suffered — his refusal to marry me after ruining me being the first. For I decided that with the money I had saved, and what he gave me on parting, I would set myself up as a Cyprian of the first water, my talents seeming to lie that way, and offering me a better living than being a governess or companion ever could. From then on, I concentrated on milking men of their money, as they have milked me of virtue and reputation. Marina St George, I called myself — the second name to punish *him*, and the first because it carried no taint for the family I felt compelled to support. If you ever read this, dear Bel, forgive me.

The ledgers and the letters proved that Marianne had carried out her intent by virtue of her sexual accomplishment and her business brain — for not only had she charged high rates and accepted magnificent presents from a select band of wealthy and titled lovers, but she had also lent money at extortionate rates of interest to those less wealthy, and furthermore, to Bel's fascinated horror, she had blackmailed many of the great men who had enjoyed her favours secretly while preserving their reputation to the world, by threatening to expose them, if not further recompensed.

Although they had not known the full extent of Marianne's career, her neighbours had certainly known that she was a courtesan, thus explaining their behaviour to Bel and that of her lawyers, as well as Mr Coutts's offer of help should she feel that she needed it. He had rightly seen Bel as the chaste and innocent girl she was — so like Marianne as she had been before she left to become the companion to a lady of wealthy family in Bruton Street.

The cedarwood box contained love-letters from a person of such high standing that Bel consigned them to the fire without reading other than the first — but it was apparent that Marianne had also acquired a fair fortune from him — and he had commissioned the Phillips portrait and presented it to her.

Oh, yes, Marianne's fortune was fully explained.

The other ledger detailed her income and its sources, and the documents consisted of the incriminating letters of her powerful lovers, who seemed impelled, thought Bell critically, to immortalise their folly on paper, unaware that each was only one of many whom Marianne was remorselessly persecuting.

What now exercised Bel was whether she should accept a fortune made by such methods at all. Was it right, was it proper, that she, a virtuous young person of good family, the daughter of a parson, the great-granddaughter, through her mother, of an Earl, should live on such ill-gotten gains, not only the fruits of vice, but of blackmail and usury? Would it not, perhaps, be better to give the whole lot to a home for fallen women, leaving herself and Aunt Kaye a pittance to live on? Would such an act be quixotic, rather than virtuous? She could not tell. Oh, dear, she thought, can Marianne's dreadful example be infecting me?

She had taken the puzzle to Mr Coutts, confirmed

from him that Marianne had indeed been a notorious courtesan — the most famous in London when
she had so unfortunately died, he said, who was
able to pick and choose her lovers. He was not
at all surprised by the fortune which she had
amassed.

'Your sister's understanding was excellent,' he
had said. 'Unlike many young women in her condition, she did not waste the — er — fruits of her
labour. She consulted me frequently on financial
matters, made many wise investments, and I see no
reason why you should refuse your unexpected good
fortune.'

Well, that was as may be, Bel had thought, but
she had listened to him carefully when he had told
her that if she proposed to retire to the country
again, as she had informed him she would, then it
might be advisable to go through Marianne's papers
and dispose of most of them.

It was this advice that she was busy carrying out
when she heard a violent knocking at the door. The
letter which she was examining was from a young
man infatuated with Marianne, to whom she had
lent several thousand pounds at an extortionate rate
of interest, and he was begging further time to pay,
having already paid over a sum in interest larger
than the principal! It was apparent that Marianne
had been a skilful usurer as well as a whore. Bel felt
quite faint at the thought, remembering her sister's
delicate charm and apparent innocence.

She kept the housekeeper waiting while she bun-
dled the ledgers and most of the documents back
into the cupboard, rapidly replacing the books,

finally calling, 'Come in,' to repeated impatient bangings.

Mrs Hatch, the grim-faced woman whom Bel suspected of being Marianne's watchdog, said, 'Lord Francis Carey to see you, madam, if you are At Home.'

And who the devil was Lord Francis Carey? thought Bel rapidly, seeing that his name had not been on any of the documents she had read, nor was he listed in Marianne's business ledger, so crammed with the names of the rich and the powerful; but, before she could ask, Mrs Hatch was brushed to one side and a large gentleman entered, saying impatiently, 'I have no time to waste, madam, even though I am sure that your day is free for all the folly you may care to carry out,' and, pushing Mrs Hatch, protesting, through the door and out of the room, he shut it behind him, and turned to Bel, to say grimly, 'And now, madam, let us come to terms, and quickly. From what I have heard of you, you are not backward in demanding your pound of flesh, so let us get down to it, at once, and no skimble-skamble, if you please, for I know exactly what you are, and am not to be bought off by anything you can offer—either your person, or your promises!'

CHAPTER TWO

WHAT Bel saw at first glance was the hardest, haughtiest man's face which she had ever encountered. A pair of grey eyes, as cold as a wintry sea, were set beneath thin arched eyebrows in a face as imperious as an eagle's. The mouth was as firm and cruel as a mantrap's jaws, and his blue-black hair was cut fashionably short, adding to an almost imperial presence.

He was slightly over six feet tall, his body was beautifully proportioned, and he held himself as though he knew it. He possessed broad shoulders, a deep chest, a narrow waist and hips, with long legs ending in the inevitably perfect boots of a youngish gentleman of high fashion. She judged him to be in his early thirties.

He moved towards her with a superb arrogance, the habit of command so strong in him that it seemed as though everyone else was put on earth to be his servant and to carry out his orders.

Bel hated him on sight. His face, his body and his clothes were all anathema to her. And to address her as he did! He deserved, and would get, no quarter.

'To what,' she enquired, her voice poisonously sweet, 'do I owe the honour of your visit, sir?'

'No honour is intended, madam,' he replied, and

his voice was acid, corrosive, vitriol to shrivel her and all that she stood for. 'I can assure you of that.'

'Oh, then,' said Bel, her voice still so sweet it was nauseating, cloying, 'to what do I owe the pleasure?' She would not be put down by insult, not at all. It was plain to her that he had mistaken her for Marianne, and she did not intend to enlighten him — yet.

'No pleasure either, madam,' he said grimly. 'I must insist that I take no pleasure in consorting with such a one as you. Only the direst necessity would bring me to this — house,' and the look he cast on the pretty room would have had it bursting into flames, so fierce was it.

'Oh, that is of all things the most convenient,' responded Bel, who was discovering in herself a fund of nastiness which she had not been aware that she possessed, but by all the gods of legend he deserved every unpleasant word which she flung back at him, 'seeing that I feel the same about you, sir, which makes us quits.'

The fine eyebrows drew together and rose alarmingly; the mouth thinned even further. 'I have no wish to be quits with you, madam, no wish to know you at all. . .other than for a quite obvious and brief purpose. . .'

'Nor I to honour or to. . .pleasure, you, sir,' Bel threw at him when he paused a little for breath, 'and it would satisfy me greatly if you quit my house on the instant. My only regret is that I possess no footmen to drive you from my presence. Pray leave at once!'

He made no effort to leave, merely said, through

his excellent teeth, 'I had not heard that you were impudent, madam; on the contrary, I was told that you dripped honey. I see that, as usual, rumour lied.'

Bel might remain outwardly cool, but she was seething inside. How dared he? Oh, how dared he? To say that he wanted her only for one purpose, and that briefly — in direst necessity, indeed! For Bel was not so innocent that she had not caught the insult.

'Come to the point, sir, I beg of you. Philosophic discussion on the nature or otherwise of my conversational powers is a digression I do not wish to encourage — unless, of course, we move on to the nature of *your* manners towards a lady — or rather the lack of them!'

'Lady, Mrs Marina St George? Lady? What lady seduces a very young man, and then gets him into her financial toils — with blackmail threatened? A whore, madam, a very whore. By God, were I not a man of some honour I would take you on the instant, unrecompensed, as your payment for criminal conduct. Be grateful that I neither do that, nor send for the Runners.'

'All this puffery, sir,' riposted Bel contemptuously, 'directed towards the wrong quarter. I fear you are a little behindhand. I am not Mrs St George. You may observe — it cannot have escaped your notice, so eagle-eyed as you are — that I am wearing black. I am, sir, her younger sister, up from the country.'

Lord Francis stared at her contemptuously, took in the whole enchanting picture — the ivory skin, green eyes, red-gold curls, enhanced, not diminished by the depth of her mourning black.

'Oh, madam, I thought by the colour and cut that it had been one of Marina's conceits! Up from the country, you say? I assume that you have been practising there the profession which your sister so successfully followed in the town! No matter, I will deal with you instead. By the state of this room you are settling your sister's affairs. You may settle this one — with me.'

'I will settle with my principal, sir, since I gather that you are not he,' Bel flung at him, white to the lips, the temper, signalled by her red hair, so strong in her that she wished that she were a man, to call him out, or 'plant a facer on him', as Garth, the vicar's son with whom she had played as a child, had gravely informed her, when he had been wild with a schoolboy's ambition to be a bruiser of quality.

'Indeed you will not. The young fool could not protect himself against your late sister, and since you seem, by your tongue, to be an even greater scorpion than she was, it is my duty, if not my pleasure, to see you off.'

See her off! By God — for Bel's internal language was growing more unladylike by the minute — she would see *him* off, if it were the last thing she did.

Tactics! Tactics! What served her on the chessboard might, inexperienced as she was, serve her in life.

She sank down into her chair, clasped her forehead with her left hand, picked up her quill with her

right, spoke in faltering accents, quite unlike her
recent fiery speech.

'Forgive me, sir,' she achieved. 'I am quite overset; my sister's sudden death, the long journey here,
the lawyers, and now. . .this. . .' And she heaved a
dramatic sigh.

Lord Francis, a man not to be easily caught by
anyone, as all London could have informed Bel,
stared suspiciously at this transformation, not
softened at all by the tear-drenched green eyes
which were now raised towards him.

'Oh, we are singing a different tune now, madam,
are we? What brought this about — the threat of the
Runners, or a sudden access of common sense?'

'Neither, sir. The knowledge that. . .shouting at
each other will not bring us to a conclusion, and I
am anxious that this transaction of which you speak
should be concluded. If you will please give me the
name of the young man of whom you speak, and
explain your relationship to him.'

Francis Carey, a man who temporised with
nobody, was certainly not prepared to be temporised with by a whore on the make, as he judged Bel
to be, but he decided that if madam's opposition
had collapsed so dramatically she was either
engaged in tricking him, or had given way before
his own intransigence. That being so, he decided to
finish by being as brutally frank as he had begun.

'My nephew, madam, Mark — Marcus — Carey,
Viscount Tawstock, who, I admit, is the veriest fool,
having been over-indulged by a stupid mother —'
Did Lord Francis Carey like nobody? was Bel's
immediate and uncharitable thought, masked by a

heaving bosom, showing for the first time a maidenly distress which she did not actually feel ' — came upon the Town last year, and among other follies became embroiled with your *sister* —— ' he almost spat the word at her ' — conceived that he was passionately in love with her, proposed to make her Viscountess Tawstock, save the mark, and was foolish enough not only to write her a proposal of marriage but to borrow money from her, having thrown away his allowance on the gaming tables.'

He paused for breath, and about time too, thought Bel, busy deciding what to do next — for the letter relating to the money borrowed by Marcus Carey was the one which she had been reading when his uncle arrived, and somewhere in Marianne's secret store she was sure his letter of proposal — useless now — existed.

No matter; Lord Francis had obviously come here, not knowing of Marianne's death — and where had he been, not to know that? — to frighten Marianne away, and was still, not knowing that she, Bel, was no threat, trying to warn Bel off, presumably frightened that she would continue with Lord Tawstock what Marianne had begun.

For one delirious moment she contemplated 'going into the business', and doing so. Her own strong sense of rectitude, her revulsion for the life which poor Marianne had apparently perforce chosen stifled the unworthy thought at birth. But this arrogant monster deserved to be taught a lesson, and somehow she would teach him one.

She fumbled among the papers on the desk, although well aware that the relevant letter was placed immediately before her. No matter; let him think her disorganised, scatter-brained. She appeared to find it at last, waved it distractedly at him. 'Forgive me, sir, I am not *au fait* with such matters. I am not sure whether in inheriting my sister's estate I have inherited the right to the monies owing to her—but whether that be so or not,' she added hastily, seeing him about to open his mouth, 'I am sure that you would not wish to see these papers, or the love-letters and proposal which he made to my sister, published to the world as an example of his folly.' And that, your haughty lordship, is a pretty threat to make, is it not? She continued rapidly again, 'That being so, I am prepared to return all the papers to you in return for some service which *you* might do *me*—but I am a little exercised as to the nature of the payment.'

She stopped, smiling sweetly at him through her tears, aware that for the first time she had wrong-footed him.

'You are?' he said glacially, but against his will suddenly fascinated by the sheer impudence of the young woman opposite him.

'Yes,' replied Bel, outwardly appearing to recover from her recent distress, and inwardly beginning to enjoy herself. Where, she thought, was all this coming from? From what hidden depths was this dreadfully devious behaviour emerging?

'You see, reading over Marina's papers, and being aware, by hearsay, of course, that to be a. . . Cyprian of the very first stare is different from offering such a. . .service in the countryside, I need a little advice if I am to carry on poor Marina's. . .

business. . .successfully. Who better than to perform such a service for me, by tutoring me, as it were, than such a one as you, so obviously *au fait* with everything as you are? And then you could have your nephew's. . .indiscretions back, and we shall all be happy, not least yourself, having performed such a pleasant and trifling service to gain your ends. Your patronage would help to ensure my success.' And she fluttered her eyelashes at him, quaking inside at her wicked daring, for his face had grown still, and slightly flushed as he took in what she was saying.

'By God, madam, are you proposing that I should be your pander?'

'No, indeed, not at all,' replied Bel, obviously prettily agitated at the very thought. 'Just the one service, small indeed, which you might. . .perform for me. And after all, you cannot pretend that gentlemen hesitate to recommend pleasing. . .ladybirds. . .to their friends. I have been instructed quite otherwise. That is all that is necessary for you to gain what you want. Our intercourse would then be at an end. . .unless, of course, you wished to be a regular client. I might allow a discount for *that*.'

Bel had the delight of seeing him rendered almost tongue-tied by her insolence. What she did not understand was that a pair of green eyes, red hair and a superb figure, allied to a ready wit, were beginning to work their magic on even such a hardened specimen as Francis Carey, who had long told himself that women, virtuous or loose, played no part in his life.

Desire roared through him, so suddenly and unexpectedly that he almost gasped. This. . .lightskirt, so fresh and seemingly virginal, had roused in him passions he had long thought extinct.

If he were honest, from the moment he had first seen her, so unlike the brass-faced creature of his imaginings, she had aroused the strangest stirrings in him. As a result of the effect the lovely eyes, the smiling mouth, the air of virtue—denied to some extent by her ready repartee with its hint of forbidden knowledge—had had on him he had become immensely taken with her, which to some extent explained the coarse cynicism with which he had spoken to her, in an attempt to deny her attractions.

Oh, no, he had no wish to be tempted by a woman again, particularly by a deceptive little bit of muslin working her practised tricks on him!

But tempted he was. His hands curled by his sides; if he had answered her immediately his voice would have been thick with long-suppressed desire—no, lust, it must be simple lust which gripped him, the result of long continence. And now that continence was at risk, and he had the most overpowering wish to take her into his arms, to make love to her until that charming face was soft with fulfilled passion beneath him. . . He must be going mad to think such thoughts, but yes, improbably, he was going to consent to what she had suggested.

He told himself sternly that he was merely doing so to dig young Marcus out of the pit into which he had been pushed by that hellcat her sister—but that was not the truth—he knew better than that, and, worst of all, he was so roused that he wanted her now, this very minute, on the carpet even, no time to wait. He savagely bit the inside of his mouth, to feel it fill with blood, anything to assuage the actual physical pain he was feeling. And now she was speaking again, mocking him.

'Silent, sir? You were voluble enough a moment ago.'

'Your impudence serves to silence me, madam, and I also need to consider your proposition.'

'Do not take too long,' Bel could not resist taunting him, her tone a trifle pert, but none the worse for that, she thought. 'The post awaits. Mr Leigh Hunt might like this prime piece of scandal for his news-sheet — another member of the aristocracy to expose.'

Francis Carey did not know which he wanted to do more — strike her, or push her against the wall to take his pleasure. His normally restrained behaviour, so long practised that it had become a habit, saved him.

She was speaking again. 'I own that I am not too sure how exactly to converse with those of the first flight. By your own grasp of language you seem to be well enough informed to instruct me in that a little, too.'

Francis found his voice at last. 'Conversation, madam? You wish me to instruct you in conversation also?'

'By all means. I understand that these days lively repartee, as well as. . .expertise. . .elsewhere, is much in demand among the gentlemen who will be my. . .clients. I know I can supply the main part of the business, but conversation. . .of *that* I am not so sure.'

Francis succeeded in curling his lip, and achieving normal-sounding speech, something of a feat in the state to which he had been reduced. 'Oh, I would not have thought, madam, that you would have any difficulty in that department, on the evidence of our *conversazione* so far,' and then before she could answer him, 'As to your proposition, madam, yes, I find it. . .agreeable to me. I am willing to. . .tutor you. At once would be. . .most pleasing to me. Fortunately I am at a loose end at the moment — I am usually a busy man. I take it that the house is in readiness for. . .visitors; we could set to straight away.'

This was not at all to Bel's taste. She had no intention of allowing this arrogant brute to as much as touch her, and in her inexperience did not know the degree to which she had stirred him — almost dangerously.

'Oh, no,' she said sadly, bringing a fine lace handkerchief into play, 'not so near in time to my discovery of my sister's death. It would be improper, as you would surely agree ——'

Not so improper, thought Francis, savagely, as leaving me in the state to which you have reduced me, but compelled to nod, since speech seemed suddenly beyond him again, as the houri's luminous green eyes did their work on him.

'No, you must allow me a week to recover. I need at least that. . .to do myself justice.'

You need nothing, was his unspoken reply, for I am the one to do myself justice, and that I could do on the instant, but decency. . .yet where was decency in all this? For she had bought him, not he her, by the promise of Marcus's incriminating papers in exchange for his body—for that was what their bargain amounted to.

Bel peeped at him over her handkerchief, and was not too innocent to understand that Lord Francis was in a fine pelter over something—surely the man could wait a week to sample her? No, she decided, ten days, time for her to arrange to get clear away, for she had no intention of keeping any bargain which she might make with him. He, and every other fine gentleman who had enjoyed her sister, and the other unfortunate women who sold their bodies for money, could pay for his lust. That she wronged Lord Francis a little she was not to know, and in the mood she was in the knowledge would have made no difference to her.

'Ten days,' she said, and then dropped her face into her handkerchief, sobbing, and the sobs were not all counterfeit, for she found that she was suddenly weeping for the lost sister whom she had never really known. 'Ten days; you can give me that, surely.'

Francis wanted to give her nothing, but the thought of the double gain—Marcus's papers, and the enjoyment of the woman before him—spurred him on. He nodded, reluctantly.

'Ah,' breathed Bel, putting down the handkerchief and picking up the quill pen again, 'we have a bargain, I see. Your nephew's papers in exchange for my. . .instruction at your hands,' and she began to write, affecting a die-away air that had him all the more hot for her, every expression on her vital face beginning to affect him strangely.

'Allow me to make a note.' And she continued to write nonsense on the paper before her, anything to keep him hanging on in suspense, since it was plain that he had changed dramatically from the violently aggressive man who had forced his way into Marina's study.

Common sense suddenly hit Francis hard over the head, stifling the demanding pangs of desire which he suddenly understood had been rendering him foolish. Why he did not know, but something in her posture, some hint of mockery affected him. With one bound he was over by the desk, and had wrenched the paper on which she was writing from her.

He read it, stared at it, then, 'Three blind mice,' he read, 'written in a fine scholarly hand—an educated whore, by God.' Rage mixed with lust, a totally delightful but potent sensation, had him in its thrall. 'Why, you bitch, what games are you playing with me?'

His aspect was suddenly so frightening that Bel quailed. She realised that she was going too far, did not want to be raped in Marianne's study, for now she could see what the poet called 'the lineaments of desire' plainly written on his face. Half of her was triumphant at the sight—oh, yes, he wanted Bel Passmore, did he not, but he would never get her, that was for sure—and the other half was fearful at what she might have provoked.

'No games,' she said. 'I was merely writing to. . . keep myself steady.'

'And if I take you at your word, madam, then you will not cheat me?'

'No,' replied Bel, and this was not, she told herself, truly a lie, for, although she had no intention of keeping any rendezvous with him, neither did she ever intend to use Marcus Carey's indiscretions on paper, or his borrowing of money from Marianne, against him or his uncle.

'So,' said Francis, much against his will, though his will, for once, was weak, 'I shall be here on the first of June at three o'clock of the afternoon, at your wish, madam, and afterwards you will give me everything on paper pertaining to Marcus Carey, Viscount Tawstock, and his debts will be cancelled.'

Bel crossed her fingers under the desk, met his eyes with her own, greenly limpid, and thinking, God forgive me, said, 'Yes, a bargain.'

'Good.' He turned on his heel, gave her one last searing look, threw at her, '*Auf Wiedersehen*, madam, until we meet again,' and was gone through the door, leaving Bel to fall forward, drained, across the desk — only for her, a moment later, to sit up smartly again.

Well, one thing was sure. There was no question of her giving up Marianne's wealth now; she would live on it in comfort if only to put out her tongue at every member of the male sex who saw fit to exploit women, and damn them all, and that self-righteous monster Lord Francis Carey the most of all. Self-righteous! Why, the brute could hardly wait to get his hands on her. Another hypocrite unveiled.

What a pity she could not see his face when he arrived to find her gone!

* * *

Francis Carey, that man of discretion, probity and, as Bel Passmore had immediately seen, damned arrogance, arrived back at Hathersage House just off the Strand, where his older half-brother, Jack, paralysed and dumb these last three years since a riding accident, still lived, leaving his unsatisfactory wife Louisa to try to check the unwelcome excesses of her son Marcus, who had gone to the dogs the moment he had achieved the age of twenty-one and been relieved of his uncle's guardianship.

The Carey family, or rather the senior members of it, comprising the paralysed Marquis of Hathersage, his wife and only child, were as poor as church mice; ironically, the only wealthy member of the family was Francis himself, the late Marquis's child by his third wife, whose vast estates had been settled at the time of her marriage on any male child she might bear.

This unusual turn of circumstances was fortunate, for the Marquis, almost in his dotage, had been so set on marrying her that he had agreed to these unequal terms, with the result that Francis's inheritance had not been swallowed up on the gaming tables where his father had spent the last years of his life disposing of his once great wealth — which he had wrongly assumed to be bottomless.

To Marcus's resentment of his uncle as guardian was added his further resentment of his uncle as the wealthy man which he was not.

He was in the big shabby drawing-room, standing over his weeping mother, when Francis came in to tell her that she need not worry overmuch, he had come to an agreement with Marina St George's sister and heiress, and Marcus's name was saved.

Marcus was not grateful. 'What the devil's all this, sir?' he exclaimed rudely. 'Who gave you leave to deal with my debts? The whore is dead, and can persecute me no longer, nor her doxy of a sister either.'

Francis winced: when another used the language with which he had recently abused the St George's sister, he disliked the ugly sound of it.

'You are mistaken, sir,' he replied stiffly. 'The woman was in a position to do you a mischief. You were not to be found, and your mother was agitated on your behalf, so I attempted to bring the sister off. I think that I have succeeded, but of course I do not expect gratitude.'

'No, indeed,' said Marcus unpleasantly. 'Interfering again, I see. What was the sister like?' he enquired eagerly, more concerned with that than with his new safety from scandal and ridicule, his uncle noted with disgust.

'What you might expect,' said Francis, lying through his teeth. He had, unexpectedly, no wish for his nephew to be chasing Miss. . . He suddenly realised that, for all his cleverness, he had no idea of the name of Marina St George's sister!

Marcus flung away. For all that he was not so many years younger than his uncle, who was the child of his grandfather's old age, he seemed a boy beside him, his mother thought dismally, remembering what Francis had been at Marcus's age. But then Francis had probably been born old and steady and high-handed, although his high-handedness had usefully saved Mark from more than one scrape. She always called him Mark, so much warmer than cold, classical Marcus, she thought.

Francis was a little worried that the name of the houri whom he was to bed in ten days' time was unknown to him. But what of that? Meanwhile Louisa moaned and sighed at him, bade Mark thank his uncle, advised him to be more like Francis, at which Marcus glowered at his uncle and flung out of the room — to the devil, his uncle supposed wryly, unaware that that same monster of truth and probity whose praises his mother was singing was glumly contemplating the acres of time which would have to pass before he saw the St George's sister again!

As in the pretty study where he had met her, he thought once more that he was taking leave of his senses. He was in England for only a few weeks, having come over from the Paris Embassy, where he was stationed as an attaché, for some instructions relating to the parlous state of Europe in the aftermath of the Napoleonic wars.

Everything seemed to be going wrong at once, he decided, both publicly and privately. How could he be in such a damned taking over a pretty little Cyprian who would always sell herself to the highest bidder; and why could he not work this unwonted state of passionate arousal off on any piece of muslin in a nighthouse, or in a private love-nest?

But he knew that he couldn't. Fastidious to a degree, he was only too well aware that after years of Puritanical abstinence the lure of a green-eyed, red-haired witch with a provoking smile and tongue had been too much for him. Oh, well, he would probably feel better in the morning, would have returned to his senses, be his usual self, might even reconsider the bargain, except that in some strange way honour seemed to be involved in that, too.

Not only could he not let Marcus down, but he had pledged his word to her, and what a joke that was — honour to a courtesan!

But he felt no better in the morning, nor the following morning, or any other morning afterwards, and while he was sitting in committee-rooms, talking with grave, black-coated gentlemen about what was happening in Spain, Italy, passing on his unsatisfactory master's messages, being deferred to by some, given orders by others, a pair of bewitching green eyes haunted him.

And on the final day, a sunny one, June the first, 'the Glorious First of June,' that great sea battle, he remembered — naturally so, because he had been an officer in the navy in the late wars — he dressed himself as carefully as a green boy going to meet his love, instead of a seasoned man preparing to bed a damned cheating whore, a phrase he used to mock at his own unlikely passion.

Driving to Stanhope Street, he doffed his hat at passers-by whom he knew, mentally rehearsed what he would say and do when he was with her, burning to see her, to hold her in his arms, to. . .do all the unspeakable things with her which he had not done to a woman for years, and finally drove down the street in a swelter of desire to the St Georges' house — to stare at drawn blinds, shuttered windows, and a board outside, advertising that the house was for sale!

He threw the reins to his tiger, Cassius, a nickname given to him in jest because of his lean and hungry look, like Shakespeare's murderer of the same name in *Julius Caesar*, and half ran to the front door, to bang the knocker on the door in a tattoo sufficient to wake the dead.

A well-dressed fellow emerged from the next house to stare at him, since no one answered, and a strange slow rage, quite unlike any he had ever experienced before, began to consume him.

He hailed the fellow imperiously, to receive an equally imperious stare in return. 'I see that the house is for sale,' he managed, with reasonable equanimity. 'Do I infer from that that the occupants have left?'

The fellow's stare grew lubricious. 'Why, sir,' he began, 'if you have business with the new doxy, you will be disappointed, I fear,' and then stopped dead in gasping fright as Francis leaned over the railings to seize him by his stock with such force that he was half strangled.

'And damn you, sir,' said Francis in a deadly whisper, 'give me a straight answer, a yes or no; I want no damned moral sermons from strangers who do not know my business.' And he released the man just enough to allow him to croak from his half-ruined throat.

'Pardon me, sir, but they all departed forty-eight hours agone, in a hired coach, and the furniture went after them, but where they went I have no knowledge, nor any wish to know. Too happy to see them go, and their gentlemen friends with them.'

Gone! Francis suddenly had total recall of that

mocking, mischievous face, and knew that she, whoever she was, had never had the slightest intention of honouring the unlovely bargain which she had made with him.

The rage which swept over him, as he stood there, frustrated, was of an order which he had never experienced before. He loosened his grip on the man, said savagely, 'Stay a moment, until I give you leave to go,' and stared at the blank windows. He did not even know her name, nor where she came from, nor how to find her. Her lawyers, her bankers, the real name of Marina St George — he was sure that it was a pseudonym — were alike unknown to him.

He only knew that in his baffled desire he felt murderous enough to kill her for the trick she had played on him, and that if he ever met her again he would make madam pay for what she had done after a fashion she would never forget.

Hell knew no fury like a woman scorned, said the old proverb, but what of the scorned man? What pity did that man stand in? What flames of frustration consumed him? And why should he feel such insensate anger towards a woman with whom he had only spoken for a few short minutes?

He turned towards the man he had cowed with his ferocity. 'Do you know by what name the woman who came to live here after Mrs St George's death passed?'

The man was pleased to thwart him. 'Indeed no, sir,' he smirked. 'I am happy to inform you that I have, and had, no wish to have truck with any such creatures!'

'Then damn you for a mealy-mouthed, canting swine, who probably takes his pleasure in alleys,' replied Francis savagely, nothing gentlemanly left in his make-up, he thought dismally when he finally returned to Hathersage House. He seemed lost to decency and proper conduct, he who was usually known for the correctitude of his behaviour and his keen sense of honour. The red-headed witch had deprived him of both.

But she had forgotten something in her desire to humiliate Francis Carey, to leave him in a cold stew of frustrated lust. The bill of sale on the house gave him the name of the agent who was selling it, and who would be aware of the owner's identity, and he drove there at speed to trace the bitch who had cheated him so vilely.

To find a dead end; for the house had been placed on the market in the name of Coutts, the banker, and Francis knew full well that were he to visit Thomas Coutts, whom he knew quite well, indeed banked with, that gentleman would tell him nothing, if such were the instructions of his client.

And so it proved. Mr Coutts welcomed Lord Francis, served him sherry and biscuits, asked after his career, but on Francis's enquiring about the property in Stanhope Street which the banking house had placed on the market Mr Coutts had regretfully shaken his head, and told him that his client had demanded strict confidentiality. He could tell my lord nothing. Another dead end: the witch had disappeared into the obscurity from whence she had emerged.

Of course, if he had ever met Marina St George,

so that he had known at once that it was not her to whom he was talking when he had thrust his way into the study, then things might, just might, have been different.

He told Marcus later that he was probably safe, and would hear nothing more of his letters or his debts, for he judged, correctly, that the vanishing lightskirt had been so careful of her name and her circumstances because she wished to disappear completely, probably to set herself up elsewhere, trap fools, and laugh at them behind her hand when she had succeeded in duping and frustrating them.

But oh, my dear madam, he promised her that night as he made ready for bed, his whole body one mass of frustrated and unfulfillable desire, if ever I meet you again, then beware, for revenge is sweet, and it shall be as slow and long as I can contrive to make it!

CHAPTER THREE

'Now, my dear Bel,' said Lady Almeria Harley to her best friend, Mrs Bel Merrick, that charming red-headed widow whom every eligible male who lived in or visited Lulsgate Spa had tried to woo or win at some time or other in the two years which she had lived there, 'you are not to make faces at me. It is time that you were married again. A pretty woman needs her own establishment, a kind husband, and a brood of handsome children. If Henry Venn is not good enough for you, then there are half a dozen delightful fellows who would be only too happy to take you in matrimony.'

'No doubt,' retorted Bel, smiling and holding up the pretty little baby's gown she was busy sewing, 'but I dare swear that when you came to marry it was not one of a half-dozen or so delightful fellows, but your own dear Philip Harley whom you chose to accept. I promise you that when I find someone who means to me what Philip so obviously does to you I will snap him up on the instant, but until then I shall remain a widow. After all, I am still not yet twenty-one, and would like to enjoy my single state a little longer, seeing——' crossing her fingers surreptitiously as she spoke '—that I enjoyed it for so short a time before I was married.'

Bel marvelled once again at her own powers of deceit. Sometimes her own duplicity, her powers of invention, frightened her, but she always felt the need to protect herself. After she had fled London, leaving behind, with the help of Thomas Coutts, no clue to her identity, she had returned briefly to Brangton with a faithful and silent Lottie, having pensioned off Mrs Hatch and given the little maid enough for a dowry, to find Aunt Kaye rapidly failing.

She never told her of what Marianne had become, and had sworn Lottie to secrecy, so that Aunt Kaye had died happy to the knowledge that dear sweet Marianne had left Bel enough to set her up for life. Bel had then decided that that life was not to be passed in Brangton—where she might be traced—but that she would retire to Lulsgate Spa in Leicestershire, where she knew that a varied and rich society obtained, where she might find a new and happy circle of friends, and a place of her own.

Being a supposed widow conferred respectability, and Lottie was sworn to secrecy over that; she was a hard-headed, silent woman who needed no telling why. After she had arrived in Lulsgate Bel had hired a companion, Mrs Broughton, to give her respectability, a quiet, vague, rather silly woman, if kind, who accepted that Bel had been married off young to a rich old man, who had soon died, and that Bel, having no relatives, had chosen to settle at Lulsgate in search of company, and—who knew?— a second husband, Bel had said to anyone who cared to listen, smiling sweetly as she spoke.

Lady Almeria Harley was the wife of the vicar of St Helen's church, set in the centre of Lulsgate, its beautiful vicarage beside it, so that Bel, looking out of the drawing-room window, could see the church's thirteenth-century spire, with its truncated top, known as the Little Stump to the locals, because it was not so impressive as the Stump at Boston in Lincolnshire.

Opposite to the church were the Baths, which Bel could not quite see, although they were visible from the small house which she had bought, The Willows. Small was perhaps the wrong word for it, it being so much larger than anything Bel had ever lived in before she had inherited Marianne's fortune.

'I am quite serious,' said Lady Almeria suddenly, after fifteen minutes' companionable silence, removing a row of pins from her mouth in order to speak without swallowing them. 'I do admit that there is no one whom I could wholeheartedly recommend to you, but I am sure that one day soon I shall be able to matchmake with a good heart — seeing that you will not wear Henry Venn.'

The look she gave Bel on saying this was for some reason vaguely conspiratorial, as though she had something up her sleeve, Bel thought, and then forgot her thought.

The Reverend Mr Henry Venn was the curate of St Helen's, who looked after the Lady Chapel at Morewood. He was moderately wealthy in his own right. 'I own,' said Bel serious now, 'that I am quite attracted to Henry, in a lukewarm way, you understand, but if I take Henry then I have to take his mama, and *that* thought I cannot stomach. Besides, his sense of humour is deficient, and I should be sure to say so many things at which they would both look sideways!'

Almeria's charming laugh rang out. Bel's ever-ready sense of humour was one of the things Almeria liked about Bel, coupled with Bel's good heart and industry. She had recently been made, despite her youth, the leader and the organiser of the church's sewing circle, 'So reliable, Bel,' being the usual comment, so that when old Mrs Harper went to her last rest no one, not even the old tabbies, as Almeria irreverently called them, who were the church's mainstay, had objected to Bel's replacing her.

Tact as well as charm and humour typified Bel, Almeria thought once more, watching her friend, and she thought that she knew a man who might appreciate her, and she hoped to introduce Bel to him one day soon, but until that day arrived she would continue to tease Bel about suitors, for she knew that despite her charm Bel was sufficiently hard-headed not to accept anyone for the sake of it.

'The town is filling up with visitors,' commented Almeria, watching the procession of fashionably dressed people walk by the vicarage windows. 'August usually brings the most, the London season being almost over. Philip says that although he prefers Lulsgate empty they bring much needed money into the town and give occupation to many. How many shops would Lulsgate support if there were no visitors? he says. Think of the sempstresses and milliners who would have no work without them, to say nothing of the lodging-house keepers, and those who rent their homes out for the summer, to pay for their few weeks at Brighton, or in London in June.'

Both women were silent. For all the wealth which Lulsgate contained, they were well aware of the poverty which the ending of the wars had brought, and that Morewood, once a pretty agricultural village, was now a small town of frameworker knitters, made desperately poor by the depression and the coming of the new machines, which produced more cloth but needed so many fewer workers to manage them.

It was those thrown out of work for whom Almeria and Bel were making baby clothes, and there were times when Bel, visiting Morewood, thought, And what should I be doing, with Aunt Kaye's small annuity disappearing with her death, and a pittance of my own, if Marianne's wealth had not saved me from penury?

In an effort to banish sad recollections she said, determinedly bright, 'And last night I finished *The Nun of Torelli*; are not you going to ask me what I thought of it?' and the face she showed Almeria was full of amusement, none of her true thoughts visible.

'Well, since you ask,' began Almeria, her own lively face responding to Bel's promptings, 'yes, what did you make of it?'

'Such a strange nun.' Bel held the little garment, now finished, up again to admire it as she spoke. 'Not that I know any nuns, you understand, but I should be astonished to discover that they passed their time running around underground crypts, spending the night alone with handsome young mercenary captains, and being rescued from pirates at sea; all that was missing was a burning windmill, a beggar who turned out to be a prince — oh, and a little common sense on everyone's part, in which case, of course, there would have been no story!'

'Of course.' Almeria was delighted to have Bel's wit in full flow again; she had sensed a quietness, almost a reserve lately in Bel's manner. She was not to know that Bel had recently been having second thoughts about her many deceptions because, since the flowering of her friendship with Almeria, she had come to hate deceiving her.

'What Bel needs,' she said later to her husband after dinner, Bel having left earlier in the afternoon, 'is a husband, someone to love her, to do for her what you do for me.'

Philip Harley poured himself a glass of wine. He was an orthodox churchman, not by any means an Evangelical, and did not see the need to deny himself the small luxuries of life, a little wine being one of them.

'I'm sure she has had, and will have, offers,' he said gently. Sometimes, he thought, his Almeria was a little impetuous and needed guidance — discreet, of course.

'Oh, offers,' said Almeria; 'there is no one in Lulsgate good enough for her. No, I was thinking of someone else.'

The telepathy of happily married couples informed Philip of her meaning. He put his wine glass down carefully, said slowly, 'No, Almeria, better not try to interfere if it is Francis whom you are thinking of, if you have invited him here to throw Bel at him, or him at Bel. He is not a man to play with.'

Almeria rose, put her arms around his neck.

'Now, Philip, you are not to scold me, but they are made for each other. He ought to marry again, and a woman with Bel's wit and fire, to say nothing of her looks, would be ideal for him. No milk-and-water miss would do for Francis; *he* would not want her, and *she* would not stand up to him.'

Philip disengaged himself gently and gave her a loving kiss. 'I don't like matchmaking at the best of times, and I don't think you really know your half-brother. He is not to be manipulated; nor, I think, is Bel.'

'Oh,' said Almeria sorrowfully, 'now you wrong me. I have no intention of manipulating them. I merely intend to have him here, introduce them, give them the opportunity to see how well they suit. Beneath all that severity Francis is, I am sure, a man who needs the softer passions, however much he tries to deny it. He is at a loose end at the moment since being seconded from the Paris Embassy to work at the Foreign Office. I have not told Bel that he is coming, nor him that I have a pretty widow waiting for him. Give me credit for some delicacy of thought. I simply hope that they will find one another.'

Philip thought of Lord Francis Carey, that rather grim man, sighed, and wondered. He did not doubt Almeria's delicacy, but she was planning to throw two people together, and experience — for he was rather older than his wife — had told him how little that sometimes answered; but he decided to say nothing further — better so.

* * *

Bel knew that Almeria's half-brother was coming to stay in Lulsgate. Almeria had let it slip one afternoon at the subscription library, or rather, she had overheard Almeria telling Mrs Phipps so. She had expected Almeria to say something to her of the visit, they were so close, but no, and Bel, who was not over-curious about other people's lives and doings, because she had no wish for them to be over-curious about hers, had forgotten the matter completely until she had met Almeria in the milliner's that morning.

She was trying on an enchanting poke bonnet, but did not like the gaudy red flowers decorating it, and was discussing having them replaced by blue cornflowers with Mrs Thwaites, who made and sold them, when Almeria came rushing in, all aglow.

'Oh, Bel, there you are. I just missed catching you before you left home. Mrs Broughton told me that you were coming here—I haven't a moment to breathe, my brother arrived late last night, earlier than expected, and I am giving a little supper party this evening for my most intimate friends to meet him. Do say you will come, I beg of you.'

'Of course.' Almeria's impulsiveness amused Bel as it did Almeria's husband, being so unlike the calm face which Bel had presented to the world since Marianne's death. 'I shall be delighted. Do I dress?'

'Indeed,' said Almeria, and, remembering Philip's injunctions against matchmaking, added, 'I shall expect all my friends to be looking their best. Wear your delightful bluey-green gauze,' she could not help adding; 'it goes so well with your eyes and hair—and now forgive me, I must rush. Between being a parson's wife and a great hostess, no time to breathe,' and she was gone.

Typical of Almeria not to inform me of her brother's name, thought Bel, amused. She knew from something once said that Almeria's maiden name had been Freville, and assumed that her brother was the Hon something Freville, Almeria's father having been an earl.

What she did not know was that Almeria's father had died young, Almeria's mother had married again, and was the Marquis of Hathersage's second wife, but had died in childbirth nine months after the wedding, and that Almeria's brother was a half-brother with a different name. Had she known the brother's name, she would have run screaming from the milliner's, but, happy in her apparently secure world, she ordered the cornflowers for her bonnet, walked on to the mercer's where she bought some book muslin for a dinner dress, and went happily home to care for her garden, talk to Mrs Broughton, enjoy a light nuncheon, and play the pianoforte while Mrs Broughton did her canvas work, to such a complacent Eden had she finally come.

'Now, Francis,' said his half-sister severely, much as she had done to Bel Merrick a few days earlier, 'you are not to make faces. Quite proper for you to do the pretty to all my friends immediately and at one go. No time wasted, and you will be at ins with everyone, and have time to decide who will do, and who will not do.'

'Useless to argue with you, I know, my dear

Almy,' said Francis lazily; he was draped over an armchair too small for him. 'You are the most managing creature I know, beneath all the piff-paff. I wonder how you stand it, Philip. No, on second thoughts I do not; such wonderful powers of execution must make for a well-run establishment, if nothing else. You are putting on weight, I see, and do not look like a managed man.'

'Oh, we manage one another,' said Philip truthfully, 'and there is a lot in what Almeria says.'

'And do I dress?' enquired Francis, still lazy, unconsciously echoing Bel Merrick.

'Of course,' said Almeria affectionately. 'Everyone will expect you to be the epitome of London polish, seeing that you are who and what you are.'

Francis laughed. He was always at ease with Almeria, and if he could find a woman like her, he decided, he might change his mind and marry again. He looked merrily across at his brother-in-law, raised one eyebrow at him. 'Now why,' he drawled, 'do I gain the impression that Almy has some ulterior motive in inviting me here? That she is determined that I shall find a Lady Francis in one of the pretty young heiresses or buxom widows who frequent Lulsgate in its high season?'

'Oh, come, little brother,' riposted Almeria, not a whit put out that, as usual, Francis had caught her at her games, 'you flatter yourself——' to have him riposte,

'Not at all, and "little brother"? Why, you are not so many years older than I am, and half my size. Do you wish me to dish the English language altogether by calling you big sister?'

'You may call me what you like,' said Almeria, leaning over and kissing his cheek, 'provided only that you stay as easy as you are with all my friends when they arrive tonight, and do not come the high-handed grandee with them!'

'Agreed,' he said, catching at her hand and pressing it, 'and tell me also, Philip, why you should be so lucky as to catch one of the few truly agreeable females in the world for a wife!'

Dressing for Lady Almeria's little supper, which would probably not be little at all, Bel found herself wondering what the brother would be like. Like Almeria, she hoped, brown and jolly, of amiable appearance; or would he possess wintry grey eyes, a hard face and a superb body?

She blinked with annoyance as Lottie eased the sea-green gown over her head. Would she never get that monster Lord Francis Carey out of her head? How was it that, whenever she read of a man in a novel, or thought of one whom she might like to come calling, he always seemed to look exactly like the brute who had insulted her so?

Why, even the mercenary captain in that ridiculous farrago *The Nun of Torelli* had in her imagination taken on the appearance of the noble ruffian whom she had cheated so neatly. She could forget him for weeks and then he would start walking through her dreams again. Damn the man, and damn the circumstances in which she had met him. Well, she was unlikely ever to meet him again, and perhaps she ought to start thinking of Henry Venn as a possible husband—and why should the odious

Francis Carey make her think of marriage, for goodness' sake? *He* certainly had not seemed to be a marrying man — far from it!

She set in her hair the half-moon jewel which Marianne had been wearing in the Phillips portrait, and placed a small pearl necklace round her neck, pearl drops in her ears, and a pearl ring on her finger. They were all that she had kept of Marianne's jewellery; the rest had, with the help of Mr Thomas Coutts, been sold, and the proceeds wisely invested.

Kid slippers on her feet, a cobweb of a shawl and a tiny fan of chicken feather, dyed sea-green, completed her toilette. There, that should please Almeria, convince her that Bel Merrick just might be husband-hunting. Mrs Broughton had cried off, so Lottie would escort her there, and would take her home — she was to help in the kitchens, having begun her career in them, and was not too proud to revive it occasionally, for the Harleys' cook-house-keeper was her best friend, and the two old women helped one another out when Bel or Almeria entertained.

The company was almost completely assembled in Almeria's drawing-room when she arrived, to be smothered in an embrace before Almeria held her off to examine her. 'Oh, famous, my dear. You should be gracing Town with your looks and presence. You know everyone here, I think, except of course, the guest of honour.'

She led Bel across the room, bowing and acknowledging her many Lulsgate friends, towards the hearth, where a group of people stood talking together. Philip was standing before the empty fire-grate, speaking to a tall dark-haired man who had his back to the room, and was bending to listen to what Mrs Robey was saying. Mrs Robey was a lady on the make with a daughter to marry off and the daughter was standing shy and embarrassed before the London polish of Almeria's brother, Bel supposed.

'Oh, do forgive me for interrupting,' said Almeria gaily, tapping the tall dark-haired man on his arm, 'but, Francis, I do so wish you to meet my dear young friend, Mrs Bel Merrick, who as I have already informed you quite brightens all my days for me.'

With a muttered, 'Pray excuse me,' to Philip and to Mrs Robey the tall man turned to give Bel his full attention, and, his having done so, they stood staring at one another.

Oh, dear God, thought Bel frantically, how can you play such a dreadful trick on me? For the face of Almeria's brother was that of Lord Francis Carey, and she saw his expression change immediately from one of polite amiability to one of an almost unholy glee as he, too, recognised the lady to whom Almeria had so blithely introduced him!

CHAPTER FOUR

His face changed again, so quickly that the stunned Bel almost thought that she had imagined what she had seen, and he was bowing over the hand she was offering to him.

'Delighted to meet you, madam,' he said smoothly, straightening up, so that she could see the mockery in his hard grey eyes, 'absolutely delighted,' and the ring of sincerity in his voice also delighted Almeria, who was innocently unaware of how two-edged, if not to say two-faced, his declaration was. 'My sister has been telling me that she has many charming friends in Lulsgate, and from the manner in which she has introduced us it is plain that you are one of the most favoured. You will not take it amiss if I inform you that I am determined to know more, much more of you—will seek by every means to improve our acquaintance.' And his eyes were devouring her, taking in every line of her body, even more curved and desirable, he noted, than it had been two years ago. How wrong he had been to delay coming to Lulsgate Spa!

Bel had thought that she would not be able to speak, had feared that he might unmask her immediately, like a villain in a melodrama, and declare, Ho, there, this woman is a fraud, a Cyprian like her late notorious sister of whom you have all heard.

53

But no such thing, and she had no time to think, simply to murmur graciously, and her cool tones astonished her, 'I am always pleased, sir, to meet a valued relative of my dear friend, Lady Almeria Harley. I hope you will enjoy your stay in Lulsgate, Lord Francis.'

Bel was trying to take her hand back, but he would not let go of it, raised it to kiss it again, said, his eyes hard on her, 'Now that I have met you, my dear Mrs Merrick, I know that I shall enjoy my stay immensely. You cannot conceive of the pleasure it affords me to meet such a charming person as yourself. And now, forgive me, I must tear myself away, return to Mrs Robey. I was informing her of the delights of the London season just passed, and of the coming trial of Queen Caroline; such a pity that virtue and beauty are not always allied, don't you think? Yes, I see that you agree with me. Let us speak again soon.'

Oh, she would die, thought Bel, as each sentence he uttered carried a double meaning to taunt her, causing one vast blush to overcome her whole body, so that she thought that everyone in the room must be staring at her.

But no such thing to that, either. Even Almeria, who had been half listening to what had passed, seemed to have seen or heard nothing untoward; was pleased, indeed, that on the face of it Francis seemed to have been attracted to her dearest friend and protégée.

'What a splendid fellow he is,' she said fondly to Bel, when Francis had returned to the group by the fire. 'I knew he would like you, and I was not wrong; he seemed quite struck. And he has a genius for saying and doing the right thing; I had no fear that you would not like him.' She seemed oblivious of Bel's unnatural silence, so pleased was she that her innocent little plot seemed to be working.

'I have placed him next to you at supper,' she murmured, 'so that you may further your acquaintanceship with him. I am determined that my best friend and my dear brother shall also be friends. He has been a lonely man recently, and I am trying to repair that — where better than Lulsgate Spa for him to recover his old spirits?'

Where, indeed? thought Bel sardonically. I am sure that he will recover his spirits completely in returning the disfavour I did him, with interest, if I read that haughty face aright, but aloud she said, 'Oh, he seems quite charming, if a little too polished for Lulsgate. London polish, I presume.'

'Oh, and Paris, too,' said Almeria enthusiastically, 'and Bright really must announce supper now. The party is all assembled, and food is the cement of conviviality, Philip always says — to say nothing of drink for the gentlemen.'

So there was Francis Carey taking her into supper, whom she had last thought of as standing on the pavement at Stanhope Street, staring at the empty house and the 'For Sale' notice, knowing that his prey had escaped him — only to find her, by fortunate accident, two years later, enthroned in respectability in Lulsgate Spa.

He was, she now had time to notice, magnificently turned out in the almost black that fine gentlemen were now wont to wear. Only his waistcoat, embroidered with yellow roses, spoilt the chaste perfection of his *tout ensemble*. He was a dandy almost, his stock a work of art, like the rest of him.

How could she have dreamed of him, seen him as the hero of *The Nun of Torelli* or any other piece of nonsense? And how could she ever have thought that she would be walking in to supper with him, her hand on his arm, feeling the living, breathing man, warm beside her, so very much in the flesh — making her uncomfortably aware of her own flesh, feeling naked almost, although she was wearing a considerably more chaste turn-out than most women had chosen to appear in?

So why, she thought crossly, did she have the impression, once he had touched her, that all her clothes had fallen off? Neither Mr Henry Venn's nor any other gentleman's touch had ever had such an effect on her before.

Did he know? She had the uncomfortable impression that he did, and once they were at table he turned to her with the utmost solicitude to ask her whether she was comfortable, and whether she needed water immediately. 'You appear a touch pale, madam. Are you sure that you are feeling quite well? Is there anything I might be permitted to do for you, any trifling service you would care for me to perform?'

'Not at all,' retorted Bel, almost shrewishly, she feared. 'I am in the first stare of health,' thinking, Oh, how dare he? Someone would surely notice; such two-edged comments could hardly escape detection.

But no, Almeria, not far from them, leaned

forward to say, 'Commendable of you, Francis, to care for Bel's welfare.'

'Bel,' he murmured, before he turned to speak to Mrs Robey on his right. 'Charming, quite charming, nearly as much so as. . .Marina. And Mrs. Do I take it, dear Mrs Merrick, that you are a widow, so young as you are?'

She must say something, she who was usually so charmingly free with her opinions, was noted for her repartee, her acute wit.

'Indeed, sir. I was married young to a much older gentleman, who unfortunately died soon after our marriage.'

He leaned forward to say, very softly, so that no one could hear him, 'Oh, indeed, I understand you completely. Of his exertions, I suppose.'

Bel was in agony. Not only from embarrassment as to what he might say next, but quite dreadfully his last comment had made her want to laugh. She was trapped, but would not be put down, said loudly, 'No, you mistake quite. Of putrid water, which brought on palpitations, other more dreadful symptoms, and death. Oh, my poor Augustus! Yes, now I do feel overset.'

There: if that did not hold him, nothing would. 'Forgive me,' he said to Mrs Robey, who might think him unmannerly if he attended to Mrs Merrick too constantly, 'but I fear that Mrs Merrick is not after all on her highest ropes,' and he called to Bright for a little brandy, to add to Mrs Merrick's water glass, as a restorative, he announced gravely.

Bel found everyone looking at her, with varying degrees of sympathy. Henry Venn, who was temperance-minded, said a little reprovingly, 'Are you sure, Lord Francis, that it is wise to ply Mrs Merrick with drink?' to which Francis, busy pouring Bel an extremely liberal dose of brandy from the bottle which he had firmly taken from Bright's hands, replied,

'I am persuaded that brandy, and brandy alone, will restore Mrs Merrick to the charming state which she was in on her arrival here. I do hope, Mrs Merrick,' he said as he handed her her glass, 'that nothing that I have said or done has brought on this fit of. . .discomfiture.'

'Not at all,' said Bel, drinking her brandy and water, and aware of every guest's eye on her. 'May I assure you that nothing you could say or do would ever overset me — quite the contrary.'

His pleasant smile at this was one of genuine admiration, and he chose to favour Mrs Robey with his conversation, after Bel had assured Almeria that her malaise was passing.

'It was only that I thought suddenly of my poor late husband Augustus,' she explained shyly to Almeria and the table, 'and I was distressed all over again. He loved such occasions as these.'

'And bravo to you, my dear Mrs Merrick,' she heard Francis murmur in her ear when the third covers arrived. 'Such *savoir-faire*, in one so young, but then, I forgot, so. . .experienced, too.'

'Thank you,' was Bel's response to that. 'I know exactly the value to place on any praise which I receive from you.'

Francis could not help but admire her. A houri, a lightskirt, passing as virtuous, deceiving his sister and the polite world she might be — but what spirit, what sheer cold-blooded courage, to defy him so coolly when he was doing everything to provoke her into indiscretion.

Oh, she was going to pay for her cavalier treatment of him two years ago, but before he enjoyed her in bed, where she belonged, he was going to enjoy her everywhere else, too, with the world watching. What a pity virtue had not been included in her many attributes!

'And was there a Mr Merrick?' he enquired again in a tone so low that no one else could hear.

'How can you doubt it, sir?' was all she chose to say.

'Oh, easily, easily. You have packed a great deal of living into a short time, my dear Mrs Merrick, since Lady Almeria informed me, just before I escorted you into supper, that you have been living in Lulsgate for almost exactly two years. I calculate on that basis that after your London adventure you must have met, married and buried your late husband in less than six weeks.'

'You forget, I might have met and married him before——' Bel paused. She did not wish to say anything incriminating, even in the low tones of the supper table, with everyone else conversing freely with their neighbours. Fortunately for her, young Amabel Robey had Henry Venn fully occupied.

'Before? Before what, madam? I am agog.'

'Which is what Mrs Robey will be if you do not attend to her a little more,' responded Bel smartly. 'I am not obliged to tell you the story of my life over the supper plates.'

'A great pity, that,' he said lazily, 'since I am sure it would be of the utmost interest. Another time perhaps.'

Oh, damn him, thought Bel, he has the most dreadful effect on my internal language, and he is as light-footed as a. . .as a. . . She could not think what he was as light-footed as, resolved to turn her attention to Henry, who was worriedly asking her whether she felt any effects from the brandy, all of which she had drunk without even noticing that she had done so!

'None at all,' she said severely, thinking how soft Henry looked after she had been inspecting Francis Carey's hard face. Was he soft all over? Was Francis Carey hard all over?

Oh, dear, it must be the brandy causing all these improper thoughts, and she tried to concentrate on Henry's tedious conversation about the next bazaar which was being held in the vicarage grounds, weather permitting, to raise money for the fallen women of Morewood, there being presumably none in Lulsgate, since the fallen women there plied a good trade among the summer visitors and did not need financial help.

If it were not the brandy which was upsetting her, thought Bel, it must be the frightful effect of sitting next to Francis Carey, who now turned his attentions to her again, and was asking her solemnly where she lived, for he would like to pay a call on her on the morrow to ascertain whether her malaise was chronic, or merely passing.

'Merely passing,' said Bel firmly. 'Not worthy of a call.'

'You must allow me to be the best judge of that,' announced Francis soulfully, his eyes wicked. 'Besides, think how pleased Almeria would be if we enlarged our acquaintanceship. Oh, yes, I do wish to enlarge my acquaintanceship with you, dear Mrs Merrick. I wish to see so much more of you; you cannot imagine how much more I wish to see of you.'

Bel could not help it. Wrong and wicked it might be of her, and oh, how she disliked him, saying all these dreadful things to her, but his appalling jokes were too good not to laugh at. She could really be no lady, she decided, between a bout of frantic giggles and her efforts with a handkerchief to pass it off as a mere consequence of eating something which disagreed with her a little.

Scarlet in the face, she allowed Francis to pat her on the back, heard Henry say, 'Most unlike you, dear Mrs Merrick, to be so distressed, and twice in a night, too.' The tactless fool, she thought indignantly, and, fortunately for Bel and everyone, Lady Almeria rose to her feet and led the ladies out of the room to leave the gentlemen to drink their port, while the ladies sat over the tea-board, settling Bel in a chair and anxiously asking her whether she was quite recovered.

'Oh, indeed,' responded Bel, giving for her what was almost a simper, 'I believe it was the August heat which affected me.'

'How unfortunate for you,' said Mrs Robey, ever one to improve the shining hour. 'Now my dear Amabel is never affected by the heat, are you, my love?'

'No, Mama,' replied that young lady meekly, but before her mama could gather any congratulatory smiles on her hardihood she added, unluckily, 'You know it is the cold which oversets me. Why, do you not remember, Mama, only last winter. . .?'

'And that will be quite enough of that,' announced her dominant mama. 'May I say what a fine finished gentleman your good brother seems to be, Lady Almeria? One is astonished that he is not married yet. Where are all the ladies' eyes? I ask myself.'

One would be astonished if such a haughty creature were to have been snared and married, thought Bel naughtily, and surprising for dear kind Almeria to have such a brother as he is. And then she recollected: half-brother only, of course. That must explain all.

Almeria poured Bel more tea and said warmly, 'You and Francis appeared to be getting on famously. I am so pleased; I felt sure that you would be kindred spirits. He has such a taste for reading as you do, and his wit would sort with yours.'

Bel nearly choked over her tea on thinking of the conversation in which she and Francis Carey had indulged over supper, so different as it was from Almeria's kind imaginings.

Mrs Venn, who considered that Mrs Bel Merrick usually had far too much attention paid to her — enough to turn such a young person's head, and she didn't want dear Henry marrying her, by no means — said loudly, 'My dear Henry has a pretty wit too, but then he does not possess a title and ten thousand a year, so admiration for *his* wit goes abegging. I consider Lulsgate has as much to offer in *that* line as any London salon.'

Bel winced over her tea at this none too veiled insult aimed at Francis and Almeria, and thought again that so long as his mama would be part of his future household there was no question of her accepting poor Henry.

Lady Almeria, though, treated Mrs Venn as though she were some gnat buzzing about — making somewhat of a noise, but not really doing any harm — her bite lacking even the gnat's venom.

'Oh, Francis rarely puts on airs,' she said cheerfully, 'and as for wit, one can hardly claim that Lulsgate is awash with it, dear Mrs Venn, though it does you credit to think so. Local patriotism is always a virtue, I think.'

Dear, good Almeria, thought Bel with a rush of affection, so perfectly formed to be a satisfactory parson's wife, quite unlike myself with my dreadful wish not to be put down, and my equally dreadful ability both to catch *double entendres* as well as to create them. What sort of man am I fit to be the wife of? I wonder. Francis Carey, I suppose, since he seems to be as disgracefully improper in his conduct and speech as I am in mine.

This untoward thought shocked her so dreadfully that she sat there with her mouth open. How could she even think such a thing? Why, she hated the monster, did she not? He thought her a lightskirt and worse, showed her no respect — no, not a whit — might be going to tell Almeria at any moment that she was not fit for decent society — indeed, she could not imagine why he had not had a private word to that effect with her already. . .and here she was, mooning about being his *wife*. Not only light in the head, but fit for Bedlam.

She had just consigned herself to a dank cell, and a bed of straw, with Almeria visiting her once a sennight, when her fevered imagination was soothed a little by the entry of the gentlemen, which if it did nothing else would put a stop to the inane conversation to which Lulsgate ladies, left on their own, were prone.

Bel had been brought up by an eccentric papa who had educated her as though she were a boy, and Aunt Kaye had been such a learned lady that she even knew Greek—which was the reason, she had once said sadly, that she had never married—and in her long-ago youth had been a pet of the great Dr Johnson himself, so that gushings about sweetly pretty bonnets and the unsatisfactory nature of servants had not come Bel's way until she had been settled in Lulsgate, and part of her attraction to Lady Almeria, and Almeria's to her, was because they were both rather out of the common run of women in their interests.

The gentlemen were all a little flushed, except for the two men of cloth, Philip and Henry, and the look on Lord Francis's face, Bel saw with a sinking heart, was even more devilish than the one he had worn at dinner. He was making straight for her, too, and she could feel Mrs Robey, and all the other women with pretty young daughters, bridling at his partiality for a widow, as he finally arrived by her side, said softly, 'You will allow, Mrs Merrick,' and pulled up a chair to sit by her, 'and perhaps you could persuade Almeria that a fresh pot of tea would serve to satisfy your humble servant's thirst.'

Your humble servant, indeed, thought Bel — what next? But she did as she was so politely bid. Almeria rang for more tea, and while he waited for it Francis Carey proceeded to tease Mrs Bel Merrick under the guise of paying her the most servile court.

Oh, if she had known she was going to pay for it in this coin, was Bel's inward response, she would have turned him out of Marianne's home without a thought, not tried to punish him for his insolence to her.

'You have relations in Lulsgate, I collect, Mrs Merrick, to cause you to settle here?'

'No, sir, not at all,' was her stiff reply. 'I have, unfortunately, virtually no close relatives since my aunt died.'

'No? Your husband had relatives here, then?'

Bel had always understood that it was grossly impolite to quiz people so closely on such matters, but perhaps, like many grandees, Lord Francis made his own manners.

'My husband had few relatives, sir, and none in Lulsgate. The reputation of the place attracted me.'

'Now there you do surprise me,' he said, bending forward confidentially, and fixing her with his hard grey eyes. 'I would have thought Lulsgate far too dull a town to attract such a high-stepper as yourself, and as to having no, or few, relations, I can hardly tell whether that would be a convenience or an inconvenience. It would depend on the relatives, one supposes. Some, as I am sure you are aware, might even be grossly inconvenient.'

'Since I have so few,' she parried spiritedly, 'it is difficult for me to tell. Now I do believe that you have a few inconvenient relatives yourself, or so I had heard, given to making unfortunate acquaintances, with unfortunate results.'

Lord Francis, accepting a cup of tea from his sister, who was up in the boughs with delight at the apparent sight of Bel and Francis on such splendid terms, chuckled drily at this, took a sip of his tea, shuddered, 'Too hot,' put it down, leaned forward again, and said, most intimately, 'Are you threatening me, Mrs Merrick? Most unwise.' And from the killing look he fixed on Bel Almeria was certain that her dream of wedding bells might yet come about.

'Threaten you?' said Bel innocently. 'Now how should I do that?'

She had no idea how the wicked spirit which was beginning to inform all her conversation with him had begun to alter her whole appearance. The slight flush on her ivory face, the sparkle in her eye, the charmingly satiric twist to her mouth were beginning to affect the man opposite to her in the most untoward fashion.

Francis Carey had begun his campaign against her with the decision that he would harden his heart against the harpy he judged her to be. He would desire her, lustfully, would feel nothing for her, but see her as a body to be won.

Alas, with every word which passed between them, his desire for her as a woman, rather than as an object to satisfy him sexually, grew the more.

Oh, he wanted the revenge he had promised

himself if he were ever fortunate enough to find her again, but more and more that revenge was beginning to take a different form from the one he had first contemplated. For he wanted her to respond to him in every way — yes, every way. He had for a moment considered exposing her to his sister once her supper guests had gone, but now he had decided that he would enjoy himself more in this dull backwater by taking on this mermaid at her own game, and beating her.

He had, after losing her, enquired of Marina St George and her reputation, but this woman was St George's best, he was sure. He had not heard that the great Marina was remarkably witty, but her sister certainly was. And clever enough to pass as an innocent, for he was quite sure from what Philip Harley had told him of her, in answer to his apparently idle questions, that she was not plying her trade in Lulsgate.

Presumably with what she had earned herself, and had inherited from her sister, she had acquired a fortune of a size large enough to keep her in comfort, for the time being, at least. He was also certain that the late Mr Merrick was a convenient invention, to confer an aura of respectability on her which she might not otherwise have possessed. Oh, he was going to enjoy himself in Lulsgate, that was for sure!

Bel could almost feel his thoughts, apparently respectful though his face was, for she read his body — and his eyes — and both were disrespectful after the subtlest fashion. How do I know such things? she thought, a little shocked at herself, for this was not the first occasion on which she had read men and women correctly, divining their real thoughts rather than their spoken ones. Had Marianne been able to do it? Was *that* why she had been such a great courtesan?

She avoided pursuing the matter further, and said swiftly to him, 'If you continue to direct your whole attention to me, sir, you may create criticism of yourself as well as of me, and I am sure that you do not wish that to occur, for Almeria's and Philip's sake, if not your own.'

Francis almost whistled. By God, she was shrewd as well, and recalled him to the proprieties. He rose, said to her, 'Oh, madam, you presume to teach me manners, such a highly qualified dominie as you are, but you are right. Provincial life is different from London life, and I must remember that. I will call on you tomorrow, madam, and we shall carry our acquaintanceship further; you may depend on that.'

It was a threat, Bel knew, but she had driven him from her successfully, and could breathe again. If that were so, however, why did she feel so desolate at the monster's going?

She watched him walk away, tall, with an air of such consequence and purpose that he dimmed every other man in the room. She was not yet aware that she performed the same disservice for all the women in the room — but Francis knew, as he knew of his own talents — and he looked forward to the future.

CHAPTER FIVE

BEL waited for Lord Francis Carey to call on her with a flutter of excitement gripping her in the oddest fashion. It seemed to be centred at the base of her stomach, and yet be able to spread at times to other, more embarrassing parts of her body. Mixed with this was a combination of fear and exhilaration. She feared to see him—but panted to see him.

The pleasantly dull tenor of her life in Lulsgate Spa, a dullness which had wrapped her round and comforted her since Marianne's death, had disappeared, presumably for as long as Francis Carey made his home with his sister. What surprised her most of all was that the fear that she might encounter him again, now that she had encountered him, had turned into something quite different, and infinitely complex.

She looked around her pleasant drawing-room, that haven of quiet which she had built for herself over two years. The little desk in the corner had come from Marianne's study, as had a large armchair; the rest was the pleasantly shabby furniture from her father's home at Brangton, even down to some of the religious tomes which sat in an alcove of bookshelves by the hearth, mixed in with more frivolous works like *The Spectre of Castle Ashdown* and *Emily Wray: A Sad History*—the last so unintentionally amusing that Almeria and she had laughed themselves into crying when reading it, so unlikely was Emily with her fictional trials.

Well, she was not Emily, whose one response to trouble was to faint upon the spot — Francis Carey would soon find *that* out; but all the same unease became the most powerful of her feelings as the day crawled by without him appearing. Oh, drat the man, why could he not get it over with?

For his part, Francis was in no hurry. Let the bitch wait; do her good to suffer, was his savagely uncharitable thought as he made a slow toilette and ate a late breakfast in his sister's breakfast-room, as pleasantly shabby in its own way as Bel's home.

Then he read a two-day-old *Times*, savouring the thought of Mrs Bel Merrick — he still did not know what her maiden name was. . .maiden name, a good joke that, he thought sardonically — waiting anxiously for him, perhaps even shedding a few tears. He laughed at himself and put down *The Times*. Bel Merrick, shed tears? Another joke, remembering the proudly defiant face which she had worn two years ago, and again last night when he had confronted her and mocked her during supper and after.

Like Bel, he had the feeling that life was going to be far from dull before he had madam beneath him, and it was certainly not going to be dull then, not at all. Strange that for the first time in years he was hot for a woman, and that woman a. . .Cyprian, a creature he had always avoided in the past. Well, he thought sardonically, Shakespeare was right again.

'We know what we are, but we know not what we may be.'

He pulled out his watch as Almeria came in, a child clutching at her skirts, watching him around them: his nephew, Frank, named after him.

'Hello, old fellow,' he said gently, putting out a hand so that Almeria might set the shy child on his knee, where he played happily with his uncle's watch. 'I thought,' he offered Almeria casually over the top of Frank's head, 'that I might pay your pretty little widow a visit.'

He was interested to see how Almeria brightened on hearing Bel spoken of. She had sunk into a chair opposite to him. She was wearing an apron, he noted, and was a far cry from the somewhat empty-headed but perfectly dressed beauty who had taken the London season by storm before accepting Philip Harley, the poorest of her many suitors, whom she had married against everyone's wishes and forebodings that it would not last.

They had not known how strong-minded and loving Almeria was. 'I am jam-making later on,' she said. 'Cook is getting old, needs a helping hand and I do not like being idle while others work. Oh, Francis, I should not say so — Philip would say that I was interfering — but I am so happy that you and Bel appear to be at ins. She is the dearest friend I have ever had, despite the difference in our ages. Her mind is so good. You will ask her to join us on our trip to Beacon Hill tomorrow, will you not? She would enjoy a jaunt there in your curricle, always providing the weather is fine.'

Francis had the grace to feel a little ashamed,

would have liked to say, perhaps, Her mind is the only *good* thing about her, but refrained, showing Frank how the watch opened, and even revealing its workings. Frank loved the little wheels he saw, and said so.

'I remember,' said Francis, amused at the small boy's solemn scrutiny, 'how when I was Frank's age poor Jack showed me his watch, and how it delighted me,' which was a way of avoiding discussion of Bel Merrick, he knew, and served to divert Almeria.

'Jack grows no better, then,' she said quietly.

'Not at all, and never will.' Francis was short. 'And more's the pity. He is a good fellow, and both his wife and son needed the guiding hand he would be giving them — particularly Marcus, who is more outrageous than ever. When he heard I was to visit you, he talked a little wildly of coming here himself — with some of his more disreputable friends, I suppose. Said he would not put you to the trouble of giving him a room, would go to the White Peacock.'

'Nice to see him at all,' said Almeria, who loved Marcus for all his harum-scarum ways, she not knowing the worst of him.

'And now I must be going.' Francis retrieved his watch from his nephew, put him gently down. He was so surprisingly good and patient with children, thought Almeria regretfully, he really ought to have some of his own. All his haughty pride disappeared when he was with them.

Francis was not thinking of children as he strolled through Lulsgate Spa, noting the Baths, the Assembly Rooms, a small classically fronted building with a vague stone god standing in front of it. Vague, because no one knew who the god was supposed to be. The less reputable but still charming house, where a private club in which one might game was established—public gaming houses being forbidden by law—also interested him, and he promised himself a visit—in the intervals between persecuting Mrs Merrick, that was.

Her own house, built early in the eighteenth century, was small by the standards of the vicarage and some others, he noted, but obviously perfectly kept, which was not surprising, as she was so perfectly kept herself, he thought with a somewhat savage grin at the pun. He knew that his savagery, if contained, was never far from the surface, and he thought—nay, hoped—that the hint of it, plus a hint of wildness which he thought he detected in the St George's sister, would give salt to their encounters. To his horror he found his breath shortening at the very thought. No, he must at all times be in control; one slip and the tigress would have him, and not the other way about.

The conceit amused him. Two tigers prowling, the one around the other. His fists clenched a little. How had the tigress convinced Almeria that she was only a pussycat?

No matter; he stared at the knocker in the shape of a grinning imp before rattling it sharply, and then standing back, to be admired in all his London finery by a passing group, who rightly identified him as a gentleman of consequence, come to grace Lulsgate Spa.

* * *

Bel was in a fine old taking when she heard the knocker go. She was stitching at her canvas work, a charming design of yellow roses, to be a cushion cover to enhance her battered old sofa. It had been Mrs Broughton's turn to read aloud, and she was sitting in front of the garden window, reading not an improving work — Mrs Broughton had no mind for improving works, nor talent for reading them aloud — but a charming piece of froth entitled *Lady Caroline's Secret*.

Mrs Broughton, who was a woman of sound common sense when not reading sentimental novels, was so distressed by Lady Caroline's ridiculous secret, and the absurd lengths to which she went to keep it, that she could barely restrain her sobs as she read of them. Bel could hardly restrain her laughter. Having a few real secrets of her own, she could not take Lady Caroline seriously, but could scarcely inform Mrs Broughton of that interesting fact.

The sound of the knocker, while distressing her in one way, saved her face in another. She really must pass poor Caroline on to Almeria — she would enjoy her for sure — but in the meantime here undoubtedly was the monster come to attack her.

She compelled herself to sit still, to yawn a little even, one graceful hand before her mouth as the maid of all work came in.

'Gemmun to see you, mum. Are you in?' A pair of phrases which it had taken Lottie a week to teach her, so shy was she.

'Indeed, pray admit him. He did not give his name?'

'It was Lord Francis something, I think, mum.'

'Oh, how too delightful!' exclaimed Mrs Broughton, who was always impressed by a lord. 'So flattering of him to visit us so soon!' She put down *Lady Caroline's Secret*. Real life suddenly attracted her more.

Both women rose to meet him. He was as splendid as ever, Bel noted, his tailcoat today a deep charcoal and his trousers charcoal also, but of a lighter hue. By his expression, one of power contained, he was out for blood, and, if so, she was ready to meet him, supported as she was by the presence of Mrs Broughton.

'Charge, Chester, charge! On, Stanley, on,' she thought in the words of Sir Walter Scott, only to remember the next bit of the quotation, 'Were the last words of Marmion.' Well, they were not going to be *her* last words, by no means, and the small defiant smile which her face bore as she thought this was noted by her enemy.

So, madam was prepared to fight, was she? Good!

'Ladies,' he said, bowing, 'pray be seated. I am come to renew a friendship, newly made. Delighted to see you both again. In good health—industrious too, I see.' His sardonic gaze encompassed Bel's tapestry.

Bel and Mrs Broughton made suitable noises in answer to this, his splendour and address, Bel noticed wryly, quite overcoming Mrs Broughton: she obviously thought him one of the Minerva Press's heroes come to life.

'I am not always the industrious one,' she answered, happy to find something innocuous of which to speak. 'Today it is Mrs Broughton's turn to read to me. We were just palpitating together over the happy accident that the hooded stranger Lady Caroline met on a glacier high in the Swiss Alps turned out to be her true father, whom she had never before met. You may imagine the affecting scenes which followed, almost melting the snow and ice in which they were set!'

If Bel could not prevent her wicked spirit from displaying itself, even to this odious nobleman whom she had decided she could not abide, then Francis Carey could not help giving a delighted crack of laughter at this piece of satire.

'Oh, now I see how you won Almeria over!' he exclaimed. 'By sharing her delight in reading such novels, but equally her appreciation of their many absurdities.'

Won Almeria over! He made her sound a worse plotter than dastardly Guido Frontini, Lady Caroline's villainous pursuer; but her reply to him was gentle.

'Quite so, and you, I had not thought you to be a devotee of the Gothic novel, Lord Francis. Blue books and red boxes are more in your line, surely?'

Better and better, thought Francis. It will be a pleasure to overcome such a learned doxy. Madam has received a good education, somehow, somewhere. It will be an equal pleasure, perhaps, to discover how.

Aloud he said smoothly, 'Blue books and red boxes are sometimes so exquisitely boring, Mrs Merrick, that relaxation is required — and then I was wont to raid Almeria's bookshelves, and the habit still endures. One cannot be constantly austere in one's reading. Even the great Dr Johnson once wrote a novel.'

'Oh, *Rasselas*,' said Bel carelessly, as much to inform Mrs Broughton, who looked a little surprised at this news, as to display her own learning, although the delightfully sardonic quirk of Lord Francis's right eyebrow served to inform her that he was perfectly aware of that learning. 'But hardly in the line of the Minerva Press. Where are the Italian Alps, the ruined castles. . .the heroine disputing with the climate in quite the wrong turn-out?'

Mrs Broughton was vaguely distressed. 'I thought,' she trembled, 'that you enjoyed what I was reading to you, dear Bel. Perhaps you would prefer something a little more serious in the future,' and she looked with regret at poor Lady Caroline, now face-down on an occasional table.

Bel's, 'Not at all, I find them most enjoyable,' was followed by Francis's comment, meant particularly for her,

'Better she disputed with the climate, madam, than with the hero. Heroes and heroines should never be at odds. Unlike their real-life counterparts, where odds are more common than evens — as you, I know, are well aware.'

Oh, dear, he is at it again, was Bel's inward comment to that. Not only will it be difficult for me to keep a straight face if he goes on, but I shall find myself responding to him in the same coin, and perhaps even Mrs Broughton will notice what we are doing.

'Oh, real life and novels are always different,

Lord Francis,' she explained, as one to an idiot, 'since in them everything is resolved at the end, and that is rarely true in life, there being no end there, except the obvious one which we shall not mention.'

'No, indeed,' he replied instantly. 'Happy to learn that you understand that. It will make matters between us so much easier if we know where we stand. You agree to that, I hope?'

'In that, if nothing else, we are in agreement,' she answered smartly. 'Plain speaking is always better. A little more of it and Lady Caroline would not be in such a pelter.'

'You really wish it?' he said, eyes wicked. 'Plain speaking? Would you wish some informed plain speaking from me, Mrs Merrick? That would remove misunderstanding, I am sure, but would it be wise?'

Oh, damn him, damn him. She knew now why he was a diplomat, so rapid in his responses, so pointed in them, but the poison disguised so neatly beneath the sugar.

Fortunately for Bel, Mrs Broughton was as charmingly and blindly amiable as she was kind and useful as a companion and watchdog, literal-minded to a fault, and she saw nothing untoward in the veiled exchanges going on between her mistress and her visitor. On the contrary, she thought how splendidly well they were doing together, and after a few more exchanges of a like nature she thought to further Bel's interests by saying eagerly, 'You are interested in gardens, Lord Francis? I saw your eyes wander to the view outside. Perhaps you would like dear Bel to show you around hers; it is a little gem, and all due to her exertions. She makes a delightful sight, potting plants, I do assure you.'

'Oh, you need not assure me, Mrs Broughton. I can quite imagine it—seeing that Mrs Merrick is a delightful sight at all times, and all. . .places.' And his dreadful eyes caressed her. 'I should be delighted to have such an. . .experienced guide to lay the delights of her. . .garden before me.'

Bel privately damned Mrs Broughton. She had absolutely no wish to be alone with Lord Francis, either in a garden or anywhere else, where his conversation would, no doubt, become even more pointed; but there was, in politeness, nothing for it.

She rose, said, resignedly, 'If you really wish to study the delights of nature, Lord Francis, then I will be your guide,' and led the way through the open doors—to Purgatory, doubtless—where else?

Bel's garden was large enough to have pleasant flowerbeds in the new informal style which was becoming popular, a small glass-house and, through an archway, a kitchen garden with a south-facing wall. James, her gardener, who came in several days a week—she shared him with other like-minded ladies—provided salad stuffs, vegetables, and fruit from the cordons on the warm wall.

They strolled at first among the flowers in full view of a beaming Mrs Broughton who could already hear wedding bells as she watched them engaged in apparently amiable conversation. Had she been nearer, she would have retreated in shocked dismay.

At first, all was proper, Lord Francis saying nothing but um and ah, as Bel gave him a short lecture on her plants, showering him with Latin names and erudite horticultural information. If his expression was even more sardonic than usual, his haughtiness a little more in evidence, they were shielded from Mrs Broughton by the fact that his head was bent to gaze, apparently admiringly, at Bel.

He had to confess that she made the most charming picture. She was clad in a simple cream dress of fine muslin with a faint amber stripe running through it. The collar was chastely high; in fact the whole of Bel's turn-out apparently sought to convince the beholder of its wearer's extreme sense of virtue. Even the red-gold curls, which he remembered as riotous in London, had been carefully confined, and the luminous green eyes were modestly veiled, and did not flash fire until he became too provoking.

Francis decided to be provoking.

He was admiring a small goldfish pond, and Bel had begun a short lecture on the care and feeding of fish, designed less to inform him than to keep him from speaking, when he leaned forward, took her by the arm, and said gently, 'You make a most damnably desirable spectacle, my dear Mrs Merrick; allow me to desire it in a little more privacy,' and he led her firmly towards the archway into the kitchen garden, away from Mrs Broughton's interested eyes, where they would be quite alone.

'So,' said Bel, who had been hoping that he might have changed his mind about her after seeing her with his sister and in the chaste confines of her home, 'by your language — for you would not speak so to a lady — you still consider me a. . .lightskirt.'

'Oh, come,' he mocked. 'Plain speaking, you said; we both know exactly what you are, and for the moment it is our little secret.' He was still walking her towards the kitchen garden, adding, 'I must confess that if it gives me greater access to you I prefer early plums and late lettuces to goldfish — though had you a mermaid in your pond I would have admired that. But the only mermaid in Lulsgate Spa at the moment is your good self, whose company I propose to enjoy until the weather changes.'

He released her, but not before he had turned her towards him, 'To enjoy the view more easily,' he informed her with lazy hauteur.

Bel stepped even further away from him; to her horror she found that his lightest touch had the most disastrous effect on her, and the sight of him so near to her was even worse. She supposed that it was fear which was causing her to tremble and her whole body to ache, not yet knowing that quite another emotion was affecting her.

He smiled and narrowed the distance between them again, his grey eyes glittering. Bel's breathing shortened still more, but she could not retreat further; she would end up inside the row of lettuces if she did.

'Why are you here?' she enquired hoarsely. 'What is the true purpose of your visit?'

'Ah, so we arrive at the meat of the matter, madam, no prevarications. It may have escaped your memory, but we had a bargain, my dear Mrs Merrick.'

'A bargain?' Bel kept her voice steady with difficulty.

'Yes, my dear houri. A bargain, freely offered by you, not by me. I was to. . .instruct you, you remember, in exchange for certain papers. I am here to. . .fulfil that bargain.'

'I did not mean——' she began, heart thudding, fear of him, she was beginning to realise, mixed with a most dreadful desire, so that she was almost mesmerised by the sound of his voice, a beautiful one, exquisitely modulated, used to command and also to enchant, although Bel was not aware that he had done little enchanting with it of recent years.

'You "did not mean"? of course you *meant*. You meant to make a fool of me, leaving me staring at a deserted house like gaby. No, I will teach you, slowly, not to make bargains which you do not intend to keep, and I hope to enjoy that charming body, usually reserved for those who pay you well — without paying you anything.'

Bel licked her lips, tried to pull her wits into some sort of order, for this was worse than she had feared, and said, as the thought struck her, 'You could gain your revenge so easily. Why have you not informed your sister — oh, not of the truth, but what you mistakenly think is the truth?'

'Tell her who and what you are, you mean? The courtesan with a blackmailer and usurer for a sister, she using her charms in bed to cheat and deceive as you used them out of bed to cheat me, with promises you never intended to keep?'

His lip curled; he was enjoying the distress he could tell she was suffering beneath her brave front.

'Yes,' said Bel, suddenly fierce, showing spirit. 'One sentence is all that is needed; why not say it?'

'Because I wish to enjoy myself. . .and you. You humiliated me, madam, and I have carried the memory around with me for the last two years. Oh, sometimes I forgot, and then at the most inopportune moment I would remember; see you again, mocking me. Oh, you roused me, dear Mrs Merrick, as you well know, held me off with promises, sobbing about your sister's death. I should have remembered how truly hard-hearted courtesans are. Now I shall make promises to you which *I* intend to keep. When I think fit I shall tell my sister exactly what I have discovered you are, a lightskirt who plies for hire most viciously; but when and where I choose to do that, and how long I shall take, I shall not tell you. . .you must live in delightful anticipation. . .as I did.'

'And which of us is the more vicious, sir, tell me that?' And then, 'No, you cannot do this. You do not know. . .you are cruel, so cruel.'

'Yes, I am cruel, rightly so.' And he laughed grimly. 'And what is it that I do not know? Pray tell me. I need to know everything about you, as I intend to make you keep the bargain you made with me — eventually — lest you betray poor Marcus, as your sister did.'

'I am not what you think.' Bel offered this sturdily, not apologetically. 'I am quite innocent, not a Cyprian at all.'

Lord Francis looked her up and down, and she followed suit by so scanning him. He was delighted at the sight, for winning a spiritless whore would have been no pleasure. The cool perfection of that lovely face, framed in its light curls — some of which had escaped from the severe style in which she had bound her hair—the careful and tasteful toilette—all presented to the world a model of apparent virtue.

'Oh, you are exactly what I think you are—' and his lip curled '—a whited sepulchre, a worm on the rose of this small town, not because you are a whore, no, not at all, but because you pretend to be what you are not. You are dishonest, madam.'

'And you are vile,' retorted Bel, 'to conduct a. . .' and she remembered, such a strange memory, *The Nun of Torelli* '. . . vendetta. Yes, you are vile even were I the creature you think I am, doubly vile because I am innocent. Oh, you are like all men, to despise what all men use and pay for. You flaunt yourself as virtuous, walk where you please, remain respected, while condemning those with whom you take your pleasure to be unconsidered outcasts.'

'I repeat: your trade is not what I protest, but the dishonesty with which you plied it—and your pretence of virtue.'

'No pretence,' flashed Bel, and suddenly was steady, a rock, her own fists clenched as she had seen his were—and why was that? 'I will not consent to this. It is war, sir, war, with no quarter. I will give you nothing.'

'On the contrary, by the time that all is over you will give me everything, beg me to take it, and I will debate whether I wish to do so.'

Oh, but she was gallant, and his fists were clenched because were he to do what he so desperately wished he would be upon her, to compel her at once to give him what he so dearly wanted. He must make her beg, if only to stop himself from doing so!

'Come,' he said—he could not prevent himself, 'a foretaste,' and before she could stop him she was in his arms and he was kissing her, and she was responding, madly, wildly, against all sense, all reason, until, remembering where they were, with Mrs Broughton perhaps beginning to wonder what they were doing, he pushed her away.

'No dishonesty there on my part. You know why I want you—and you, were you practising your usual arts—or were you being honest too?'

He held out his arm, and perforce she took it, so that when they came into view again he was passing on to her his sister's invitation to the picnic on Beacon Hill, 'and Mrs Broughton, of course,' he finished, giving that lady a gallant bow which had her admiring him all over again. 'I look forward to seeing you both; I shall call for you at eleven of the clock.' For he had told Bel he would brook no denial, and she dared not offend him, lest he tell Almeria her secret straight away.

'So charming, so gracious,' gushed Mrs Broughton when he had taken his leave. 'If only all fine gentlemen were like him!'

And thank God that they are not, was Bel's response to that, but so steady was she, so much herself, that nothing of her distress showed.

One art she was rapidly learning was that of consummate self-control, and she thanked Lord Francis for that, if nothing else.

CHAPTER SIX

As HE walked back to the vicarage, Francis Carey's thoughts were a strange mixture of an almost savage pleasure, frustrated desire and, astonishingly enough for such an arrogant, self-assured man, a feeling which was almost shame.

Nonsense, he told himself firmly, she deserves all that I care to hand out to her; but he was almost relieved when he reached the Harleys' to discover such a brouhaha that it was enough to drive Bel Merrick temporarily out of his head.

Little Frank ran to meet him, pulling at his hand, three-year-old Caroline toddling behind. Frank was holding a miniature wooden horse, and Caroline was dragging a new rag doll behind her. 'Oh, Uncle Francis!' exclaimed his nephew. 'Ain't it jolly, Cousin Mark has come, with presents; now we shall have some famous times!' for heedless Cousin Mark was quite naturally a roaring favourite with equally heedless small fry.

Francis lifted little Frank up, walked into the drawing-room to discover Marcus sitting there, as carelessly turned out as ever, hair and stock awry, drinking port while Philip Harley drank water, and Almeria was exclaiming, 'No, really!' and, 'Never say so, Mark!' at every other sentence.

'Oh, there you are, Uncle,' cried Marcus, as though the last time the two had met they had parted as bosom bows, and not, as usual, at daggers drawn over Marcus's ever-growing debts. 'I'm sure that you'll be pleased to hear that I have decided to come and retrench in the countryside, leaving Town to improve my financial situation as well as my health. I am at the White Peacock with a couple of friends, have no mind to add to poor Almeria's expenses,' ignoring the fact that he had already added to them, since Almeria had just asked him to bring his friends along to dinner.

'I have been asking whether there are any pretty young girls here, with good competences,' he rattled on gaily. 'The pretty part is essential, the competence would be an added virtue. Almeria informs me that, while there is no one here to rival Miss Coutts in terms of the available tin, there are some quite decent belles, including of all things a pretty young widow with more than a competence, but she's saying hands off to that — reserved for you, I gather.'

Now why should that careless reference to Bel Merrick make Francis clench his fists and want to strike his inoffensive nephew? For it was Bel whom he did not want to be exploited, he oddly discovered, not Marcus whom he felt should need protection!

He stared coldly at his nephew. Did this idle lounger really resemble himself? He supposed he did. They both possessed the same grey eyes, dark hair, and somewhat straight mouth. But where Francis was severe, Marcus was slack; where Francis looked like a grave Roman senator of the old school on a coin, Marcus rather resembled a dissolute young Roman emperor in the last days of that Empire's decline. Not that Marcus was vicious, Francis decided wearily, simply idle and stupid, the spoiled son of a silly mother.

'And who are these friends you are inflicting on us?' he enquired sternly.

'Oh, jolly good fellows both,' said Marcus rapidly, knowing quite well that his uncle was bound to dislike them. 'Rhys Howell, lately a captain in the Lifeguards, and Fred Carnaby—you know Fred, he was in the Diplomatic himself until recently.'

'As well I know,' remarked Francis glacially, 'until he was sent home for drunkenness and mislaying important dispatches. Hardly the sort of friend to bring here.'

'Well, too late now,' said Marcus cheerfully. 'Invitation already gone out.'

'And Howell, so-called captain,' pursued Francis determinedly, like a confounded dog with a juicy bone, thought his nephew irreverently. 'I have heard nothing good of him. A man is known by the company he keeps, Marcus, and your company is not nice.'

'You have forgotten what it is to be young, sir.'

'Oh, come, Mark,' interjected Almeria, trying to keep the peace. 'Thirty-four is hardly old, and you are already twenty-four yourself. Francis is right to wish you to settle down.'

'I'll make a promise,' said Marcus earnestly, who had made many promises before, and never kept one of them. 'If I find a splendid young woman here, I promise to pop the question and settle down myself—in Lulsgate Spa, perhaps! Will that do, sir?'

Francis regarded him with distaste. Perhaps he ought to throw him to Bel Merrick; it was all the young fool deserved. Question was, did she deserve him? And what an odd question that was to ask himself, he thought crossly.

'And I am to meet the pretty widow and some of the Lulsgate belles soon,' continued Mark, 'for Almeria has asked us all to accompany her on the trip to Beacon Hill tomorrow, and fortunate it is that I have brought my curricle with me. If I fall on my knees and say, Pretty please, Almeria, my angel, may I escort the charming young widow?'

'No,' said Francis coldly, before Almeria could answer Marcus, 'you may not, for I have already asked her to accompany me, and you are not a safe enough whip to escort any young woman. Confine yourself to conveying your disreputable friends about Leicestershire. Their loss, should you over-turn the curricle and them, would not be felt by their relatives or by society.' He turned to his half-sister. 'If you will excuse me, I will leave you to change for dinner.'

'And what's the matter with him?' exclaimed Marcus frankly, when his uncle had left them. 'What burr sits under his saddle? Pretty widow not coming up to scratch? More chance for me, then. Think I'll change myself.' And he left whistling a cheerful tune, the words of which were not known to Almeria, and just as well, thought Philip, giving his wife an absent kiss as she rolled her eyes at him, not knowing which gave her the vapours most, silly young Marcus, or his unbending uncle.

One reason for wanting Francis to marry Bel was

that she might take some of the starch out of him—
but it would not do to say so!

Bel, waiting for Francis to arrive the next morning,
was quite unaware that the plot was thickening as
yet more actors arrived on the scene. Mrs
Broughton beside her was all of a delighted flutter.
Francis had said that he would come for them in the
Harleys' carriage, and Bel would then be transferred
to his curricle, the Harleys' coachman taking over
the responsibility of the carriage in which Mrs
Broughton would sit with the Harley family. Henry
Venn was driving his mother and Mrs Robey in
their carriage, and several other equipages of varying age and fashionability would make up the party.

Fortunately the day was fine, and even if Bel's
spirits were a little low at the prospect of being
persecuted by a haughty nobleman all day, the other
prospect of a picnic and a stroll in good countryside
could still attract. She would not allow him to
destroy the pleasure which she had come to feel in
living at Lulsgate Spa.

But he behaved himself perfectly when he
arrived, handed Mrs Broughton in, and later out of,
the carriage in fine style, and confided in them both
that his and Almeria's nephew, Marcus Carey,
Viscount Tawstock, had arrived with friends, and
would be accompanying them on their jaunt.

Marcus Carey, the young fool who had proposed
to Marianne and to whom she had been lending
money! And what would *his* friends be like?

They were all assembled in Almeria's drawing-
room, congratulating themselves on the fineness of

the weather. Francis's hand was firmly on Bel's arm when he led her in, as though she might be about to desert him again at any moment, and she knew at once which of the three men whom she had never seen before was Marcus, the blurred likeness to Francis was so strong.

Marcus's candid appreciation of her when he was introduced did a little to mollify the spirits which Francis's treatment had wounded.

'Why, you dog, Uncle, is that what brought you to Lulsgate?' And he bent over Bel's hand with as much gallantry as he could muster, straightening up to stare at her in admiration, adding, 'We have not met before, I know, but I have the feeling, almost, that we have. You have a sister, perhaps? You certainly possess the look of someone I have known, but I should never have forgotten that divine shade of red-gold hair had I met it before!'

Bel could almost feel Francis's sardonic and mocking stare at Marcus's artless words. She was well aware that, although she had not greatly resembled Marianne in looks, there had been an indefinable resemblance between them—something in the expression, perhaps?—and that Marcus had seen it!

She judged it politic merely to smile; anything she said would be a lie, and, worse, might hang her later—and then she was being introduced to two men whom she instinctively knew were Marcus's toad-eaters, mere hangers-on whom only Marcus's presence there could have brought into the vicarage.

Fred Carnaby was nothing, but, unworldly though she was, she disliked Captain Rhys Howell on sight—and did not know why. He was handsome in an easy, obvious fashion, quite unlike Francis's severe and harsh haughtiness, and his manner was as warm and soothing as Francis's was abrasive. He held her hand a trifle too long, smiled a little too easily, and she decided that she disliked soft blue eyes and curly blond hair. Besides, by his manner, she thought, Captain Howell was a deal too fond of himself, and did not need anyone else to be fond of him.

But she was all courtesy, and when Francis had handed her into his curricle, a beautiful thing, picked out in chocolate and cream, drawn by two matched chestnuts, and they were starting off towards Beacon Hill, Cassius up behind them, he said coolly to her as he manoeuvred her through the light traffic of Lulsgate's main street, 'A lady of great discretion, I see. First to be such a diplomat when Marcus committed his unintended gaffe, and then your reception of the dubious captain—I must congratulate you. Such *savoir-faire*. A pity that you did not choose to settle in London; you could have gone much further than your sister, been a great man's public ladybird, the queen of the *demimonde*, no less.'

'Am I supposed to be flattered by that?' said Bel curtly. 'Your compliment is as dubious as the captain's.'

'Keep on remembering what you are is my advice,' was his only reply, 'for, resourceful though you are, I hardly think you carry enough armament to keep the captain in order. And now shall we declare a truce? I have a mind to enjoy my day in the sun,' and the look he gave her as he said this was so warm and caressing that it altered his whole face, transforming it so that Bel had a powerful and sad wish that she could have met him in different circumstances, and then their whole intercourse could have been different, too.

She shook herself mentally, said coolly, 'If you wish. I have no desire to distress Almeria, who is goodness itself, and Philip also deserves consideration, to say nothing of the children.'

This last sentence gave her a pang. She dearly loved little Frank and Caroline, who in return loved Aunt Bel, and the pang grew worse as she suddenly thought that this renewed meeting with Lord Francis Carey might yet mean that she would have to fly Lulsgate and give up the happy life which she had created for herself.

'Good,' said Francis, and then applied himself to driving, for the roads around Lulsgate were not good, and this part of Leicestershire, near Charnwood Forest, was a little hilly — 'For we are not so far from the Pennines, after all,' he remarked, smartly negotiating a difficult corner.

'I suppose you are what they call a whip,' offered Bel, who had, much against her will, been admiring the whole athletic picture which he presented.

'After a fashion,' he returned lazily. 'I have no pretence to being a name in any way. My life has been too busy for me to indulge myself in following fashion's dictates — I have never wanted to rival a coachman on the road or a pugilist in the ring. They are the pursuits of men without occupation. Merely to do ordinary things well is an aim worth following.'

Bel was suddenly determined to know more of him. 'And your occupation—what was, or is that?'

'At the moment,' he returned, 'I am a diplomat of sorts. I was at the Paris Embassy, but I have been recalled to act in an advisory capacity at the Foreign Office, a duty which is neither here nor there, and if that is what I am doomed to then I shall seek other duties. I suppose I ought to sit for Parliament at the next election and find my future there. The idea does not particularly attract.'

'And you have always been a diplomat?' Bel was curious. Something about his athleticism, the habit of command strong in his voice, had suggested quite otherwise.

'Oh, I see why you, and she, were so successful,' he remarked, breaching their truce a little. 'This gentle interest in a man's affairs, flattering as well as soothing. No,' he said hastily, seeing her expression grow stormy, 'I will answer you. I was in the navy, until there was no ship for me—was seconded to the admiralty, and from thence, by degrees, ended up in my present position.'

'The navy!' exclaimed Bel. It explained so much about him. His cold certainty—she could imagine him commanding a crew of recalcitrant sailors, quelling them with a look. 'Did you see action in any of the great battles in the recent wars?' and her voice was as eager as a boy's, not a girl's. 'Lord Nelson was quite my favourite hero. I used to dream of running away to sea and being a midshipman!'

'And a deuced hard life you would have found it,' was his answer to that, giving her a surprised glance on hearing this unlikely revelation. 'I was at

Trafalgar, and allow me to tell you that sea battles are most unpleasant things, not romantic at all. You are better reading of them with Almeria, rather than taking part.'

'All the interesting doings in life are reserved for the male sex,' remarked Bel, a little aggrieved, 'such as being a sailor, driving a curricle, or a thousand other things. We are left with such milk-and-water occupations as sewing and tatting, no comparison at all!'

'But so much safer,' riposted Francis, using his whip to touch his horses lightly to make them turn more tightly than they wished. 'One rarely ends up with one's head removed by a cannon-ball while making baby-clothes.'

Bel could not help giving a fat chuckle at this. She had a vision of herself and Almeria sitting decorous in the vicarage drawing-room, dodging bullets, balls and grenades. Could one dodge them? She thought not. They 'arrived', one supposed, willy-nilly. She remarked so to Francis, who, rapidly looking sideways at her, registered a pang at the sight of her vivid face.

'Indeed, you are perceptive to understand that — there is no avoiding them — and I may add that driving a curricle is not the easiest thing in life. There are daring ladies who do, although most confine themselves to perch, or ladies' phaetons.'

Bel had a vision of herself, seated behind a pair of milk-white unicorns — for if one were using one's imagination one could surely imagine that — driving a curricle whose body was silver gilt, rubies set in

the wheels, and the harness gold cord, and all the
metal connected with it silver and gold, too.

Her face took on such an expression of pure
happiness that Francis, despite himself, was
touched. How did she do it? He had met many
ladybirds, and not one of them could assume that
look of enchanting innocence.

The day pleased Bel as well; the sun was at its
kindest, golden and warm, with the faintest hint of
mist in the distance taming the summer's heat. The
greenery which surrounded them had achieved its
final perfection before it began to fall into a golden
or dull-ochre decay, the grasses becoming straw,
losing their lushness.

Beacon Hill now rose before them. They were
not to mount in their various carriages to the top,
but to draw up on a flattish meadow at its base; last
of all to be wheeled into position was the landau
which contained the cold collation and the servants
who would prepare and lay it out for them, once
their masters had taken their pleasure, either by
sitting in the shade or strolling up to the top to look
out across the countryside towards Cold Ashby in
Northamptonshire where the previous beacon to
herald the Armada's coming had been lit, or north-
wards to the next.

'Stirring days, were they not?' remarked Bel to
Francis, after his tiger had handed her down, and
he had taken her arm, most proprietorially, she
noticed. Anyone watching them would have
assumed that Lord Francis Carey was indeed smitten by the widow's charms.

'And fortunate that the great Elizabeth and her

sea captains won,' was Francis's answer, 'seeing that
if they had not done so we should hardly be jaunting
here — or might be speaking Spanish at the very
least.'

'Only think,' said Bel, 'it would have been in the
Channel that you won your spurs — if naval captains
win spurs — and not Trafalgar, if you had lived then.'

'Spurs are for knights,' said Francis, 'of whom I
am not one, not sailors.' And was that a reminder
of their true situation? thought Bel, but she deter-
mindedly made nothing of it, particularly when little
Frank, happy to be free again, came running to his
uncle.

'You will give me a ride in your curricle one day,
will you not, Uncle Frank?' he exclaimed. 'Perhaps
you would let me sit on Aunt Bel's knee? She is
quite my favourite aunt,' he went on, 'even if she is
not a true one — a friend-aunt, Mama says. Perhaps — ' and he screwed his eyes up at his daring
' — you would make her a real aunt, and then I could
have her all the time. Oh,' he said sadly, 'Mama
told me not to say that to you, Uncle Francis, and
now I have forgot — but,' brightening, 'I am sure
you do not mind,' and he ran off again, his legs
itching, his mama later said, after being confined in
the carriage during their longish journey.

Bel, all blushes at the little boy's artless remarks,
hardly dared to look at Francis, particularly when
he remarked drily, 'You have won one male animal
of the Carey family over, Mrs Bel Merrick, that is
plain to see.'

Pricked, she could not help retorting, 'Oh,
indeed? I thought, by your behaviour, that I had

won two. One hardly pursues with such determination those to whom we are indifferent!'

Where all this was coming from Bel did not know. Ever since she had first met him, two years ago, she had begun to change from the milk-and-water creature who had gone to London and who had nearly been extinguished by the revelation of Marianne's career. The speed of change had slowed down during her time at Lulsgate, but since Francis had arrived so dramatically in her life again its pace had increased equally dramatically. There was something about him to which she responded, and whether that would have been so if she had met him as the respectable unknowing young lady she had once been she had no means of knowing. She only knew that in order to cope with him at all she needed all her wits about her, and those wits were sharpened every time she met him.

Marcus was approaching, Miss Robey on his arm, and Captain Howell with another pretty young thing on his — Kate Thomson, a manufacturer's daughter, visiting Lulsgate with her clergywoman aunt, and part of Almeria's circle in consequence, the clergywoman's late husband having been Philip's tutor at Oxford. And a less suitable partner than Captain Howell for a virtuous young woman Bel could not think of, but she assumed that Marcus had done the introductions and Almeria was helpless before them.

'Ah, Carey,' murmured Captain Howell, 'you had a good journey here, the roads not too tricky for a good whip?' And he waved a negligent hand at his own rather showy phaeton. 'And now for a walk to see the panorama—I am assured by the ladies that it is worth subjecting oneself to the sun and the insects to enjoy it. We shall shortly find out.'

Even his most innocuous remarks, thought Bel, appeared disagreeable when offered with such oily knowingness. She could almost feel Francis stiffen when addressed so familiarly by such a toad-eater, but there was nothing for it, and it was really, thought Bel unkindly, a little amusing to think that for once the great Francis Carey was being put down, even if she had to thank such a cad for doing so!

Almost as though he had divined her thoughts, Francis gave her arm a light pressure, similar, Bel thought, to that which he applied with his whip to his horses, saying, 'Shall we find our own way to the top, Mrs Merrick? Will Mrs Broughton allow you out of her sight? Surely in such a public view, with such a large party, I may be allowed to escort a young gentlewoman without adverse comment.'

Even as he spoke, Mrs Broughton walked towards them, fanning herself, her face already scarlet; being somewhat plump, she felt the heat of the day more than a little.

'You will forgive me if I do not accompany you both, but I wish to rest; the sun afflicts me, and I may help Lady Almeria with the collation. She needs to oversee it, she says, and I am to bid you to be back not later than two. The servants have placed the wine bottles in the stream, and the sandwiches will be greasy if you delay overlong. You may tell me of the view when you return, Bel. Philip, who has already set out, has promised to sketch it for me.'

Matchmaking, matchmaking, thought Bel of Mrs Broughton and dear Almeria both; if only you knew the truth! Almeria—Frank and Caroline running about her—waved her hand to them and made shooing motions in the direction of the path up the hill. Henry Venn, a disconsolate look on his face, his mother by his side, proprietorial as usual, was apparently about to escort the Harley children to the top, in default of being allowed Bel.

'I like my niece and nephew,' remarked Francis, as they set off, 'but feeling as I do they would be distinctly *de trop*. I shall endeavour to make up for my defection later. Almeria has packed a cricket bat and ball so that we may have some lively entertainment when we have recovered from luncheon, or nuncheon—I am not sure what one calls what one consumes at two in the afternoon, in the open.'

'A new word is needed, perhaps,' suggested Bel, as they began their upward march after Marcus and his companions, who could be heard laughing and talking together, Kate and Miss Robey not finding Captain Howell and his witticisms as unlikeable as Bel did. She was aware that, since discovering what Marianne had become, her knowledge of the world had increased so greatly that she could never again be so young and innocent as they were.

Curiously, the knowledge did not depress her. Young women ought not to be kept in the same state as fools, she decided, and this redoubled her intention not to be cowed by Lord Francis Carey. Not that he was doing much cowing of her at the moment, and when they reached the top of the hill, where Captain Howell was pretending to look for ash from the beacon — after over two hundred years! — she noted that Francis was careful to keep her away from Marcus and his friends — whether this was for her protection, or theirs, she could not decide.

In deference to the ladies, the whole party — a large one, for others beside the Harleys' immediate friends and relatives had come along — now sat for a moment. Parasols were opened, and Bel's, a frivolous lemon-coloured specimen, to match her loose gown, served to protect Francis as well as herself. They sat at a little distance from the others, and he pointed out to her the various landmarks around them, and in the warmth of post-noon Bel felt delightfully sleepy and relaxed, muttering um and ah at him, rather as he had done yesterday when she had been telling him of the plants and the fish.

'Why do I gain the impression that *you* are funning *me*?' he said, the loose expression coming oddly from him — his speech was usually precise, devoid of the slang which Marcus and Captain Howell used so freely, making the young women about them giggle and titter, with cries of 'Never say so!', 'You are teasing me!', and 'Who would have thought it, sir?'

'Funning you? Never!' replied Bel calmly as though she were discussing parliamentary matters with him. 'No such thing. I would not dare. Perfect respect is what you always demand and are invariably given, I am sure.'

'Said like that,' he returned lazily, 'it can only

mean that you are offering me perfect disrespect, secure in the knowledge that, here, no condign punishment can immediately follow. Take care. My memory is long and payment will be required — later.'

The grey eyes mocking her were no longer cold, his face, usually so set and stern, soft; whatever else, there was no doubt that Francis Carey was enjoying himself, and, had Bel but known, was doing so after a fashion which he had not felt for years. The only flaw, he considered, in the delightful sensation that being with her was producing was the knowledge that consummation of it might take a little time.

Oh, the siren that she was! She need do nothing, but nothing, to engage and trap him. She had captured him from the moment he had walked into the study at Stanhope Street, had merely needed to look at him and he was lost. Oh, the pity of it that she was what she was. To have paid court to her properly, enjoyed her wit, beauty and fire in due form, *that* would have been something. And yet was not this sparring even more delightful with its undertones of the forbidden and the wicked carried on as it was in the presence of those who had no, or little, suspicion of what was going on in front of them?

If Bel were truthful, and had been informed of how Francis felt, she would have been compelled to admit that she shared much of his feelings. The spice which their unwilling conspiracy gave to all their encounters was having its effect on her — There must be more of Marianne in me than I thought, being her response as he helped her to her feet, and with one last look at the splendid view beneath them they set off for lunch, the last to leave.

'Come, we will follow a different path from the others. I don't want company,' commanded Francis, and, taking her hand, she following, he led her down a secluded track, shaded by some scrub, and, once well into it, out of view of the rest, he turned, took her parasol from her unresisting hand to place it on the ground, and before Bel could prevent him — did she want to prevent him? — took her in his arms, saying, 'First payment for me, Mrs Bel Merrick, a foretaste of what is to come,' and began to plunder her mouth.

Untried, unkissed, never before even touched by a man, Bel felt her senses reel. Beforehand she would have quailed at the thought of such an intimate caress as his mouth teased her own mouth open and his tongue met hers, causing such a roaring wave of sensation to pass over her that her knees sagged and she almost fell against him.

She should be shocked, revolted; she had not asked for this, did not want it, no, never — but yes, oh, yes, this was delightful, and when his palm cupped her right breast, stroking it through the light muslin, his thumb finding her nipple and doing dreadful things to it, so that this time the sensation produced had her gasping aloud, his mouth having progressed to the creamy skin below her slender neck, almost to the shadow of the cleft between her breasts, Bel said aloud before she could stop herself, 'Yes, oh, yes,' so that he withdrew, laughing, saying,

'The first plea of many from you, madam, I trust,'

and the mockery in his voice rendered her wild—
with rage now, not with passion.

'No,' she panted, 'no, not at all, you are quite
mistook. Yes, you must stop, was what I meant.'

'Not, No, you must go on?' he riposted, eyebrows
wickedly raised. 'I am sorry I may not pleasure you
further now, but we risk comment. Later, perhaps,
we may continue where we left off.'

'No, never!' raged Bel. 'I should not have come
with you at all. I shall ask Almeria for protection.
You are not to treat me so cavalierly. I do not
deserve it.'

'But you wanted it as much as I did. Never say
that you did not. A most willing encounter, by my
faith. It augurs well for our future dalliance. Come.'
And he picked up her parasol. 'Open it again, not
to shield us from the sun, but the rest of the world
from the spectacle of a well-roused woman. You
look delectable, madam, but ripe for bedding at the
moment.'

Oh, horrors! Bel knew the truth of what he was
saying. Her whole body had become slack, relaxed,
her mouth, even, had become almost slumbrous.
She wanted more. Her body was on fire, not from
the heat of the day, but from the heat of him.

This would never do. She opened the parasol and
looked away, suddenly almost in tears at her body's
betrayal of her. However much she thought that the
cold mind ruled, once exposed to the fires of passion
the body had taken its own wilful way. She could no
longer deceive herself. She desired Lord Francis
Carey most desperately, but if she could not have
him in honour she was determined not to have him

at all. He could not win his disgraceful campaign, however powerful the broadsides he fired at her.

This unintended nautical metaphor restored Bel's self-command and her ready humour. How apt it was to think so of a sailor. Did Lord Francis have a girl in every port? she wondered, and, thinking so, the face she showed him was one of Bel restored. Humour had replaced erotic passion, and he marvelled at her self-command. A mistress, a very mistress of the amorous arts, to recover so quickly. She was wasted living a pure life in Lulsgate; such art, such self-command would compel a fortune in London — and all to be enjoyed for nothing by Francis Carey. . .when he was ready.

Nonsense. He was ready now, but the open meadow was before them, cloths were spread on the grass, the food was waiting, the wine already being drunk, the ladies' lemonade being poured from glass pitchers, and he was handing Bel down, saying lazily in response to Almeria's slightly raised brows at their latecoming, 'I was enchanted by the view, persuaded Mrs Merrick to remain while I took my fill of it and beg pardon for dilatoriness.'

But the view which Francis Carey had been enjoying was that of Bel Merrick's enchanting profile, and for the life of him he could not have told his half-sister what he had seen from the top of Beacon Hill!

CHAPTER SEVEN

EATING in the open, delightful though it sounded in prospect, for she had never engaged in it before, was not so remarkably pleasant as Bel had thought it would be. True, the food tasted delicious in the open air; it was the other aspects of picnicking which were not so attractive.

First of all there were the wasps and flies, which were attracted by the food; secondly there was the difficulty of eating gracefully without making one's fingers unpleasantly sticky, or ruining one's gown; and finally the position was not so comfortable as one might have expected.

She said so to Francis, who was busy eating a chicken wing, and saving his glass of sparkling white wine from overturning on the ground.

'Alfresco meals sound delightful in novels,' she informed him, 'but are not so remarkably pleasant as I thought they would be.'

'Exactly so,' was his reply to that. 'Boring though it might sound, I always think food best eaten at a good table. One's cravat,' he said, rescuing a portion of chicken from his own perfectly tied butterfly fall, 'takes less wear and tear.'

Pleased to agree with him over something, Bel, who had recovered from her inward confusion after the encounter on the hill, began to listen to the conversation of the others. Inevitably, the news

106

being what it was, the company had begun to discuss the delightfully scandalous business of the Bill of Pains and Penalties, instigated by her husband, King Geoge IV, against Queen Caroline, the wife he loathed, accusing her of low behaviour culminating in repeated acts of adultery.

Discussion over this interesting event, sure to provide gossip for months, centred not on the question of the Queen's innocence, but on political grounds, those Tories favouring the King being adamant on the Bill's passing, and those Whigs who wished to see the King and the Government embarrassed wishing to see it fall.

The liveliness of the gossip was assisted by the fact that Marcus, Fred Carnaby and George Hargrove, another amiable but light-minded youth, had removed all the young unmarried girls, once lunch was over, to the other end of the green, and were playing childish games with them, leaving the seasoned men and women to gossip at will, Bel as a widow being included in the number.

Even Mrs Venn, that austere matron, was not averse to joining in, wagging her high-dressed head, her coiffeur a relic of her long-lost youth, deploring everybody, King, Queen and lords.

'And is the poor creature truly innocent, do you think?' asked Almeria of her brother. She could never bear to think ill of anyone.

'Hardly,' was Francis's dry response to that. He normally avoided joining in with such idle gossip, but the Queen's trial was more than that, it was politics, and who knew what might happen? Some doomsters had even suggested that the King's unpopularity might result in revolution, if the mob grew too restive. 'No one, not even those who support her, think that. I was at a dinner party, seated near Viscount Granville, George Canning's friend and adviser, and his comment was that the Bill indicting her would not pass the Lords, there not being sufficient evidence. Besides, he added, the majority would be for her, not on the grounds of her unpopularity, but of his. The answer to "Is she bad?" is "He is as bad". Guilt and innocence, he indicated, do not enter into it, and I fear that he is right. All the same, his friend George Canning fled to the Continent when the Bill was to reach the Lords, for fear that his relationship with the Queen might cause him damage, even though it was years ago.'

Captain Howell, not loath to show his own acquaintanceship with society gossip, commented, 'One wonders that Granville himself did not fly the country, since the Princess of Wales, as she was then, was one of his many conquests.'

'Ah, but Granville does not wish to be Prime Minister one day, and Canning does,' returned Francis unarguably, 'and he is now quite reformed—which Mr Canning is not.'

He did not add that it was reported that Lord Granville's clever wife had commented that if the qualification of the members of the House of Lords entitled to judge the Queen was that they had not had an affair with her then the House would be remarkably empty when the Bill designed to judge her was brought in!

Almeria said, 'One would like to believe her

innocent. It is not right that vice should occupy the throne itself,' and then thought sadly that if that were so, then the Queen's husband, George IV, ought to consider abdicating.

'Yes,' said Francis, sanctimoniously for him, 'vice should never flourish; one wishes to see it gain the punishment it deserves. You agree with me, I am sure, Mrs Merrick?' he added, turning to Bel, who sat beside him, a little wary as this conversation had continued, waiting for some two-edged comment from him, and sure enough here it came.

She would not be daunted, not she. 'Oh, I do so agree with you,' she said. 'The wages of sin, as the Bible says, are cruel, and none of us, however high in rank, should be exempt from them. Although if there is an element of revenge in the King's pursuit of his poor Queen then I must add that I deplore that, too. A most unworthy sentiment, revenge.' That should hold you a little, she thought.

But no. 'Bravo,' said Francis, 'a most Christian sentiment and exactly what I would have expected from you, Mrs Merrick, so absolutely does it sort with your character as I have come to know it,' and this was said with such apparent sincerity that not only Almeria but others thought how partial Lord Francis was growing towards the pretty widow.

Henry Venn, indeed, ground his teeth, seeing beauty and a modest fortune slipping from him; Captain Howell, still with the wine glass in his hand, sipped from it thoughtfully and turned inscrutable eyes on the subject of Lord Francis's apparent admiration.

The Reverend Mr Philip Harley, that saintly but

shrewd man, was the only person who did not quite take Francis Carey's apparent compliment to Mrs Merrick at its full face value. But he said nothing, being wise as well as perceptive. Instead, tiring of this lubricious gossip about a woman whom he considered to be as unfortunate as she was ill-advised, he said gently, 'You suggested a game of cricket, Francis, to entertain Frank as well as the ladies. Enough time has passed since lunch to enable us to perform without difficulty.'

'Then we must round up Marcus and the rest,' drawled Captain Howell, rising from his recumbent position on the grass, to give him his due, thought Bel, as ready to join in childish games as the less sophisticated of the party. The servants were to be pressed in, the coachman being a useful bowler for the Lulsgate team, and the audience was to consist of the ladies, and little Caroline, young Frank being allowed to field under the eyes of his papa and uncle.

Somewhat to Bel's surprise, that haughty gentleman, Francis Carey, joined in as enthusiastically as anyone else, taking off his beautiful cravat, his tight, fashionable coat, and rolling up his shirt-sleeves. She had not thought it of him, but Almeria, seeing her surprise, said, 'Oh, dear Francis excels at all sports and pastimes. He is a fine shot, and although he does not care for it Philip says he was a good pugilist—only practises it now to keep himself in trim.'

In trim he certainly was, was Bel's response. Losing a little of his outer clothing had served to reveal what a splendid body he possessed, emphasis-

ing its strength and its masculinity. Soft, self-indul-
gent Marcus looked almost effeminate beside his
uncle. He, too, shed his coat and stock, and gave
Bel his dazzling smile; she had to admit that he
possessed his own charm, even if it were different
from his uncle's, as he said, 'You will cheer for me,
will you not? Francis must not be the only one of us
here to gain your approval.'

'Bravely said,' remarked Rhys Howell, who had
come up to them while Marcus was talking. 'Lord
Francis must not be allowed to monopolise the only
real charmer in Lulsgate Spa. You will allow me to
call on you one afternoon, Mrs Merrick, will you
not? I mean to further my acquaintance with you,
to both our advantages, I hope.'

Was she mistaken—Bel hoped she was—but was
there something a little two-edged in this remark of
Captain Howell's; or was her doubtful association
with Francis Carey beginning to colour every word
said to her by anybody—however innocent they
meant those words to be?

Bel shivered a little, bright though the sunshine
was, but forgot her malaise in watching the men
enjoy themselves. All boys again, was her reaction,
as it was Almeria's.

'Difficult to think how serious Philip is and how
severe Francis is,' she said to Bel, 'when one sees
them at play. I do believe all men remain boys at
heart.'

Bel could not but agree with her. They were
seated at some distance from the one stump at
which the bowler was aiming, and she joined in the
cheering when someone was out, or scored a good

run by dashing towards Almeria's parasol, set upright in the ground instead of another wicket, there not being enough players to justify two batsmen at once, Philip said.

When Francis came to the wicket, the fun began. Almeria had been correct to describe him as adept at all sports, and despite herself Bel rose from her seat, the more easily to see him perform. Frank was jumping up and down, shouting 'Huzza!' every time his uncle lashed the ball into the distance.

'Bravo!' he shouted, after one splendid shot had sent the ball into the undergrowth and the fielders had spent some time looking for it, and the next ball Francis treated with even more disdain, striking it high into the air, towards the bevy of applauding women.

Bel never knew why she did it, but as the ball reached the top of its flight and began to arc towards her the memory of jolly days in Brangton with Garth were on her. She had purposely worn a dress whose skirts would not confine her, whose hem was unfashionably well clear of the ground, showing, as Francis had already noted, a pretty pair of ankles, and so she began to run towards the spot where the ball would land.

And then, as it was almost upon her, she saw that she would have to throw herself forward to catch it, and to catch Francis out was suddenly the most important thing in the world, so she launched herself forward, caught it, held it high, and then landed flat on her face, all the wind knocked out of her body, but the ball safely clear of the ground and Francis dismissed, stars in front of her eyes, and joy in her heart.

The only person not nonplussed by her extraordinary action was Francis himself. He flung down his bat and ran towards where she lay prone in the grass, unmoving, his face white. He threw himself down on his knees beside her, and why should it matter to him that Bel Merrick was not hurt? But all the same, before anyone else could arrive to help, he was assisting her, saying hoarsely, 'You have taken no harm?'

'No, none,' said Bel faintly, still holding tightly to the ball, 'and I have dismissed you, have I not?'

They were face to face, closer than they had ever been except for the brief embrace on the hill. So close that Bel could smell the warm masculine scent of him, the scent of a man engaged in powerful exertion, touched with a little fear for her safety, a smell uniquely that of Francis Carey; while he was equally aware of the unique flowery scent of Bel Merrick, and, all unknowing, his face was soft with love and concern for her.

Bel later thought that had they not been interrupted there might have been the beginning of healing between them. But then the world, in the shape of Captain Howell, was on them.

'Madam not damaged, eh, Carey?' he said, his face hard and knowing. 'A splendid catch, that, Mrs Merrick; should be a cricketer yourself. Bound and determined to get him out, were you?'

Their moment was over. Francis's face resumed its normal haughty aspect, and Bel's her look of slight withdrawal.

All in all Mrs Bel Merrick was quite the heroine of the afternoon, particularly so far as the gentlemen were concerned. The ladies, especially the younger ones, were not so sure. The pretty widow had stolen their thunder again.

'Oh, famous,' cried Frank, jumping up and down on the spot while Bel was tenderly carried by Francis to where Almeria gently straightened her dishevelled appearance, removed the dry grass from her hair, and generally restored her to her usual state of calm order. 'That's the very first time anyone has ever got Uncle Francis out when we've played cricket, and it was Aunt Bel who caught him! Would you like a go with the bat, Aunt Bel? Oh, do have a go with the bat—and then Uncle Francis can try to catch you!'

Everyone laughed at the little boy's enthusiasm, not least Uncle Francis and Aunt Bel, who laughingly declined, saying, 'I have had quite enough excitement for one afternoon, dear Frank, without putting myself in the way of allowing your uncle to gain his revenge. Another time, perhaps,' and she hardly dared to look at him while she spoke, helped a little by his nephew who flung his arms around her and tried to climb on her knee, disputing the favour with Caroline, who wished to offer Bel her new rag doll to play with.

'Pray, children, allow your aunt to rest,' instructed Almeria; 'she has had quite enough excitement for one afternoon,' amusing Bel a little, for she felt tremendously invigorated, if not to say uplifted, after giving haughty Francis his comeuppance—except that she could not forget the expression on his face when he had come to rescue her—so strange and gentle, almost loving.

Well, enough of that, she thought briskly, amused to note that Francis was so proprietorial with her, glaring at Rhys Howell when he tried to comfort her by saying, 'A fine opportunity for you to take Lulsgate waters tomorrow, to restore youself, Mrs Merrick. I understand that they are full of that rare stuff, sodium chloride.'

'Very rare,' snorted Francis, almost forgetting himself by being openly uncivil to a man he detested, 'seeing that sodium chloride is nothing but common salt, and would hardly restore Mrs Merrick to anything. . .other than giving her what I am sure she does not wish—a monstrous thirst!'

Captain Howell did not glare back, but said, rather wittily and pointedly, Bel thought—this was suddenly not Francis's day—'Well, Carey——' and she could almost feel Francis grind his teeth at this unwanted familiarity '—since the nobility and gentry see fit to rush to Brighton to bathe in and drink the salt sea-water there, it would not come amiss for Mrs Merrick to do the same, perhaps. Do I hope to see you there tomorrow, madam?' he queried. 'We could take the waters together; overfeeding in Town has rendered me a little bilious.'

Bel did not care for him at all—there was something false in his obsequiousness to her—but Francis Carey needed to be taught a lesson; that he could not dictate to Mrs Bel Merrick whom she should meet, and how she should conduct herself. So she smiled sweetly at Captain Howell, fluttering her eyelashes after a fashion she usually avoided, and said softly, 'Should I feel sufficiently up to an excursion to the Baths tomorrow, Captain Howell, you will be sure to see me in the Pump Room, and, if so, I shall be pleased to take the waters with you.'

She hoped that this would end the matter. The cricket match resumed again, for a short time only; the afternoon drawing on towards evening, and a late dinner beckoning, the party regretfully assembled for home, all the picnic stuff and cricketing paraphernalia having been packed. Francis, on his sister's instructions, came forward to escort her home, Captain Howell being fobbed off with lesser attractions.

He said nothing until she was safely tucked in; for some reason both he and Almeria thinking that a young woman who had engaged in such minimal exertion as running to catch a ball and then falling over needed the utmost in tender, loving care — to the degree that they thought fit to muffle her in a blanket on such a warm day!

Bel was something in agreement with Cassius, whose sardonic expression before he hoisted himself on to his small seat behind them both told her what he thought of the coddling of such fine ladies as herself.

Coddling did not stop there. Having started off once more, Francis remarked in his most lordly voice, not so loud as the one he used on the quarter-deck to be sure, but full of the same command, 'You would be wise to have as little as possible to do with Captain Howell, Mrs Merrick. I tell you so for your own good. His reputation, particularly with women, is deplorable.'

'Oh!' Bel almost gasped; she was not to be
lectured on proper behaviour by a man whose
declared intent to her was so determinedly
improper. 'For a man whose stated intentions
towards myself are so dishonourable, I find such
an. . .objurgation insufferable indeed. Am I to suppose that to be. . .deplorable to me is reserved
strictly for you? Such hypocrisy! What would your
poor sister say if she knew of the lengths to which
you are going to reserve my ruin to yourself? Why
should you care what Captain Howell does with and
to me?'

She was well aware that Cassius was probably
listening to every word she uttered, ears flapping,
for she had not attempted to keep her voice down,
but she did not care about that, not she! Nor
apparently did Francis.

A look of fury crossed his haughty face; the hand
holding his whip upright—they were driving along
an easy stretch of road, his horses needing little
direction—was shaking a little.

'Rant on, madam,' he said at last. 'I thought that
perhaps you were a little nice in choosing those on
whom you conferred your favours—or so you have
suggested. I see that I was wrong—paddle in the
mud with Captain Howell if you will; it is probably
no more than I should have expected. I thought to
help you.'

'Paddle in the mud! Thought to help me!' Bel was
running out of exclamation marks. 'The public
spaces of the Pump Room are not exactly muddy!
And as to your notion of helping me—well, words
fail me!'

'I cannot say that I have ever noticed any such phenomenon,' said Francis through his teeth. 'On the contrary, a longer-tongued shrew I have seldom encountered. You lack gratitude, madam. Stupid of me, I know, but I was only speaking for your own good.' He knew perfectly well that in the light of what he had promised to do to her he must sound ridiculous, but the mere idea of Rhys Howell, or any other man, laying a finger on Bel Merrick made him feel quite ill, and as for all the men she had. . . entertained before he had met her, well, he could have killed the lot of them. . .slowly.

The very last thing he had expected had happened to him. Standing there, his bat in his hand, watching her run to catch the cricket ball he had launched into the air, her beautiful face alight with joy, seeing her fall, had produced in him the most astonishing sensation. Inconveniently, against all reason, he knew that he had fallen hopelessly and desperately in love with a Cyprian of Cyprians, a woman whom, as he had seen this very day, men had only to look at to want. Henry Venn, young Marcus and his silly friends, Rhys Howell, and the rest of them, married and single, had all walked around her, their tongues hanging out, panting at the sight of her, and he was no better — no, much worse — than the rest.

How could such a thing have happened to him?

Oh, he must possess madam, and soon, to anaesthetise himself, to cool this terrible fever which he now knew had been burning him up since he had first seen her two years ago. *That* was the reason for his rage against her. But worse even than that was the dreadful thought that even to have her in his arms might not assuage his desire, but would merely serve to inflame him the more! For he hated every man who spoke to her, not simply the dubious semi-criminal he suspected Howell to be.

A mistress of the erotic arts, sitting beside him in his curricle, arguing with him wittily and unanswerably, refusing to be put down, robbing him of honour and common sense—how could he deal with her? He could go to his sister, tell her the truth about her friend, destroy her socially and for good—and make Almeria and all her family unhappy into the bargain. He told himself that he could not do it, because it would deprive him of the revenge which he had promised himself he would have if he ever encountered the sweet cheat again, but there was more to it than that.

He was drowning in love's cross-currents, for astonishingly he did not want to ruin her in *that* way, if he did in the other. Indeed, he hardly knew what he did want.

Why could she not have been chaste, so that he could have gone on his knees to her, instead of wanting her on her knees before him, to ask her to be—what? His wife? The second wife whom he had vowed he would never take, so determined was he to be faithful to the memory of his dear, lost Cassie.

His dear, lost Cassie! For the first time in years he had ceased to think of her; ever since he had first met Bel Merrick her poor shade had grown thinner and thinner; the years had done their work on him, and the boy who had loved and married and lost her was as dead as Cassie.

No! He would not be caught by madam; he had

made his intent known, and by God he would have her, and on his terms.

The silence between them stretched on and on. Francis's eyes were on the road, Bel's on her hands, now lax in her lap, now gripped together, for, like Francis, the terrible trammels of love were netting her about; she was a fish or a bird, caught in the meshes, unable to move in any direction. And, also like him, she hardly knew what to think, feel or do.

She told herself that she hated him, but knew that she lied, or rather knew that love and hate were now so inextricably blended that the power of decision had almost gone from her. As in the moment she had caught the cricket ball and had held it aloft she had felt regret for catching him, mixed with her triumph, so now she hardly knew where detestation ended and obsession began.

Oh, why could she not have met him in Lulsgate for the first time, been introduced to him as Miss Anne Isabella Passmore, the Reverend Mr Caius Passmore's virtuous daughter, on whom he could have smiled, with and to whom he would have spoken honourably, so that he would have been gentle with her, not reproached her in fierce despite?

They were entering Lulsgate again, passing the first new houses, and the even newer half-finished ones lining the road, tribute to the developing wealth of this part of Leicestershire. They were passing the Baths, reaching her home, he was setting her down, Mrs Broughton was being conducted home, too, and the day, so fraught with incident, was over. Lottie was coming out to greet her, exclaiming, 'Oh, Miss Bel, what have you done to your bonnet?' and Francis was bowing over her hand, saying in a low and stifled voice,

'I had forgot the truce I proclaimed; pray forgive me,' and she was replying, wearily, because although so little had happened on the way home she felt as though she had lived through years of emotion,

'And, I, too, forgot myself, Lord Francis. I thank you for the journey and,' she could not help herself, 'for the cricket. I had not played it for years, and found it strangely satisfying to catch a ball again.'

His strong face lightened at that, filled with somewhat unexpected humour as she lanced the tension which had lain between them. 'Oh, yes, you triumphed mightily, did you not? One act only, all afternoon, and you are immortalised in Lulsgate's annals. Allow me, if you would, to escort you to the Assembly Ball tomorrow evening,' and before she could reply he bowed over her offered hand as courteously as though they were what they appeared to be; a lady of spotless reputation and her loving cavalier—living for a moment, thought Bel, in the world of make-believe.

CHAPTER EIGHT

LULSGATE society called the next morning, either in their own person, or sending a footman, to ask whether Mrs Bel Merrick was fully recovered from her exertions of the previous afternoon.

Bel's amusement that such a mild event as her catching a cricket ball and falling over had caused such paroxysms of excitement was tempered by the thought that life in Lulsgate Spa was so tame that it needed only for a lady to be a little unladylike and take the consequences to send everyone into such regal fantods!

Only she knew what really lay behind her own respectable façade — that she was the sister of one of London's most notorious courtesans, and was being persecuted by a man whom everyone in Lulsgate Spa thought was her dearest admirer.

She had decided to take Captain Howell up on his suggestion that she join him during the morning in the Pump Room, and was debating whether to ask Mrs Broughton to go with her, that lady being truly overset after a day in the open and eating and drinking too much in the fresh air.

She lay wheezing on a sofa, and it was Bel who was tending her, rather than the other way round, when the knocker on the front door sounded, and the maid came in to tell her that Lady Almeria Harley was a-calling.

122

'Oh, I see you are in splendid fettle!' kind Almeria exclaimed when she entered, and then, remorsefully, to Mrs Broughton, 'I see that you, and not Bel, have been rendered *hors de combat* as the result of yesterday's adventures. You must not sit in the sun again, dear madam. Not wise, not wise at all. Have you taken Epsom's Salts? I am persuaded that they are the very thing for the bilious.'

'Epsom's, and every other variety of salts, my dear,' replied Bel briskly; 'however, nothing but rest will answer, I fear.'

'I came to offer to escort you to the Pump Room, dear Bel,' offered Almeria, looking dubiously at Mrs Broughton. 'Shall you feel happy at leaving your companion?'

'Oh, pray, do not consider me,' said Mrs Broughton faintly. 'Dear Bel needs restoring, too. A cup or so of Lulsgate water will set her up for the day.'

Bel privately thought not. She thought Lulsgate water vastly overrated, but did not care to say so. Everyone in Lulsgate was convinced that drinking very salty liquid was a recipe for perfect health, long life, and a good complexion.

Mrs Broughton was, indeed, asking Bel to bring her a bottle back — 'seeing that I have not the energy to go there to drink it in its proper surroundings. And you will change my book for me at the subscription library, will you not, dear Bel? Although I fear that you will not find anything to equal *Lady Caroline's Secret*; that was not only sweetly pretty, but exciting, too. So sad, poor Lady Caroline, but to marry dear Belfiori in the end, that was the best

thing of all! I could not have endured it if he had
continued to think the worst of her because she
dared not tell him her secret.'

Bel wondered what unkind god in the Pantheon
was arranging matters so that everything said and
done these days seemed to cast its shadow on her
own unfortunate condition. What Belfiori would
spring from what trapdoor to rescue her from
Francis's vengeance? And perhaps from Captain
Howell — there was something in his manner to her
which she did not like — and now she was being
fanciful.

'Dear Mrs Broughton,' said Almeria affectionately, as they left the house. 'I sometimes wonder
whether you are her companion rather than the
other way round. She is so easily overset and needs
so much shepherding. It is you who wait on her,
fetch and carry her library books, correct her tatting. You are a good soul, Mrs Bel Merrick, and
Philip agrees with that verdict, I must tell you. He
was praising you at dinner last night to Francis,
almost as though he thought Francis needed to be
told what a good creature you are, when he can see
so for himself.

'Shall we go to the library first, and find something
we can both enjoy, and which Mrs Broughton will
cry over? Secrets, indeed! Real life contains very
few, thank goodness, and Lulsgate Spa is not the
place where people have them. Goodness and virtue
may be dull, but think, my love, how appalling it
would be to nurse a guilty secret. I am sure that I
could not sleep if I did!'

This lengthy speech did not end until both women

were safely inside the library and checking through the bookshelves, Bel reflecting sardonically that those like Lady Almeria who were born into wealth position and security could have little idea of how the rest of the world fared, so easily could she deny what lay all around her, for Bel was certain that others beside herself would not care for their entire life to be exposed to public view.

Filippo's Tower was finally decided on as a suitable book to comfort Mrs Broughton by making her flesh creep and her eyes drip salt tears, and which would serve to sustain her through her malaise; and then their destination was the Pump Room.

'I tried to persuade Francis to come with me,' remarked Almeria reflectively, 'but he says that an old sea-dog friend of his has settled near here, and that he proposed to visit him. He said that not even Lulsgate water could reconcile him to meeting Captain Howell for two days in succession!'

And I really do not want to meet him either, thought Bel. He makes me shiver, and I do not know why. He is not ill-looking after all, and although his manner is a little oily it is no more so than that of many other self-consequential men.

They finally entered the Rotunda, with its high glass dome, classical archways and statues of various gods and goddesses disposed in niches around the walls. The well was in the centre of the large room, and a series of spouts in the shape of shells were set in its high sides from which water flowed, to run into a low trough, be conducted away, or be caught in suitable receptacles to be drunk by those, like

Bel, who might find it health-giving—not that Bel really thought any such thing.

Beyond them were the big double doors through which visitors who wished to bathe in the life-giving waters took their way. Bel had once surrendered to her doctor's wishes and gone there, but the springs which fed the baths contained a great deal of sulphur as well as salt, and she found them distasteful. She concluded that she was not at Lulsgate for its waters, whether sulphur-laden or not.

Fortunately for Bel, Captain Howell was not alone. He and Marcus and other young bloods were standing in one corner of the room, quizzing the passers-by, and laughing openly at some of the old men and women who chose to frequent the Pump Room, often daily. They were discussing the evening's dance at the Assembly Rooms—they were held twice weekly.

Entry to the Rooms was by a large subscription to keep out riff-raff, and, although Lulsgate had no powerful Master of Ceremonies to rule the spa as Beau Nash had once done at Bath, the MC who ran the Assembly Rooms, Mr Courtney, organised the events staged there very strictly, so that Lulsgate should not deteriorate socially, as some spas had done, losing their attraction for wealthy visitors and depriving the growing town of money.

Bel and Almeria both accepted glasses of Lulsgate water, Almeria being greeted by one of the church-warden's wives with demands to discuss the decoration of the church when Harvest Festival time arrived, and, offering Bel a smile of apology,

Almeria was led away, leaving Bel to drink her water alone.

Rhys Howell must have had eyes in the back of his head, Bel thought crossly, for the moment Almeria was swept away he came over to greet Bel, and bowed extravagantly to her. 'Come, you must not be solitary, Mrs Merrick, when there are those who wish to entertain you.' And he escorted her towards some armchairs in the corner of the room, near to his cronies—he was one of those men who always attracted a small court around them—made up of victims as well as toadies of someone who they mistakenly thought was a man in the first stare of fashion.

'You are in looks today, madam,' he proclaimed. 'I am happy to inform you, Mrs Merrick, that you show no signs of yesterday's exertions. You hardly need the restorative properties of the water you are drinking.'

More compliments followed until Marcus, restless, said, rudely, Bel thought, 'You are as bad as Uncle Francis, Howell—and that is saying something—for monopolising Mrs Merrick. Allow me to entertain her for a little.' And he pushed Howell to one side, and sat in the next armchair to Bel.

'Have you lived here long, madam?' was his opening gambit. 'I would have thought Lulsgate a dull spot for such a charmer as yourself to grace for long. Were you ever in London?'

'A short visit, once only,' replied Bel, determined not to lie more than she need.

'Forgive me for quizzing you——' Captain Howell was taking the conversation over from Marcus

Tawstock, whom he undoubtedly had in his toils,
'—but you did not go into society, I collect.'

'No,' was Bel's short answer to that. She *did*
object to his quizzing her, would much have preferred to speak with artless young Marcus, but could
not say so.

'I thought not,' he said, offering her his wolfish
smile. 'I should have been certain to have remembered you, so distinctive as you are, but I have been
out of England these last few years — on business —
and thought I might have missed you then.'

Bel gave him an ambiguous smile, which she also
offered to his next remark. 'You intend to vegetate
here, madam, not grace London with your. . .inim-
itable presence? One wonders why.' And again Bel
did not like the expression he assumed when he had
finished speaking.

'I enjoy country living,' was her short reply.

'Oh, indeed, so do I. For a short time, that is.
And, of course, you gather useful admirers round
you here, as you would in Town, do you not?'

Bel was suddenly certain that this conversation
was, on his part, by no means innocent. She shivered a little, and was grateful when Mark intervened
again.

'You are an inconsiderate devil, are you not,
Howell? You knew that I wished to converse with
Mrs Merrick, and here you are again, cutting me
out. I particularly wished to ask her whether she
would allow me to escort her to the Assembly Ball
this evening, and since you will not leave us alone
you compel me to ask her publicly, for if I leave you

with her much longer, you are sure to be there before me.'

'Oh, indeed,' said Captain Howell and favoured Bel with his vulpine stare this time — she thought that perhaps with that tinge of red in his hair he was more fox than wolf, 'I shall ask her now, seeing that you were more concerned to reprimand me than to make your offer directly to her. Tell him, my dear Mrs Merrick, that you would much prefer me as a partner — seasoned men are always preferable to raw boys, as I am sure you are well aware.'

There was something so brutally suggestive in his manner of speech to her, so unpleasantly coarse, that Bel was sure he was offering her a double meaning — suggesting that she was a courtesan, or very knowing, at the least. She would much prefer Marcus, and began to falter, her usual calm on the verge of breaking down, as Captain Howell plainly saw, so that he said, quite softly, 'It would be wise, I think, Mrs Merrick, to accept my offer for tonight's Assembly, rather than Mark's here.' And this time his smile was almost a leer.

'Forgive me, Howell,' announced a new voice in the conversation glacially, 'but Mrs Merrick will be attending this evening's Assembly with me. I was beforehand, although you have not given her time to say so.'

It was Francis Carey, turned out completely à point, not for a cross-country journey as his half-sister had suggested, but wearing Town clothes of the most exquisite perfection.

'So you say, Carey,' said Rhys Howell smoothly. 'But Mrs Merrick has mentioned nothing of this. He seeks to pre-empt you unfairly, does he not, dear madam? Pray tell him either that you have changed your mind, or that he took your consent for granted!'

'Oh!' Bel was suddenly quite outraged by the behaviour of all three men, for Marcus, unseen by either Francis or Captain Howell, was mouthing something at her and pointing to himself, while Francis and the captain faced one another like a pair of mad dogs disputing a particularly juicy bone. And what was Francis doing here, anyway? Why was he not, as Almeria had said, jaunting about Leicestershire, rather than rushing here to tease her again?

She could think of nothing better to say than to ask him that!

'What are you doing here, Lord Francis? Almeria said that you were paying duty calls about Leicestershire.'

'I changed my mind,' he announced curtly. 'And, for your sake, a good thing too. I will not have you throw me over to go with another man.'

'Mrs Merrick does not confirm that she agreed to attend with you,' Rhys Howell began. 'I think you must be mistook —— '

'No,' snorted Francis. 'It is you who are mistook, Howell. In decency you had better retire.'

'Oh,' cried Bel, suddenly beside herself at all this, and stamping her foot. 'I have not agreed to attend with anyone yet. You are both intolerable, Lord Francis for taking my agreement yesterday as read, without waiting for an answer, you to persist, Captain Howell, so mannerlessly, and as for

Marcus, making faces at me behind you both, with such examples before him as the pair of you, I am not surprised at *his* conduct. No——' as both men opened their mouths again. '—I shall be going with. . .with. . . Mr Henry Venn,' for poor Henry had been besieging her for weeks to attend with him, and now she would inform him that she would be his partner this evening if he wished.

She had not the slightest wish to go anywhere with Henry, with or without his mother, for she was sure that Mrs Venn would attach herself to them this evening, but she was suddenly so enraged with both of them, and the attention which this altercation was causing, as their voices grew louder and louder, that she wanted nothing from either of them!

Both men suddenly realised that there was nothing left to fight for, and both said together, 'Then you will do me the honour of allowing me to wait on you this afternoon,' to which she replied shortly,

'Indeed no. I never receive on Wednesday afternoon. I have other duties to attend to, other matters to occupy me.'

Both men, unknown to each other and to Bel, were immediately struck with the same thought.

Other matters to which to attend! What could they be? Could it be that madam was still plying her trade in Lulsgate, discreetly, of course, but keeping in practice and earning a little money on the side? Both opened their mouths to try to make other arrangements. Francis's fury with both Bel and Captain Howell made him behave most uncharacteristically, as he later told himself dismally, Mrs Bel Merrick having such a devastating effect on his manners as well as his morals, but Bel was before them again.

'If you are trying to make an appointment with me,' she said crossly, 'you must both call at my door and take your chances, and that goes for you too, Lord Tawstock,' she added, seeing Marcus look hopeful at the prospect of cutting out his seniors. 'And now you will excuse me. I must return to Mrs Broughton with her latest novel, and you, Lord Francis, will proffer my excuses to your sister, for not returning with her, but I feel the need for something stronger than Lulsgate waters to restore me.'

She was completely unaware that, slightly flushed, her face animated, she had never looked so desirable, so that both men before her were in the grip of the strongest desire to enjoy the little widow whether she would or no.

Fortunately unknowing, Bel bowed and retired, anger lending grace to her carriage, elegance to her walk and fire to her eyes, so that every head in the room turned to see her go.

Well! she thought on emerging into the street again. If I had thought to ensure for myself a quiet life by coming to Lulsgate, I certainly committed the biggest mistake of my life. What with Francis promising me ravishment and surrender in the distant future, and Captain Howell uttering veiled threats in the present, it seems that I must have all my wits about me, or I shall be sunk with all hands by Lord Francis, and be charged to destruction by

Captain Howell. A plague on you both, gentlemen. But, oh, dear, she knew that that sentiment did not apply to Lord Francis Carey, however much it did to Captain Rhys Howell!

CHAPTER NINE

'So,' SAID Lady Almeria to her half-brother, 'you changed your mind about your day's activities.'

'Yes.' Francis was brief. He had no mind to explain to Almeria that he, who had dismissed women to the edge of his life, had been so haunted by Bel Merrick that he had been unable to leave Lulsgate Spa that morning knowing that she was likely to meet that ineffable swine Rhys Howell at the Pump Room.

Even Almeria, less so her husband, was surprised when, over luncheon, a cold collation as usual, Francis remarked, apparently idly, 'I understand from Mrs Merrick that she never receives on Wednesday afternoons, is otherwise engaged. With you on parish matters, I suppose.'

Almeria, as well as Philip, looked at him sharply. 'I really don't know, Francis. I only know that Bel is never available on Wednesday and Friday afternoon, and it has not occurred to me to question her on her activities. I know that everyone in Lulsgate likes to think that they know what everyone else is doing, but it is a cast of mind which I deplore.'

Nothing more to say on that, then! was Francis's glum internal comment. Nothing for it but to set Cassius to watching her, an ignoble act of which he was ashamed, but then his whole conduct lately had become shameful, and he shuddered a little at what

Almeria might think if she knew, not only the truth about Bel, but how he was virtually trying to blackmail her into his bed—for he had to acknowledge that his actions justified no other description.

Luncheon passed without further discussion of Bel Merrick, Philip contenting himself with discussing local matters, and commenting on the latest news in *The Times* about Queen Caroline and matters European, being determined to pick Francis's good brains while he was staying with them.

Only, when Francis had excused himself, ostensibly to change into riding clothes, but actually to brief Cassius—who had performed several such missions for him in Paris on behalf of some diplomatic subtleties, and was consequently able to disguise his tracking of others successfully—Philip looked up at his wife and said quietly, 'A private word with you, my dear.'

Almeria's expression showed her surprise when in response to her nod he said, 'Tell me, my dear, you know him well. Do not you think that there is something a little odd about Francis's interest in Mrs Merrick?'

'Odd?' repeated Almeria. 'Well, only in the sense that it is as long as I can remember since Francis showed an interest in any woman.'

'I think there is more to it than that,' observed Philip thoughtfully. 'I may be mistaken, but there is something in his speech and manner to her which is—to me, at least—a little strange, not at all like his usual conduct towards women.'

'I cannot say,' answered Almeria, 'that I have

noticed anything untoward—and why should there be? Bel is a dear, sweet girl, and that should gain her nothing but approbation from Francis, surely.'

'Exactly so,' said Philip mysteriously, and decided to let the matter drop. He did wonder why his brother-in-law had bolted so rapidly from the room after asking pointed questions about Bel Merrick, and also wondered what he was doing now.

What Francis was doing was briefing Cassius, that close-mouthed Mercury, the messenger whom Francis could trust, who would never gossip, however bribed or tempted, because Francis had saved him from ruin and transportation some ten years ago, and he had served him devotedly ever since.

'Watch the house,' Francis concluded, 'and if Mrs Merrick leaves it follow her discreetly, find out where she goes, and then come and report to me immediately.'

Cassius nodded, saying aloud as he set off on his mission, 'And what's got in to you, cully? Never seen you so hot after a skirt afore. Not to say that this one ain't a prime piece of meat—and if you think she's a lightskirt, which I suspects as you do, then you're fit for Bedlam, sir, though I'll not tell you so!'

Francis, unaware of his judgemental servant's thoughts, decided to change, then rest a little in Philip's study until Cassius should return, hopefully with some useful information. Could Bel Merrick really be plying her trade in Lulsgate Spa? And if she were, why should it trouble him?

* * *

Bel set off on her usual Wednesday afternoon errand unaware that Cassius was on her tail—as he would have said. She had, he noted, no one with her, was plainly dressed in dove-grey and walked briskly along. She carried a covered basket, and took the road out of Lulsgate in the direction of that small and poverty-stricken village, Morewood, where the long depression after the late wars, coupled with the new machinery, had virtually destroyed the livelihood of the framework knitters there, so many fewer men being needed to operate the new machines, which were also capable of knitting much wider and longer pieces of cloth—a fact which still further depressed the wages of those fortunate enough to be employed to work them, whose old standard of living had been destroyed.

Occasionally some of those who had no work intruded into Lulsgate, their ragged children behind them, to try to beg from rich visitors to the spa, but the constables officiously ordered them back to their 'proper dwellings' and told them not to annoy their betters.

Well, thought Cassius sardonically, if m'lord thought madam was after trade, which Cassius suspected he did, then she was visiting an odd place to find it; and when Bel finally reached her destination he gave a long whistle before investigating further. The smile on his face as he hurried back to report was even more sardonic than it usually was, and the report he finally made to Francis more cryptic than it need have been—for Cassius was not averse to teasing the master who had saved him, but who he sometimes thought was too high-nosed for his own good!

Morewood! She was visiting Morewood! What the devil was she doing there? The sketchy report which Cassius had made had told Francis only that Bel had visited a small house on the further side of the little village, and that Cassius had no idea what she was doing there, or to whom the house belonged, he not liking to ask questions and draw attention to himself.

Francis had driven through Morewood once, and the place had depressed him. It contained only a few good homes, the whole village being given over to cottages with long windows in their upper rooms, the typical sign of framework knitters' homes, their machines always kept on the upper floors. The air of poverty saddened him, as it did Philip Harley, who tried, through Henry Venn who looked after the Chapel of Ease there, to alleviate the villagers' dreadful conditions. To small avail, for the villagers had turned away from the established church and favoured a Methodist ministry whose chapel was a tin tabernacle, very unlike the graceful Gothic building for which Henry Venn was responsible.

He decided to take his curricle to Morewood and reconnoitre; the word sounded better than spying, somehow—which, after all, was what he was doing, but all in a good cause, he told himself sanctimoniously. But what good cause was that? The cause of Francis Carey's insatiable curiosity about everything which concerned Bel Merrick, of course.

The journey to Morewood, a silently gleeful Cassius up behind him, was soon accomplished, and just outside the village he left the curricle and the tiger concealed in a side-lane and began to walk briskly to where Cassius had told him Bel had made for.

The little house was modest enough—surely not a worthwhile customer there—and he stopped a sullen old man to ask him to whom it belonged, and his jaw dropped when the man said, 'Gideon Birch, the Methodee minister, o' course. Everyone knows that!'

The minister? What the devil was Bel Merrick doing with a Methodist minister? He stared at the little house, and then, on an impulse, hearing voices, he walked down the lane by the side of the house, to glare over a hedge at the garden from whence the voices—and now childish laughter— were coming.

There was nothing for it. That grandee, Lord Francis Carey, the pride of the Corps Diplomatique, was reduced to standing tiptoe in a lane and peering over a hedge. Worse was to come, for what he saw shamed him.

Sitting on the lawn, a group of small children facing her, was Bel Merrick. The children, of all ages from five to about twelve, so far as he could judge, were equipped with slates and pencils, and an impromptu spelling bee was in progress. The laughter was because as each child correctly spelt the name of an animal Bel was drawing it on the slate before her and showing it to them.

And while he stood there, fascinated, she drew an animal and then asked a small child in the front row to tell her its name, and spell it for her.

Something strange seemed to happen, something passed from him to her, for as the child finished Bel turned her head slowly, to see him watching her.

A tide of colour washed over her face. She looked defiantly at him, said loudly, 'See, children, we have a visitor. Pray join us, Lord Francis, seeing that you have tracked me down. I could do with an assistant.'

Francis had never, in his whole life, felt so miserably helpless and ashamed. He shook his head, disembodied, he knew, the rest of him hidden by the hedge, only for her to cry, 'Never say you are shy, sir, nor that you have no feeling for these little ones. You have a duty to *me* now, having followed me here; pray fulfil it. There is a gate a little further on by which you may enter.' And now it was her look which challenged him, so that he shrugged; nothing for it. He could not retreat like a whipped cur — which was, astonishingly, how he felt, there was such a world of difference between what he had thought she was doing and what she was actually doing!

Bel felt indignation roaring through her, for how dared he spy on her, and follow her, especially after this morning? So that when she rose to meet him her face was brighter than ever, with a mixture of anger and scorn.

'Come, sir. You must meet my pupils. They are some of the poor children who have no work to go to. You do know that these little ones work long hours, and shame on us that we allow it. They need to learn to read and to write, and there is no school here, no dame to teach them, nor could their parents pay to keep one, so Mr Birch, the minister here, whom I met some few months ago, accepted my offer to teach these little ones, he having no aptitude for the task and having so many other duties.'

Francis tried to revive his scorn by assuming that Mr Gideon Birch was some handsome young fellow of the artisan class turned preacher who might have some attraction for Mrs Bel Merrick, she presumably having come from that class of persons herself, but he despised himself for the thought, and sat on a white-painted wooden garden seat— 'where,' said Bel, scornfully, 'you may remain if you do not disturb us.'

The lesson continued, Bel, watching him, occasionally asking him a question, to include him in the lesson. One of the children read a small passage from the Bible, the story of Joseph, and then Bel asked them questions about it, as Francis remembered his governess similarly questioning him, long ago, in the schoolroom at the top of Tawstock House, something which he had long forgotten.

Outwardly calm, Bel was in turmoil. What business did he have to track her here? Could there be nothing left to herself, nothing private? For she had not even told Almeria of this. In her middle teens she had run, at her late papa's suggestion, such little classes for the poor children of Brangton, but Lulsgate, rich, important and comfortable, did not need such amenities; accidentally meeting Gideon Birch, she had discovered the need in Morewood for such help as she could give, and had offered to give it.

The little meeting ended, as Mr Birch always wished it, with all the class reciting the Lord's Prayer, heads bent, hands held together, and then the children filed out, the little boys bowing to Bel, and the little girls curtsying, and before they left through the gate they extended, at Bel's instructions, the same politeness to Francis.

'And now, sir,' she said, turning to him, 'why are you here?'

He had the grace to look awkward, she thought, and said, 'I was annoyed—I know that it was wrong of me—when you said that you were not at home this afternoon. I. . .was determined to find out what you were doing.'

'And now you have found out,' said Bel, almost contemptuously, thinking that for the first time the initiative in their meetings had passed from him to her, 'I think that you should leave, don't you? Unless you feel that there is some ukase, some edict you might like to pass to prevent me from lightening these children's lives a little.' Here, in this quiet garden, where she could see Gideon Birch through his kitchen window preparing to come outside, there was no place for his aristocratic scorn.

'Now you are being unfair,' he protested, watching an old man leave the house and come towards them, carrying a tray on which stood a pitcher of lemonade and three glasses. 'I can have no conceivable objection to the errand of mercy on which you are engaged.'

'No?' said Bel fiercely. 'I thought that you might protest that my presence might pollute them,' but, suddenly hearing Mr Birch approach them, she said

more coolly, 'I think that I ought to introduce you
to Mr Birch, even if I cannot explain your presence
here to him, since I have no inkling of the reason
for it myself.'

Mr Birch had placed his tray on a small wooden
table, painted to match the bench. Francis rose as
he did so, and bowed, saying—and it was all that he
could think of in his very real distress and embarrassment, 'I have come to escort Mrs Merrick
home,' after Bel had performed the necessary
introductions.

No virile young suitor, Mr Gideon Birch, but an
elderly man with a warm, concerned face, who said,
'You will do me the honour, Lord Francis, of taking
a glass of my sister's good lemonade with us. She is
unfortunately absent, so cannot welcome you. I am
happy to learn that Mrs Merrick will have an escort
today. I am never easy that she comes alone,
although I understand why she does. She does us a
great kindness in offering her services to us, free of
charge, especially as she is not a member of our
church, although I am one of those Methodists who
likes to think of himself as still part of the Church
of England's fold, as John Wesley was.'

Bel noted that Francis was rapidly recovering his
savoir-faire and spoke interestedly and informedly
to Mr Birch, so that that gentleman thought what a
gracious person he was, unlike many of the mighty
whom Mr Birch had so far encountered.

'So,' said Francis, 'you were an Oxford man
yourself before you heard George Whitfield preach
and were converted.'

'Yes,' said Mr Birch mildly. 'I was offered a

preferment in South Yorkshire, whence my family is sprung, but once I had been converted, had endured my private encounter on the road to Damascus, there was nothing for it, I had to follow my Master's call. Besides, there are many to succour the rich, few the poor. They need the Lord more in places like Morewood than in Lulsgate Spa.'

'Well spoken,' said Francis, now the grandee who could accommodate himself to any society, and plainly both interesting and pleasing the old man by displaying his knowledge without flaunting it, as Bel noticed.

She realised again, as she had often done before, that men were quite different when not with women, spoke differently, and had a range of interests rarely displayed in social intercourse. Whether she was glad or sorry at this she did not know, only that it was true, and wondered why so few women seemed to realise that it was so.

She was aware of Francis's eyes on her, answered a question of Mr Birch's, drank his excellent lemonade, and promised to be back on Friday to take the class again.

She made her adieus to the old man, picked up her plain bonnet, and put it on, and tied its ribbons, retrieved her parasol and the empty basket which Mr Birch had brought from the house.

'Mrs Merrick,' he informed Francis, 'always brings us some excellent cake. She says that it is surplus to her wants, would be thrown away if we did not accept it, but I suspect by its excellence that that is her way of bribing us not to refuse it, not letting us seem to sponge upon her kindness. She is a true friend—does good by stealth. I trust, sir, that you will not reveal to others what you have discovered.'

'Indeed not,' Francis replied, sincerity in his voice. 'if that is what you both wish.'

'I would not discommode her, sir,' said Mr Birch, 'for there are those who would not be pleased at what she does, and would gossip unpleasantly of it, and I am happy to learn that you are prepared to be discreet, will be careful to consider her interests,' and the old eyes on Francis were shrewd. 'We may meet again some time, sir, I hope. It is a long time since I was privileged to talk with a person as informed as yourself.'

They all bowed their farewells, Mr Birch retaining the formal manners of the eighteenth-century days when he had been a young scholar at Magdalen, Oxford.

'So,' said Francis, a little heavily, Bel thought, on their leaving the pleasant garden, 'I owe you an apology, Mrs Merrick.'

'For what you thought of me,' returned Bel shrewdly, 'or for following me?'

'Both,' said Francis, 'and I think you must agree that I could not possibly have guessed what you are doing. You will not hold it against me, and refuse a ride home?'

Bel looked about for his curricle, noting that when he added, 'I have it down a side-street, Cassius attending,' he had the grace to blush.

'Diplomatic treachery at work, I see,' she commented sardonically. 'Was it Cassius who followed me? I am sure that it was not yourself!'

Francis chose to ignore this, saying instead as they rounded the corner to see Cassius staring at them, a knowing expression on his wrinkled face, 'I shall say nothing of this to Almeria and Philip, for had you wished them to know I am sure you would have told them. I do not think they would be displeased, you know.'

'Perhaps not,' said Bel a little curtly as Francis helped her up, Cassius attending to the horses, 'but I have no wish for gossip as Mr Birch says, and you must know as well as I do that the Methodist connection is not well seen, even if the Countess of Huntingdon has established a Connexion of her own. But I am not a countess, and my patronage would not be so honoured as hers, by no means.'

They were off, Bel's now empty basket on her knee, both of them unwontedly silent. Francis was wondering again about the strange nature of the courtesan he was driving home, and Bel was wondering about him. He had behaved so simply and properly to old Mr Birch; could it ever be that he might behave so to herself?

CHAPTER TEN

HENRY VENN, unable to believe his luck, did take Bel to the ball at the Assembly Rooms, and of course Bel was right: his mother did accompany them. Captain Howell and Marcus also claimed her for dances, but not Francis Carey.

Francis, in the oddest state of mind it had been his misfortune to suffer after the afternoon's contretemps—for that was the only way he could interpret it truthfully—could not bring himself to see Bel Merrick in public until he had recovered his usual haughty equanimity—if he could ever regain it, that was!

He hardly knew how he felt, and could not have believed the confusion of mind which he found himself in, and if anyone had told him a month ago that he would be in a mad frenzy of desire for a ladybird, was refusing to slake it by buying her, was not sure that he was other than in love with her, and was determined to have her in love with him, desperately and beyond reason, he would have called them a liar.

Seeing her in the garden with the children and later with Mr Birch had brought a new dimension to their relationship. What a paradox she was! He supposed that he should not be surprised to find that a loose woman was a practical and practising Christian, but he was.

147

Bel, for her part, was surprised to discover how sorry she was that Francis was absent. Whatever the reason, when he walked into a room she felt that he brought passion and vitality in with him, never mind that he despised her. All the other men she met seemed third-rate beside him.

'So, you have taken pity on poor Henry, then,' Almeria said to her in the interval between dances when Bel was alone. Henry had gone to fetch her a cooling drink, and his mama was busily engaged with three other mature matrons, destroying the reputations of any who incurred their displeasure, in the intervals of playing a game of whist in a small room opening into the ballroom itself.

'Francis refused to come,' she continued. 'He sent you his compliments, and hoped to attend, but said he was weary, needed an early night. Although what,' she added, 'he can have been doing in Lulsgate to weary him neither Philip nor I can think. London never seems to tire him so.'

'The country air this afternoon too strong for him?' said Bel, cryptically if a little naughtily.

'Perhaps,' said Almeria doubtfully. 'He did take a drive this afternoon — I believe he gave you a lift at the end of it; he seemed *distrait* when he returned.' She hesitated. 'He was a little as he was when his wife died. I feel that perhaps it would be right of me to inform you of his sad story. I know that he will never tell you, and Philip would say I was interfering, but I think that you ought to know; it explains him so much.'

She fell silent, and Bel said nothing. Francis was, or rather had been, married! She wondered what had happened, and her heart beat rapidly as she waited for Almeria to continue.

'He was only nineteen when he married his childhood sweetheart, Cassie — Cassandra Poyntz, Sir Charles Poyntz's daughter. They were so in love, and Francis was not a bit as he is now — a little forbidding, I must admit. He was so happy and jolly, rather like a more responsible Marcus. He was in the navy, as I suppose you know. They only had five happy months together, then Francis had to go to sea and left Cassie in Portsmouth; she was two months pregnant. He was on HMS Circe, which was sunk in action; he was transferred to another ship going to a West Indies station, and, what with one thing and another, instead of being back with her in a few months to be there when the baby was born it was a year before he saw Portsmouth again.

'And when he reached home she was five months dead, and the baby too. She was a little thing, very sweet and gentle, and the birth was something like poor Princess Charlotte's and the outcome was the same. Mother and child both dead. Poor Francis. You can imagine what it did to him. He quite changed. Jack, our brother, said he grew up in an hour, and that it was a pity it was so quick, for he refused all consolation, would never speak of her, and took occupation and duty for his wife, would hardly look at a woman — indeed, he has spoken to and shown more interest in you than in all the other women in his life since Cassie died put together.'

Almeria fell silent; she had promised Philip that she would not interfere, but she had felt that Bel should know the truth about her half-brother.

Oh, poor Francis, what a terrible story! was Bel's immediate and pitying reaction. It gave him no right to treat her as he did, but she could understand why he would never give his heart away again, seeing what had happened to him when he had done so before — everything gone in an instant when he had been looking forward to wife and child both.

She guessed, too, and guessed correctly, that duty and shunning the fair sex had brought Francis to the point where he had come to see women as enemies, waiting to hurt him again.

She grew quiet, thoughtful, and when Henry returned the bright sparkle of her early evening manner had gone, so much so that on Henry's showing his displeasure at Captain Howell for coming to claim her for their dance she dismissed it as absently as she did his further criticism of the raffish captain, as he termed him, after he had returned her. In the same *distraite* fashion she had agreed to Rhys Howell's insistence that he visit her the following day.

That night, lying in bed, she thought over her relationship with Francis, and bitterly regretted the anger which had seized her when he had burst in that first day, and the reckless deceit with which she had cheated him. She was compelled to admit that her own conduct had helped to provoke him into believing that she shared her sister's profession, and that at no time had she given him any reason to think otherwise than that she was a courtesan, too.

Well, in the words of her old governess, she thought ruefully, You have made your bed, Bel, and must lie on it, and then her usual bright wit conquered her ridiculous self-pity, as she added the gloss, and you must try to prevent Francis Carey from lying on it, too. Unless he offers you a wedding-ring, that is. And, thinking of him, she let sleep take her into a land where regrets and hopes were transformed into other symbols and she was running through a wood, tears streaming down her face, looking for something — what? — and, panting, woke to the realisation that, treat her as he might, it was Francis Carey, so sadly bereaved, for whom she was weeping. Or was it herself?

Bel had no desire whatsoever to entertain Rhys Howell. She felt an instinctive distrust of him and all his works, and was sorry to see what a firm friend he was of silly young Marcus's; for all her youth, she had discovered that she possessed the power to read people aright. She wondered again if Marianne had shared it, and wondered further if it had helped to make her so successful.

She waited for the sound of the knocker all morning, quite distracted, causing Mrs Broughton to say mildly, 'You are hardly yourself today, my dear. I do hope that you are not sickening for something.'

'No,' said Bel rapidly, and to stop further comment picked up *Filippo's Tower* and said, 'Pray allow me to read to you, madam,' only for Mrs Broughton to look at her, scandalised, and remark,

'In the morning, my dear?' for she had been brought up in a household where novels were allowed to be read provided only that they were indulged in in the afternoon, when all one's duties were done.

'Oh, yes,' sighed Bel, and picked up the little nightdress she was working, and began to hem industriously, an occupation which had one drawback: she had the time to think both of Captain Howell's unwanted visit, and of Francis Carey's being either cold and haughty, or unwontedly amorous—both expressions seemingly reserved for Mrs Bel Merrick!

The doorknocker duly reverberated through the house. Mrs Broughton looked up from her plain sewing—canvas work, like novels, being reserved for the afternoon, and said hopefully, 'I do hope that that is dear Lord Francis come a-calling. I do declare I am quite in love with the man. Oh, to be twenty-five again!'

But it was, as Bel expected, Captain Howell whom the maid announced, and Captain Howell who came in, his black cane with its ivory top in his hand, his clothes just that little bit too fashionable in a flash way. Indeed, in another world, of which Bel knew nothing, he was known as 'Flash Howell' and valued accordingly.

'Ladies.' He was all good manners this morning: he put down his hat and his cane beside the chair which he was offered, made small talk for a moment, and then said, almost carelessly, leaning forward to give Bel the full benefit of his smile, 'My dear Mrs Merrick, I wonder if you would allow me to have a few words alone with you? I have some private messages for you, from your sister, which she has asked me to deliver, concerning your family. You will forgive us, madam, will you not?' he said, turning his doubtful charm on Mrs Broughton.

'My sister?' queried Bel, trying to keep her voice steady. She had had but the one, Marianne, also known as Marina St George, and to hear Captain Howell speak of sister and messages filled her with nameless dread.

'Your dear sister Marianne,' said Rhys Howell sweetly. 'You have but the one, I believe.'

Had was the proper tense, thought Bel distractedly, but looked at Mrs Broughton; if Rhys Howell proposed to speak to her of Marianne — and how had he tracked her here, and how did he know that she was Marianne's sister? — she had no wish for Mrs Broughton to be present.

'No matter,' smiled Mrs Broughton, determined to love every gentleman who seemed to possess a *tendre* for dear Bel. 'I will take a turn in the garden. I see our neighbour is there; we may discuss the prospect of a good plum crop together. Plum tart is a favourite delicacy of mine,' and she drifted through the glass doors to the garden.

'What an obliging soul,' remarked Rhys Howell, looking after her, an unpleasant leer on his face.

'My sister, you said,' offered Bel, desperate to get this over with, an indelicate expression used by her maid Lottie for anything from taking physic to listening to a tedious sermon in church.

'Ah, yes, your sister,' drawled the captain. 'Dear Mrs Marina St George, such a high flyer; you may imagine how I felt when I came back from urgent business on the Continent to discover her unexpectedly dead, her sister inherited, the house sold. I was desolate. We were partners, she and I. I cannot for the world understand how she came to forget

me in her will. Why, she owed her start in her. . .
way of life to me, and an apt pupil she certainly
was.'

He paused. 'You were about to say something,
Mrs Merrick?' and he trod hard on the word Mrs,
his expression sardonic.

Bel would not be put off by his odious mixture of
innuendo and familiarity.

'Mrs Marina St George?' she began. 'I know of
no such person.'

'Oh, come, my love,' said Captain Howell, closing
one eye in a wink so lubricious that Bel shuddered
before it. 'No need to try to flim-flam me, my dear
Miss Passmore. A useful invention, Mr Merrick, I
am sure. You share your dead sister's wit and
inventiveness; we should be splendid partners, you
and I. Clergymen's daughters make the best whores,
should they decide to go to the bad, and your sister
went to the bad most spectacularly. Now you, you
could rival her — you have managed to preserve a
delicacy and innocence which are quite remarkable.'

'You have lost me,' said Bel, rising. 'I ask you to
leave. I have no idea of what you speak.'

'Won't do, you know,' leered Captain Howell
confidentially, putting a hand familiarly on Bel's
knee. 'Father the Reverend Mr Caius Passmore,
sister the late and talented Marina, servant named
Lottie, who was close-mouthed, for a woman, but
felt compelled to write to her great-nephew, upon
whom she dotes, where you are and what you were
doing. . . You see I speak no lie; your sister and I
were so close she told me everything of you. Now
what, I wonder, would that upright gentleman Lord

Francis Carey think, if informed that the virtuous little widow was the sister of the fair Marina, and probably a dab hand at the game herself? Wouldn't like him to know, would you — eh, would you?' And his voice rose menacingly.

Bel had a desperate desire to laugh, seeing that Lord Francis also shared the delusion of her lack of virtue with Captain Howell, and would not be in the least surprised at whatever Captain Howell chose to tell him.

'And the aristocratic sister, and the parson husband — what would they think of their pious home's being a haven for such as yourself, my dear? Worth something to keep me quiet, do you think? That is if you don't want to resume Marina's partnership with me, eh?' His wink grew more grotesque by the minute.

Had Marianne really been this low rogue's partner, thought Bel, and did it matter if she had? In the here and now he was perfectly able to ruin her socially and financially, and would have no scruple about doing either.

She rose, deciding to put on a brass face and deny everything. 'I am still at a loss,' she replied, her voice freezing, 'and I ask you to leave immediately. I am not accustomed to being insulted in my own home.'

Captain Howell put his finger by his nose. 'Oh, I'm patient, sweet, patient. I mean to stay in this dull backwater a while longer, and you, you'll go nowhere, for you've nowhere to go. I shall remind you of my wishes, madam, until reckoning day, when you'll either give me what your sister morally owed me, or I shall tell Lulsgate Spa of the serpent in their bed of flowers. Until then, madam, adieu.'

He picked up his hat and cane, walked to the door, bowed mockingly and added, 'Allow me to congratulate you, madam. I do believe that you are as cool a piece as the great Marina herself, and you deserve his haughty lordship as a prize, yes, you do. But beware, madam, beware. I know these high-nosed gentlemen. Should he discover who and what you are. . .' and he wagged his head commiseratingly at her '. . .*that* would be an interesting day, a most interesting day. Till we meet again, madam, for meet we most assuredly shall — to do good business together, I hope — you must not keep all the rewards to yourself!'

CHAPTER ELEVEN

BEL hardly knew whether to laugh or to cry: to laugh at Captain Howell's notion of the shock which Lord Francis Carey would receive over the knowledge that Bel's sister was Marina St George, something which he already knew, or to cry over the fact that two men now knew her secret — and the second a malignant creature who would not hesitate to harm her in any way he could in order to get some, or all, of Marina's fortune for himself.

And there was no one whom she could tell or to whom she could turn for advice or help. She was quite alone, and the strange thought struck her that the vile way in which Captain Howell had spoken to her, not only the manner of his speech, but the way in which he had looked at her, held his body, revealed how different a man Francis Carey was from the unpleasant captain, even though he despised her for being, as he thought, a courtesan.

Bel even realised that in other circumstances she might have gone to Francis for help and protection, something which was now impossible.

Pondering this, she heard the knocker go again, and voices in the hall. The door opened and the little maid stood there, only to be swept aside by Francis, his face ablaze, saying, 'I must see Mrs Merrick, and at once.'

Bel wanted no more scandal, and said coolly,

feeling that she had exchanged one tormentor, Captain Howell, only to gain another, Francis Carey, 'Yes, you may see me, Lord Francis,' so that the little maid bobbed at her and departed. She turned to him, lifted her brows and, still cool, said, 'Well, sir, what brings you here in such a pelter that you have forgotten your breeding?'

Francis made no response to this last. Lip curling, he said, 'So, you have been entertaining the captain alone? Remarkable, seeing what a pother you made over walking with me in the garden with Mrs Broughton playing nearby dragon!'

'It is no business of yours. . .' began Bel, only to have him fling at her,

'It is not only your reputation for which you should have a care, madam, but your safety which you should also consider. The man is, I am certain — nay, I have reason to know — little more than a common criminal. He left the Life Guards under the most dubious circumstances, was forced to flee England because he cheated his criminal associates, performed the same unwise act in France, and was compelled to return — which is why he is here, rather than London, to escape vengeance, one presumes — and you, madam, see fit to entertain him alone!'

He ran out of breath, and about time too, thought Bel, the courage with which she always faced life strong in her as he moved towards her. She had been standing by the glass doors when he entered, about to rejoin Mrs Broughton, whom she could see, head bobbing, talking with their neighbour — about plum tart probably! This prosaic thought, against all the suppressed violence which had been

going on in her quiet drawing-room, made her want
to giggle.

Francis saw the smile blossom on her face, misinterpreted it, and said furiously, 'A joke, madam?
You think Rhys Howell's unsavoury reputation a
joke!'

'I am wondering,' said Bel, her heart hammering,
'why, knowing this of him, you do nothing about it.
The man should be before the Justices, surely, if
half of what you say of him is true.'

'Oh, indeed,' he almost snarled, 'I should have
known that your light-footed wit would have you
firing broadsides at me. Well, let me tell you, my
legal-minded lady, that I have no evidence of this to
satisfy a court, but, being in France when he was,
and at the Embassy, I knew a deal more than I
should about such. . .persons, even if little enough
to do anything about it, except to be wary, and warn
my friends.'

'Your friends!' Bel's contemptuous snort of laughter would have graced a Drury Lane melodrama, so
fine was it. 'Am I, then, to count myself one of their
number? You surprise me, sir. I thought that I was
only fit to be thrown on a bed and ravished, or tied
to the cart's tail as a common whore to be whipped!'

'Oh.' Poor Francis was breathless. Armoured
with rage at both men who were in their different
fashions blackmailing her, Bel had never looked so
lovely. Her luminous green eyes flashed fire; even
her red curls seemed springier; the tender mouth
quivered voluptuously; her whole beautiful body,
although she did not know this, seemed to be
straining against the light muslin dress she wore. It

was enough to drive any red-blooded male mad with desire. Francis Carey felt a very red-blooded male indeed. 'I come to warn you, help you, madam, since you seem to need it, and what reward do I receive? A lawyer in skirts, instructing me of my duty.'

He was almost upon her, and a dreadful mirth, akin to hysteria, Bel knew, began to inform her. She dodged away from him, into the room—she dared not let him pursue her outside, for fear that the anger which consumed him might cause him to be unwise before Mrs Broughton and reveal all, which would never do.

In her haste to remove him from the revealing window she caught against the little occasional table on which her workbox stood and knocked it over, the child's nightdress and the contents of the box cascading across the floor, pins, reels of cotton, her thimble, crochet hooks and all the paraphernalia which accompanied a lady's sewing spread out between them.

To Bel's surprise this minor disaster seemed infinitely more important than all the dreadful threats which the two men in her life had thrown at her.

'Oh, no,' she wailed, 'now look what you have made me do!' and she fell plump on her knees on the carpet, grieving over each pin and hook as though she were recovering the treasures of Midas, at least.

Francis was nearly as fevered as she was. Jealousy, desire and frustration held him in thrall, and the sight of her on her knees on the carpet, lovely face distressed, overset him further.

To his own subsequent astonishment — what could have got into him to behave so uncharacteristically? — he found himself on his knees before her, to the ruin of his breeches, his boots and his common sense, none of them assisted by the violence which he was doing to them. 'Oh, no,' he crooned, clumsily trying to pick up pins, 'do not grieve,' and then, as she stared at him astonished, the little nightgown in her hands, a crystal teardrop running down one damask cheek, he was going mad, wanting to write poetry — to a whore, yes, a whore, but what did that matter? He put up his hands to clasp her face in them, saying tenderly, 'Oh, do not cry, I beg of you, do not cry, pray let me kiss that tear away,' and before she could stop him he licked up the salty pearl and began to suit his actions to his words.

He had forgotten that he had promised himself that she would be on her knees begging him, not the other way round, but no matter. While Bel. . .

While Bel what? She should be thrusting him away, telling him to take his mouth where it was wanted, but each delicate moth-like kiss made it harder and harder for her to do any such thing. She was so near to him that she could see that his eyes were not a pure grey but had little black flecks in them, like granite. Could granite melt? It seemed to be doing so.

She gave a little moan, dropped the nightgown among the scattered pins and needles, and gently, very gently, as he lifted his mouth from her eyes to transfer it to her mouth, she kissed him back — and then sanity prevailed.

Mrs Broughton might come in, and she hated him, did she not? He thought her a whore and would shortly, if she were not careful, be treating her as one, here on the carpet, among the pins and needles; and what would Mrs Broughton think? For his hands had left her face and were beginning to pull her dress down. So she pushed him away before her body could betray her, and sprang to her feet, to leave him among the needles and pins; it was all that he deserved.

'Oh, you are all the same,' she raged at him. 'Show a little weakness, and you are all over us. And how can you, with all that you have said to me, be in the least surprised that I should wish to favour Captain Howell? If all diplomats are such muddled thinkers as you are — and naval captains, too,' she flung in for good measure, 'no wonder it took us so long to win the war, and to win allies, such mad heedlessness as you show, with Mrs Broughton in the garden and likely to interrupt you at your work any minute. Shame on you!'

Francis, still on his knees, stared up at her. Paradise so near, and now so far away. He wanted to pull her to the carpet, but Mrs Broughton's name was like cold water to him, whereas the sight of the angry Bel served only to rouse him further. He ached, yes, he did, and damn his treacherous body which had now overtaken the cold mind which had ruled it for so long, and mastered it quite, so that Bel Merrick walked through his days as well as his dreams.

And that came, he tried to tell himself sternly, from over-continence; Marcus was right, he should have indulged himself more, pleasured a few bits of muslin, and then this one bit of muslin would not inflame him so.

Useless talk — it was Bel Merrick he wanted and none else, and now she must know it, the witch, and would tantalise him the more, if he knew women.

He rose, conscious that for once all his haughty pride had fled from him — and she had done that, with one tear; one damned tear, and he was undone.

'You wrong me,' he began, and what a stupid thing to say — could he think of nothing better? 'I had meant to console you merely, but you do not seem to need consolation.'

'Oh!' exclaimed Bel. 'Consolation! I am not so green as to think that *that* was what you were about. Unless you were consoling yourself, that is!' She was rather proud of that last statement; it was quite fit to be one of La Rochefoucauld's witty *Maxims*, she thought.

Francis said, through his teeth, 'You are pleased to reproach me, madam. Believe me, you cannot reproach me more than I reproach myself.'

'For failing in your fell design to ravish me, presumably,' flashed Bel, on whom adversity seemed to be bestowing the gift of tongues. 'I cannot believe that you are feeling ashamed of so accosting me — *again*!' And her eyes flashed fire and ice.

That usually resourceful nobleman Francis Carey had no answer to this. He had never found himself in such a position before, and had certainly no experience to call on to advise him. God help me, he thought, if I were the womaniser she must think me, I should know what to do—unknowingly in the same case as Bel, who was as innocent as he was!

They stared at one another, each crediting the other with a past as lurid as it was imaginary, and each so strongly attracted to the other that they were compelled to call the emotion they were mutually experiencing hate, for they dared not admit that it was love.

'I think that you had better leave, at once, sir,' declaimed Bel, all dignity, rivalling Mrs Siddons in her best dramatic fit, to have him reply humbly, for him,

'You will remember a little what I said of Captain——' to have Bel retort,

'Oh, this is brave, sir, brave,' more in the line of Dorothy Jordan expressing grief at a wanton social misunderstanding than Siddons as Herodias about to demand John the Baptist's head on a platter.

Francis walked to the door, head high, past Bel, also head high, both principals congratulating themselves firmly on their recovered self-command, both painfully aware that in their recent passage they had given themselves away completely.

To think that I could find myself in love with such a haughty peacock who thinks all women are fair game, raged Bel inwardly, as Francis reproached himself for falling for a lightskirt, and then behaving towards her like a bullyboy whom Captain Howell might despise.

'Oh!' Bel let out a long breath, sank into a chair, as Mrs Broughton finally arrived, to prattle vaguely of plum tart, Lord Francis missed, *Filippo's Tower*, the changing weather, and how delightfully well Bel looked.

'All this social junketing must agree with you, my dear. You never looked so when we led a quiet life. You bloom, you positively bloom, I do declare!'

Lord Francis Carey was not blooming. Furious with himself for his loss of self-control — or was it that his loss of self-control had not gone far enough? — he strode down the main street of Lulsgate Spa, cutting everyone right, left and centre in his determination to reach his nephew and warn him of the captain. A letter which he had sent to London had brought him a reply, giving him further, worse information about the man — hence his visit to Bel, and his anger at seeing Howell visit her, apparently in her confidence.

He strode into the taproom at the White Peacock unaware that his expression was thunderous, and whether his rage was directed at himself, Marcus, Captain Howell or Bel Merrick he did not know.

Marcus was seated at one of the tables, a tankard in front of him, smoking a clay pipe, an experiment he was beginning to regret. There was no sign of his usual court of hangers-on. He looked up in mild surprise as his uncle entered.

'Didn't know you favoured this sort of entertainment, sir,' he offered almost reproachfully.

'I don't.' And Marcus could not help noticing that, saying this, his uncle was even more glacial than usual. Oh, Hades, another sermon, he thought glumly, and prepared to be lectured again. What was it this time? He did not have long to wait to find out.

'I am glad to find you alone,' began Francis, refusing the chair which Marcus pointed out to him. 'Thank you, no, I have no intention of staying. I have come to warn you that Captain Howell is not a fit person for someone of your station and expectations to make a friend of, never mind a boon companion,' he continued, his temper not helped by Marcus's eyes beginning to roll heavenwards.

'I know that I am no longer your guardian——'

He got no further, for Marcus said petulantly, 'Amen, to that, sir, and, that being so, I am in no mind to be lectured by you. Rhys Howell is no better and no worse than a hundred others in society, and I find him amusing.'

'Then your taste is deplorable.' Francis was not prepared to give way on this. 'I must warn you not to play cards with him. I know that you frequent the tables at Gaunt's Club on Bridge Street, and it has come to my attention that you have already lost large sums to him; you must be aware that you cannot afford to do so.'

'Win some, lose some,' yawned Marcus aggravatingly. 'I won last week, he wins this week, next week the luck will turn again. All square at the end, Uncle, the odds see to that.'

'They do if all the players are honest——' began Francis, only to be interrupted again.

'Oh, damn that for a tale, sir, begging your pardon,' said Marcus. 'No reason to think Rhys other than straight. Sing another tune, sir, this one's flat.'

Francis could think of no tune which he could sing that would please anyone he knew. Even Almeria and Philip were looking at him a little sideways these days, especially Philip, and as for Bel Merrick. . .so it was not surprising that Marcus was recalcitrant—he should have expected nothing else.

'Very well,' he said, preparing to leave. 'I have done my best to warn you, but if you refuse to listen. . .' And he shrugged his shoulders. 'I would have thought that the man's character shone on his face—that, and the fact that he has come to Lulsgate at all.'

'He came because I did,' returned Marcus impudently. 'Is it so very strange, Uncle, that someone likes me, does not spend his time dooming at me like some messenger fellow in that damned dull Greek stuff they forced down my throat at Oxford?'

Francis turned and stared at his nephew, wondering how his clever brother Jack could have spawned such an ass. 'If you had listened to that damned dull stuff more carefully,' was his cold reply, 'you would have discovered that fools in them got short shrift for their folly. I leave you to Captain Howell. You deserve one another.'

And I was no more successful with Marcus than I was with Bel Merrick, he thought, but at least she was intelligent in her waywardness, whereas Marcus. . . All that he possesses to recommend him is a pretty face and a willingness to be cozened.

Listening to Mrs Broughton read *Filippo's Tower* to her did absolutely nothing to restore Bel to her normal tranquil state of mind. The determined silliness of Bianca dei Franceschini's every response to the predicament in which she found herself roused her, for once, to tears rather than laughter.

How could she be so stupid as to take refuge with vile Federigo Orsini and fly the noble and improbably virtuous Rafaello degli Uberti? Real people did not behave like that, not at all. Why, even she, inexperienced as she was, could recognise Captain Howell for the villain which Lord Francis had confirmed him to be.

Her anger with Francis Carey was not for pointing out to her what she already knew, but because he seemed to think that he was the only one allowed to prey on Bel Merrick! Not that she saw Francis Carey as wicked; no Federigo Orsini he — that role was reserved for Rhys Howell. It was merely that he was morally blind when it came to reading Bel Merrick. And that was partly her fault, was it not? That blind moment of temper in Stanhope Street had unleashed all this on her.

Not that she could blame Rhys Howell's villainy on Francis Carey, since the captain would presumably have tracked her down even if Francis Carey had never existed, and she was now caught in two nets, not one, with no idea of how to extricate herself from either.

But one way or another, she promised herself, I will. And how inconvenient life was, that real people were not hopelessly virtuous like Rafaello, but more of a mixture, like Francis; and presumably, then, even Rhys Howell was not as completely villainous as Federigo Orsini was, even though he might be so towards herself and Marcus. . .

Bel gave up, allowed Mrs Broughton's soothing tones to pour over her, like treacle from a jar, and when that lady put the book down, sighing, 'Oh, how delightful, even better than *Lady Caroline's Secret*,' Bel did not scream at her, Oh, what bosh you talk, madam. You know as well as I do how ridiculously improbable all that we read to each other is. For it passed over her in a wave, or even as a revelation, like one being smitten by God, as Mr Birch would have said, that Mrs Broughton and all those who read the Minerva Press's productions were seeking refuge in them from the intolerable demands of a world in which Mrs Broughton, if not employed by Bel, would have slowly starved to death in genteel poverty.

To live in a world where right always triumphed and virtue was its own reward — but also gained a fair share of the world's goods as well — must always be not only soothing to the nerves but an aid to sleep; and happiness achieved that way felt no different from happiness achieved in any other.

Bel could not help smiling to herself as she thought this. I am truly a parson's daughter, she decided, to moralise and think such things, and I don't believe, although pray God I shall never be put to it to find out, that I could ever have followed Marianne's way of life.

And then, again, revelation struck. But suppose I had been tempted by Francis, without the cushion of Marianne's ill-gotten wealth behind me; how

would I have behaved then? For face it, Bel, if he
desires you, as he plainly does, then you desire him,
and if that were a way out of poverty and misery,
what then, Bel Merrick, what then?

CHAPTER TWELVE

OF COURSE, life had to slow down a little, Bel thought; it could not go in the same hectic fashion that it had done since first Francis Carey and then Rhys Howell had arrived in Lulsgate Spa.

Neither of them made a move in the strange three-cornered game she was playing with them — or they were playing with her. The somnolent peace which had prevailed in Lulsgate during the two years in which she had lived there resumed; it was as though nothing had happened, or would ever happen.

Bel attended the St Helen's sewing circle, arranged the flowers in the church, took her daily walk, visited Lady Almeria and Philip, spoke coolly to Lord Francis when she met him, bowed distantly to Captain Howell — she could not afford to cut him — joked a little with Marcus, finished *Filippo's Tower*, took out *The Hermit of San Severino* — the Hermit being someone who vaguely resembled Francis Carey, all haughty pride, straight mouth and hard grey eyes, as well as his overbearing rectitude towards everyone except the heroine.

The heroine was not a bit like Bel; true, she was virtuous, but she had no spirit at all, allowed the Hermit to walk all over her, scorning her, although she was so determinedly proper that she was only fit for a saint. Bel was quite out of patience with her.

She really ought to give the Hermit what for, as Garth used to say.

Coming out of her little class at Morewood one day, the late August rain pelting down, she found Francis Carey waiting for her at Mr Birch's gate, a large green umbrella in his hand. This unromantic sight amused her — was this part of his strategy to bring her to her knees before him? If so it seemed a strange one.

'You will allow me to drive you home, I trust? It is really not at all wise for you to walk through this downpour. You will catch a cold.'

What could Bel say? She could not bring herself to send him away when he had been standing in the rain waiting for her. She could see Mr Birch hovering in his little bow window; he had expressed his distress that she should be going home without proper protection. 'You will be soaked before you get very far.'

Bel could not make out the expression on Mr Birch's face as Francis held the umbrella over her head and walked her to the curricle, Cassius, his withered face impassive, water dripping off his little top hat, standing behind.

'Poor Cassius,' she said. 'He will be soaked through by the time we reach Lulsgate.'

'His fault,' said Francis curtly. 'He insisted on coming. I told him that he was not needed. He said that he was always needed.' His expression lightened a little. 'I could not make out who Cassius thought needed the chaperon, you or me.'

'Oh, you!' exclaimed Bel, relieved that matters

were light between them. 'He does not heed me, I am sure. He is protecting you from me.'

Francis knew this not to be true. He had been aware ever since they had reached Lulsgate that both Cassius and his man, Walters, disapproved of him and his dealings with Bel. Cassius had said to him, indeed — and how he knew of Francis's belief as to Bel's lack of reputation Francis could not imagine, 'You're wrong, you know, *sir* —— ' and the 'sir' was insulting. 'She's a good woman, Mrs Bel Merrick, none better,' and then had turned his back on his master.

'I,' Francis had said frostily to the turned back, 'am not interested in your opinions about any woman, good or bad.'

Cassius had muttered something rude under his breath, and when ordered to fetch the cattle, and see them properly harnessed, had announced that he would be up, 'whatever.'

Francis rarely pulled rank with his servants. They and he usually knew exactly how they stood with one another. 'A hard man, but fair', was Cassius's usual description of him to the staff in the houses which they visited. Faced with this act of mutiny, he said coldly, 'You will do as I order you, man. For God's sake, who is the master here?'

Cassius, already donning his hat and its red and white cockade, Francis's colours, said, 'You'll do without me, then, for good, sir,' and turned steady eyes on his master.

Francis drew in his breath and readied himself to use his best quarterdeck voice, designed to make

Satan on his throne quail, but something in the steady eye Cassius turned on him stopped him.

'I do believe,' he said, face and voice incredulous, 'that you are constituting yourself her protector when I drive her in the curricle.'

'She needs one, then?' returned Cassius, giving no ground at all. 'You wish me to leave your service, *sir*?'

Francis cursed beneath his breath. He had no mind to lose Cassius, and why that should be was another mystery. The little man always went his own way, and this was not the first time such an act of insubordination had occurred.

'Get up, then, damn you,' he finished. 'You may have the privilege of being soaked to the skin, and if you take a rheum do not expect me to nurse you, or give you sympathy!'

Cassius rolled his eyes heavenwards, did as he was bid, and all the way to Mr Birch's home and back again Francis could feel his beady eyes boring into his back.

'You have thought of what I told you of Captain Howell?' And then, seeing Bel's face flush with anger, he added hastily, 'I have reason to believe that Marcus has begun to lose large sums of money at Gaunt's gaming house to the captain and his dubious friends. Howell allowed him to win when he first came here — a common trick to catch pigeons and pluck them, and now Marcus sits about waiting for his luck to turn, which it never will.'

He did not know why he was telling Bel this — except to reinforce his warnings about Howell, and when she said, 'Have you spoken to your sister of this?' he replied wearily.

'Yes, and he will take no note of *her* warnings, either. The trouble is, the man comes from a reasonably good family, and Marcus is innocent enough to think that that alone is a guarantee of his good behaviour. But Howell tarnished his good name and reputation long ago, although that has never prevented him from ending up with some young fool in tow.'

Bel thought for a moment. She was genuinely sorry for Almeria's sake that Marcus was being so stupid, but could not help saying, 'When we first met, you were of the opinion that I was about to pluck the pigeon myself. Does this confidence mean that you have changed your mind?'

'Only to the extent,' he said kindly, but with his usual air of effortless superiority, 'that I do not think that Marcus is now your target — not rich enough, I think.'

'Oh', said Bel, exasperated, 'then who, pray, is my target? I should like to be enlightened. I hate to think that I am working in the dark.'

Overhearing this, Cassius gave a series of strangled coughs, like a small horse neighing.

'Myself, of course,' said Francis, pulling back on the reins to indicate that they were to stop, Bel's front door being reached. 'Richer, more of a prize; not such a good title perhaps, but better than you might have hoped to achieve. Not that marriage is necessarily your —— '

At this point what he was about to say was drowned by a coughing fit from the dripping Cassius, so noisy that Bel turned, said sympathetically, 'Oh, poor Cassius. How heartless of you,

Lord Francis, to drag him out in such weather,
without any means of protection. You must see that
he has a hot lemon drink with rum in it when he
goes in.'

Francis turned to stare at Cassius, and said grimly,
'His fault entirely if he dies of a rain-induced fever.
He insisted on riding behind, in defiance of my
orders. I have to say that it is bad enough to be
bullied by my tiger, without my would-be doxy
putting her oar in, and requiring me to nurse my
servant, instead of the other way about.'

'You have not been sitting in the rain, inad-
equately clothed,' replied Bel incontrovertibly, 'so
the question of his nursing you does not arise.'

'No more,' said Francis wrathfully. 'I insist,
Cassius, that you hand Mrs Merrick down before
she orders me to carry you to bed. I do believe the
pair of you are hatching some damned conspiracy
against me.' And then, seeing Bel's laughing
naughty face at having provoked him to lose his
temper, 'Why, madam, do I understand that you
are roasting me? Has your impudence no limits? I
should marry you off to my tiger here as a suitable
punishment for the pair of you.' Then, on hearing
the tiger's coughing laughter as he prepared to hand
Bel down, he was seized—again—with the most
dreadful desire to do her a mischief—the sort
of mischief which involved removing her clothes
and. . .and. . .

Francis thought that he was going mad. He
pushed Cassius to one side, took Bel by the arm,
and half ran down her little front garden to her own
door, and, regardless of watchers, said goodbye, or

rather kissed her goodbye, tipping her face up to do so.

The kiss, contrary to usage, began fiercely and ended gently, and when Bel said, eyes wicked as he straightened up, 'You had best hurry, Francis, or Cassius will drown,' he replied with a half-sob,

'Oh, you witch, Bel, you witch. What is it that you do to a man? When I am with you, all sense, all honour flies away from me.'

'I?' said Bel innocently. 'I do nothing, Francis. And while you are about it you have provided Mrs Venn with enough ammunition to aim at us for the rest of the season. If you have no care for your reputation, Francis, you might consider mine. I know that you think I do not possess one — but Lulsgate is my home, and so far I have led a spotless life. Should she say anything, I will inform her that she was mistook — you were removing a smut from my eye. Her sight is notoriously bad.'

'And you, my dear doxy,' said Francis, delighted at her quick wit, 'are as devious as you are desirable. You are right to remind me not to be over-fierce with you publicly. I have no mind to ruin you — yet; but if you smile at me like that I shall not answer for the consequences,' and he bent towards her again.

'Cassius,' said Bel firmly, and pushed him towards the gate, where Cassius stood patiently, holding the horses, his eye on his master. 'He thinks that you need protecting from me, in which of course he is quite wrong, the reverse being true.'

But you, my dear Mrs Bel Merrick, thought Francis, striding back to his curricle, do not have the right of that, for, improbably, Cassius had constituted himself your protector!

'Bel,' said Lady Almeria carefully as they sat side by side in the Harleys' drawing-room, working busily away, waiting for the rest of Lulsgate Spa's sewing circle to arrive, 'a word to the wise. Mrs Venn is a little of a viper for gossip, as I'm sure that you are aware, so it would be better not to give her occasion to circulate any.' She fell silent again, staring at her hem stitching.

Bel knew at once that Mrs Venn had been busily spreading the news of Francis Carey's public and stolen kiss around Lulsgate, that some kind person had gleefully retailed the gossip to the vicar's wife after such a fashion that Almeria felt that she had to counsel a young friend.

The sturdy independence which lay behind her decorative appearance reared its head; she bit her thread in two and said quietly, 'Perhaps such advice ought to be offered to your brother rather than myself, the man usually taking the lead in such matters. I think I know to what Mrs Venn referred, and she was quite mistook.' She was astonished at how easily the lie flowed from her lips, but she was not about to be destroyed by a combination of Francis's folly and Mrs Venn's jealousy of herself as a possible wife for her son—self-preservation was the order of the day. 'Francis gave me a lift home the other afternoon. He saw me to the door where he removed a smut from my eye for me. Doubtless Mrs Venn, in her enthusiasm to spread gossip around Lulsgate, misinterpreted what she saw.'

'Oh, dear.' Almeria coloured to her hairline, looked distressed, and put down her sewing. 'I should have thought before I. . . I should have known you both better, but I only wished to help you; you are after all so young, and Mrs Broughton. . .' She almost began to stammer, and Bel felt remorse that her lie should overset poor Almeria, but she had not asked for the kiss, or, rather, she *might* have done so, but never in such a public place. She knew that Francis had lost control for a moment, but could hardly tell his sister so.

She put out a hand to Almeria, the younger woman comforting the older one — there were times recently when Bel felt that she was ninety — and murmured gently, 'Do not distress yourself; you were right to counsel me if you thought that I was being indiscreet. I promise you, my dear friend, that I know how to treat your brother — or any other man, for that matter. Trust me.'

Almeria's face changed again. 'Oh, dear Bel,' she said, 'you are so alone, with no relatives to whom you may turn for advice, and, although you have always behaved with the most perfect discretion, as a woman you are vulnerable, and as your friend I would always wish to help you. Forgive me if I have hurt you by believing a falsehood.'

Bel, from being cool, a little distant, was herself again, charmingly impulsive, even if her impulses were controlled. She rose, kissed Almeria on the cheek and went to stand before the window, looking out across the garden, which backed on to Bel's own, tears filling her eyes, hating herself for the lie and at having caused Almeria distress by telling it.

Oh, Francis, she thought, if only we could have met after a proper fashion, introduced at a ball or in a drawing-room where the strong attraction we feel for one another could have taken its due course. Or if only I *had* been a lightskirt, so that we could have taken our pleasure together, heedless of consequences. As it is, we are trapped in a situation nearly as fraught as those of the novels I take home for Mrs Broughton, and with no easy way out, no author to wave a magic wand and bring all to a happy conclusion.

She resumed her seat, for she could hear the others arriving, and when they came in, Mrs Venn among them, she was her normal self again. Bel was not to know that when Francis entered the vicarage drawing-room later that day, telling Almeria that he would not be in for dinner, he intended to spend the evening at Gaunt's gaming club, she said quietly to him, something which Bel had said having struck home, 'Francis, a word with you.' She was a little fearful at his reaction to what she was about to say, for he was a formidable man, and no mistake. 'Lulsgate Spa is a small place, and gossip abounds, some of it not nice. I know that you seem attracted to my good friend, Mrs Bel Merrick, and I trust you to do nothing which would hurt her, or destroy her standing here.'

Francis stood stock-still, rigid. What could he say? Like Bel, he was reduced to a lie. He could not reply, The woman is not what you think, and, being what she is, has no reputation to destroy, and sooner or later I intend to take my long-deferred pleasure with her, and damn the consequences!

To his horror, shame ran through him. He tossed the gloves he was holding on to an occasional table, and, like Bel, walked to the window, but saw nothing. Through numb lips he said, 'I will never do anything to hurt a lady, Almy, dear, you may be sure of that.'

He hated himself for the equivocation. What a weaselling declaration! Bel Merrick being far from a lady, he might treat her as he pleased, but his half-sister would take his statement at its face value.

Like Bel, he wished that things had been different. He could, he knew, solve his problems by leaving Lulsgate Spa, forgetting her, but he could not. He was in her toils; what had begun as simple revenge had become something much more complex—he wanted Bel Merrick, most desperately, all of her, and he wanted her to come to him; he would not go to her, he would not, never.

Thinking so, he turned. 'Any more good advice, my dear?' And, although he did not know it, the face he showed her was hard, inimical, the face of a man staring down an enemy.

Almeria was horrified. Philip had warned her against meddling. She had meddled, and—what had she done?

'Oh, do forgive me,' she stammered, 'I had not meant. . .'

Like Bel, he leaned forward, face softening a little, to kiss her on the cheek. 'I know,' he said. 'But the road to hell is paved with good intentions—and there is a limit to what vicar's wives may or can do.'

It was a rebuke, Almeria knew, and one more

proof of Philip's wisdom. She would not meddle with Bel and Francis again, and she would listen to her husband's quiet advice in future — in the present she must learn to live with the knowledge that something more than simple mutual attraction lay between her friend and her brother.

Gaunt's gaming club was, as usual, well patronised: husbands, fathers, brothers and lovers were busy enjoying themselves. Francis looked around for Marcus and his low friends when he entered, but there was no sign of them. There were a few persons present whose acquaintance he had made in Lulsgate, including an old friend from his boyhood days, George Stamper, now a fat squire with a fat wife whom he had deserted for the night, having met Francis earlier in the day and offered to introduce him to Gaunt's.

'Good to get away from the women,' he sighed. 'See you had the common sense not to marry, Frank.' He had no knowledge of Francis's short marriage to Cassie, and Francis did not choose to enlighten him. He agreed to make up a four for whist with two cronies of George's, and looked around Gaunt's while introductions were being made.

It was quite a reasonable gaming hell, as hells went, and if one had to gamble outside one's home, seeing that it could only be done in clubs in private these days, Francis supposed that Gaunt's was as good a place as any.

The room he was in was respectable enough, although there was another down a short corridor,

George told him, where there were girls and 'other possibilities'—to do with the girls, presumably. Francis wondered, briefly, if Marcus was already there, but the 'other place' did not open until nine of the clock, and it was now only seven.

Along one wall a huge sideboard ran, on which were set out plates of excellent food, which came free, once the heavy entrance fee had been paid. On a small table stood a large silver wine cooler, full of bottles of good white wine; red wine stood on a shelf beneath the table, and rows of glasses were stored in a cupboard whose doors were perpetually open.

The four men about to play whist ate and drank first. Francis attracted a good deal of attention. A member of a distinguished noble family, he was something of a pasha in this company, and his very air of cool indifference to others added to the impression of effortless superiority which he always gave off.

Even George Stamper was affected by it, and sought to dispel the unease it created in him by clapping Francis on the back and behaving as though they had been uninterrupted boon companions in the sixteen years since they had last seen one another.

Eating over, they carried their wine glasses and a plate of ratafia biscuits to their table and began to play. Francis's luck was as good as his skill; his attention was not on the game, however, but on the door, and it was almost with a sense of relief that he saw Rhys Howell enter.

Marcus did not, at first, appear to be with him.

But, suddenly, in the small group which comprised Howell's raffish court, and which followed him in, Francis suddenly saw his nephew being held erect by two knowing rogues. Marcus was half-cut already, his face flushed, and as he walked, or rather staggered, to the table where hazard was being played it was evident that he was a pigeon ripe for the plucking.

Rage with Howell, coupled with annoyance at Marcus for being such a weak young fool, consumed Francis, but little of it showed. He kept an unobtrusive eye on the goings-on at the hazard table, and became convinced that Howell and the man who ran the table were in collusion, and that Marcus was their joint victim. Marcus was playing against Howell, and Francis could hear the rattle of the dice box behind him, and Marcus's blurred voice cursing as luck constantly favoured Howell.

'Dammit, Howell, the devil's in the dice that I do so badly,' floated across the room towards Francis as the round of whist ended.

'Excuse me, gentlemen,' said Francis, rising, his face hard and angry. He pushed the money he had won into the centre of the table. 'I fear that I must leave you, and you may share what I have won between you as a recompense for spoiling your game, but I have a duty to perform.'

He turned towards the hazard table, where Marcus, face purple, was sprawled in his chair, peering angrily at a smiling Rhys Howell, who was plainly sober. The whole scene was reminiscent of a print from a sequence rightly called *The Rake's*

Progress, showing the young fool of an heir being despoiled by his hangers-on.

On impulse Francis picked up a bottle of wine and a glass as he passed the wine table on his way towards Marcus. He ignored Rhys Howell, who stared at him insolently, saying, 'Want to throw a main, Carey? Thought you was only interested in old lady's games like whist, haw, haw!'

'Marcus,' said Francis, not quite in his quarter-deck voice, but near it. 'Time to go home, I think. You're hardly up to hazard or any other game in that state.'

Marcus peered at him owlishly and muttered, 'Death's head at the feast again, Uncle, are you? Want to stay until the luck changes. You go home to bed if you want. . .'

One more drink, thought Francis dispassionately, might have him unconscious, judging by his appearance. He disliked Howell intensely, but did not want an open fight with him; however, behind Francis's back, Howell was saying in a jeering voice, 'Man's of age, Carey. Can do as he pleases. Not yours to run any more.'

Francis decided on another ploy. He poured a bumper of what he suddenly saw was port, not a light red wine, from the bottle he was holding, and held it out invitingly to his nephew.

'Come on, old fellow,' he almost crooned. 'I'm not such a bad chap after all. Drink a toast with me. No heeltaps, and God bless Queen Caroline, and all who sail in her.'

This was so uncharacteristic that Marcus took the proffered glass with a crack of laughter, and, throw-

ing his head back, drank the lot down, watching his
uncle swallow his share from the bottle.

Francis's own draught was smaller than any of the
spectators realised, and as Marcus, the drink safely
down him, shuddered and fell forward, his eyes
rolling, and purple face turning ashen, Francis,
praying that he had not overdone things, caught
him, and swung his nephew over his shoulder, head
on one side, legs on the other.

Even Rhys Howell, he thought, could hardly
complain at his removing a victim who was now
dead drunk; but he underestimated the captain.

One hand plucking at Francis's sleeve as he
manoeuvred his way to the door, he hissed for the
room to hear, 'Damn you, Carey. You did that
deliberately. He owes me this game.'

Francis, enraged at the hand on his arm, and
Howell's unwanted familiarity, swung round to face
the man who was robbing and exploiting his nephew.

'Oh,' he said, his face ferocious, the face of the
man who had boarded French war ships, pistol in
one hand, cutlass in the other, 'you mean that you
wanted him drunk enough to fleece, but not so
drunk that he was unconscious and you couldn't
ruin him?'

Everyone in the room heard the insult. A deathly
quiet fell. Howell's face turned black with fury, and
Francis, who had broken his own rule of not provoking trouble, was so buoyed up by anger that he
hardly cared what he said or did.

'Satisfaction!' cried Howell. 'I'll have satisfaction
from you for that, damn you, Carey. No fine gentleman insults me with impunity.'

'No?' said Francis through his teeth. 'Well, let me inform you that I have no need to prove my courage, and I have no intention of fighting such as yourself. Rummage through the gutter if you want a fight, but don't come near me.'

'You'll pay for this. I swear you'll pay for this, Carey.'

'By God,' said Francis, swinging around again, treating Marcus's dead weight as though it did not exist. 'Call me Carey in that familiar way once more, and I *will* kill you. Now be quiet, and let me get this young fool home to his aunt's. Tell the White Peacock he'll not be returning there. My man will call for his traps tomorrow.'

He was out of the door and in the street, his companions holding back the raving Howell, Francis's late whist partners staring after him.

'Well,' said George Stamper, happy at this interesting diversion which had lightened the drab domesticity of Lulsgate Spa, 'I heard that Frank Carey had turned into a tiger when he went into the navy, but this beats all. That feller,' he said, pointing at Howell, 'ought to be glad Frank won't fight him. A devil with pistol or swords, they say. A man would be a fool to provoke him.'

Which was the general epitaph agreed to by those present as the evening now settled back into its usual calm, and George Stamper treated himself to one of the girls in 'the other place' as a reward for having introduced Frank Carey to Gaunt's gaming club, and given the company there a rare treat.

* * *

'Oh, Bel,' wailed Almeria to her friend, 'we have
never had such goings-on in Lulsgate in all the years
we have lived here. So quiet and, yes, dull. And it
is all Francis's fault—and he is usually so proper.
First of all he excites everyone just by being here—
Lulsgate is not used to such fine gentlemen—and
then Mrs Venn accused you and him of kissing in
public, and now this to-do over Francis, Marcus and
Captain Howell at Gaunt's! You have heard about
it?'

Yes, Bel had heard about it, as who had not?

'I suppose it has all been exaggerated—like the
kiss,' Bel offered, and she was devious enough to
laugh at her own duplicity—for the kiss had been
true, and doubtless Francis had done all that gossip
said he had in Gaunt's—not less.

'I cannot think what has got into Francis. There
is a look about him which I have never seen before.
It is as though——' and Almeria hesitated, but she
had to speak to *someone* '—as though he is sowing
all the wild oats he never sowed in youth. Not that
he is chasing women, not at all, he seems interested
only in yourself, but otherwise, I mean. Do I know
what I mean?' Almeria finished distractedly.

Bel knew only too well what had got into Francis
Carey. It was Bel Merrick, and the fact that she was
refusing him herself. It had got into her, too, and
was affecting everything she said and did, especially
since, being virtuous, although Francis thought that
she was not, she could not offer him herself. Of
course, being a woman, she had learned self-control
in a hard school; but Francis, she suspected, was a
passionate man who had held his emotions on a

tight rein for so long that now that he was sorely tempted and unable to do anything to satisfy himself his passion was taking its revenge by provoking him into unwise action elsewhere.

But she could hardly tell Almeria that, simply said gently, 'I suppose that Francis thought it was the only way to protect Marcus — who really does seem to need protecting.'

'Hush,' said Almeria feverishly, not wanting to be thought to be interfering again, but if she did not talk to Bel about all this she would burst. 'Here they come, quarrelling as usual.'

They were sitting in a little open-fronted summer-house, set at an angle to the path, so that they could hear the men's approach, but not see them, as Francis and Marcus were equally unaware of their presence. It was plain that they were, as Almeria had said, quarrelling.

'I tell you, I won't be kept in leading strings, Uncle.' Marcus's voice was petulant. 'You had no right to do what you did. Rhys told me that you deliberately gave me that drink to push me over the edge. A fine way to go on.'

'It was necessary,' Francis said coldly, one difficulty in arguing with him, Marcus found, being that Francis rarely lost his temper, which made his recent conduct the more baffling, 'quite necessary, if you were not to be fleeced by the cheating toad-eater you call friend. I would prefer that you stay here, at the vicarage, and not return to the Peacock.'

'You cannot stop me. . .' began Marcus, and then hesitated, on Bel's giving a giant cough to warn them they were overheard. 'Oh. Excuse me, Aunt

Almeria, Mrs Merrick, I did not see that you were there.' And he gave them both an embarrassed bow.

Francis also bowed, the marks of anger plain on his face. Anger conferred even more power on him, thought Bel, fascinated. She had a sudden dreadful wish that she had seen Francis in Gaunt's, Marcus, dead drunk and incapable over his shoulder, insulting Captain Howell, his face on fire, power radiating from him, she was sure. It certainly made a change for him to be insulting someone other than Bel Merrick!

But how strong he was, how impressive! She had another vision of him, jumping on to the deck of a ship in battle, waving a pistol—or would it be a sword?—magnificent in anger against the French.

Almeria, desperate to mend matters, said nervously, avoiding looking at Francis, 'I could not help overhearing what you were saying, Marcus. I do beg of you to stay here. Philip and I would like it of all things—so much better for you than an inn.'

This emollient request had a stronger effect on Marcus than Francis's stern orders. It was hard for him to be rude to kind Almeria.

'I am imposing on you, I know,' he began, only for Almeria to respond rapidly,

'Not at all. Philip was saying that you really ought to be with us, one of the family as you are. You could put your groom up at the Peacock, for we haven't really room for him here.'

She thought ruefully that since her passage with Francis she had rarely quoted her husband so often, and even he had noticed that her usual cheerful and managing habits had changed lately.

Marcus looked at the two women, said doubtfully, 'Well, if you really say so, then I will, but you are to turn me out if I become a burden, mind.'

'Good,' said Almeria, regaining a little of her normal cheerfulness. 'Now you may take me for a walk into Lulsgate to visit the mercer and then the apothecary, and Bel, my dear, perhaps Francis might like to visit your shrubbery for a turn there; there is an entrance at the back through our dividing fence, Francis.' And this, she thought, would give Francis a chance to recover a little of his normal self in Bel's company — and did not know how much she was deluding herself.

She and Marcus set off down the path away from them, leaving Bel and Francis face to face.

'You heard my sister,' he said. 'The least that you can do is entertain me as she wishes. Now how I might wish you to entertain me is, of course, a little different. But lead on, my dear Mrs Merrick, pray do. Of all things I wish you to provide me with enjoyment in your shrubbery.'

'Oh!' gasped Bel, thinking how right Almeria was. The devil was in Francis these days. One eyebrow cocked at her, his head bent in mock-humility, his arm held towards her with exaggerated and mocking courtesy, safe in the knowledge that none could overhear them, he felt free to indulge in his passion for her.

Last night he had woken up in a fever of desire, his whole body roused, her image in his mind; and now, seeing her, only the strongest exercise of self-control was preventing him from falling on her at once. He wondered how private the shrubbery really was, and how long it would take Almeria and Marcus to do Almeria's few errands.

There was nothing for it, thought Bel exasperatedly. Almeria was sure to ask him of the shrubbery and would think it odd to learn that Bel had refused him his treat. His treat? Inspecting the shrubbery, a treat? Bel suspected that Francis's notions of what a treat in the shrubbery was did not encompass a mere oohing and aahing and recital of Latin names, and admiring the gloss on the leaves and the state of the few blossoms.

Oh, no, it would be the gloss on Bel Merrick and *her* state which would engage him, she was sure, and as she led the way she prattled as lightly as she could of the difficulties of the true gardener she was in restoring a garden which the previous owner had neglected.

Talking so, she felt Francis bend down and deposit a kiss on her sun-warmed neck, and she said crossly, 'Now you are to stop that at once, sir. I cannot properly explain the garden if you carry on so.'

They were by now through the opening in the fence, always left there so that Bel and Almeria could visit one another freely, and were standing on a secluded path, surrounded by plants of all sizes and shapes, overlooked by nothing, as secret a place as even Francis Carey might wish to find himself in with his prey.

'I have not,' murmured Francis, 'the slightest wish to have the garden explained to me. Gardens are made for other purposes than botanising, and it is those purposes which I wish to explore.'

'Almeria,' said Bel severely, 'told me to show you the shrubbery, and that is what I am about to do.' They had reached a cross path where an old wooden bench, painted green, stood, where they would, Bel knew despairingly, be even more secluded.

Even the shade was green, and here everything was quiet, the scents of late August were all about them, the summer visibly beginning to die. Francis said, still gentle, although at what cost to himself only he knew, 'Pray, let us sit, my dear Mrs Merrick. I wish to be at one with nature — in every way known to man.'

And that is what I am afraid of, thought Bel, but allowed him to seat her gently, hoping perhaps that what he was saying might be more aggressive than what he might be about to do, and so it proved — at first, that was.

'Now I wonder why you are in such a pother, my dear doxy?' he said, leaning back and surveying her enchanting face and form lazily. 'Can it be that you are a trifle hopeful that dallying in gardens might be productive in other ways than gathering flowers fruit and vegetables?' And he picked up her hand and kissed it.

Bel pulled it away furiously. 'You are not to call me that, sir.'

'No? But that is what you are, is it not? A doxy, and dear to me, for the moment at any rate,' and as she rose to leave him, crying,

'I have shown you the shrubbery, and so you may tell Almeria,' he caught at her to detain her, saying,

'But I wish to see so much more than the garden,' and, using his strength, pulled her on to the bench again, took her in his arms and began to kiss her, gently at first, and then more and more passionately.

Bel began by fighting him off — or trying to, but as his kisses began to stir her, so that his arousal fuelled hers, she found herself drowning in the strangest sensations, quite unlike any she had experienced before.

They involved her whole body, not just her mouth, and then, when his kisses travelled down her neck, found the cleft between her breasts, and he began to caress her there, she threw her head back so that without her meaning to not only did she give him a better access to her body, but she was able to gasp her pleasure the more easily.

Reason had fled, and she felt that she could deny him nothing. Worse, her hands were beginning to caress him, and when he lifted his head for a moment she began to kiss him in the most wanton manner.

He had stopped kissing her only to give himself easier means to pull her dress down, as he had done on Beacon Hill, and this time she did not stop him, and he did not stop either, so that he was now stroking and kissing her breasts, taking them into his mouth, so that the sensations which he produced in her were so violent that Bel thought she was about to dissolve.

She writhed beneath him, so that he gave a soft laugh, and now, lifting her slightly, he began to pull her skirts up, his right hand travelling up her leg, beyond the garter on her stocking, to stroke the soft inside of her thigh—and she was not stopping him, no, not at all; she wanted him there, wanted the hand to travel further still, so strongly did she ache for him; shamefully she wanted all of him there—not just his hand—there, where no man had ever been.

Oh, madam is ready for me, thought Francis exultantly; she is as on fire for me as I am for her, and she is as sweet as I had thought her—sweeter—and it is she, Bel, I desire and none other, no one else will do—and then he remembered his vow that she should plead for him, and not he for her, and now, so wet and wanton was she, so far gone, that surely this, too, he would have.

'Feel me, Bel, feel me,' he said hoarsely. 'Feel how I need you,' and he took her hand and pressed it against his naked chest where she had unbuttoned his shirt, so that she could feel the fever which gripped him. 'And you, I can tell how much you need me. Say it, Bel, say it; say, Francis, pleasure me, please, beg me to do so, and then we may be in heaven together.'

As before, his voice broke the spell. In agony as she was, body trembling, on the very edge of a spasm of pleasure so strong that it would consume her quite, wanting most desperately the man in whose arms she lay, some strong core of integrity, so powerful that it willed her to refuse to be used by him as an instrument of revenge when she wanted to be an instrument of love, asserted itself.

'No, Francis! No! Never! I will not be used in despite, to prove what you think of me is true. I will not plead. You must plead for me, and in honour, not take me here as you might the doxy you call me, to boast later of how you had me — without payment.'

And the last phrase was the cruellest thing that she could think of to say to him, and as he pulled away, face blind and soft with desire, she added, 'Such a man of honour as you are, to save your nephew one day, and then despoil me another.'

The pride which ruled him, even at the last fence of all, was strong in him. Believing her to be otherwise then she was, he had told himself that he could not love a whore, but every fibre in his body told him that he did. That it was not, as he wished, mere lust which moved him, but that, against all reason, he loved Bel Merrick — and did not wish to hurt her.

And, that being so, he could not do what many another in his case might have done, and that was to take her as she lay before him, whether she consented or no, since, she having consented so far, a man might do as he pleased with the whore with whom he lay.

He could not resist saying as he sat up, and allowed her to free herself from his grasp, 'Not honest of you, madam, to progress so far, so willingly, and then refuse me at the last gasp of all.'

How to say, I am not experienced, did not know how quickly we should arrive at such a pass that my very virginity was on the point of being willingly lost? Had you not spoken, reminded me of how matters really stand between us, that I love, and that you only desire — for Bel had no knowledge of what time and propinquity had done to Francis —

then I would have been lost in an instant, no better than poor Marianne—indeed worse, for she was betrayed by a man who she thought loved her, whereas I. . .I know perfectly well that that is not so.

Instead Bel lowered her head, said numbly, 'I am sorry. I was carried away.'

Francis stared at her. 'Carried away! You cannot expect me to believe *that*?'

'Believe what you please,' she returned. 'And now you have had what you came for, or most of it, and you may safely tell Almeria that you have seen the shrubbery, without the necessity of lying.'

Bel was straightening herself, repairing the ravages of passion as she spoke, and Francis was feeling the worst pangs of passion die within him, the physical pain which refusal had produced abating a little.

'You will excuse me,' she said, on the verge of tears, not wishing to shed them before him. 'I must go. You know the way back, I believe.'

Francis had one final parting shot for her like a crippled ship able to fire one last ball at the enemy. 'Oh, yes, my dear doxy, I know the way back; you have made me take it so often now.' And the smile he gave her as he left was rueful, not reproachful, no enmity in it.

And Bel? She knew now beyond a doubt that blindly, inconveniently, what she felt for Francis was love, and that what had begun in light-hearted mockery of him at Stanhope Street was ending on quite a different note in Lulsgate Spa.

CHAPTER THIRTEEN

LULSGATE SPA had not known such a season for years. Bumbling along in its quiet middle class way, few great ones visiting it, it was a haven for minor gentry and tradesmen; the aristocracy, the upper gentry, the flash coves and Cyprians of the *demi-monde* usually passed it by. But in 1820 all were present and sensation followed sensation.

Marcus provided the next delightful bit of gossip. Living at the vicarage, he could not drink and ruffle as he had done, and, being sober most of the time, he suddenly, as Francis had hoped he might do, saw through Rhys Howell and his cheating ways.

Smoking was not allowed by Almeria, and his boon companions stank of smoke as well as drink, which he came to find distasteful. Clear-eyed physically, Marcus became so mentally, and one evening at Gaunt's it was Marcus who challenged the captain over his honesty at dice and cards, and not his uncle.

According to rumour, high words followed, and Marcus, imitating Francis, declined to give the captain satisfaction. 'You have had enough of my tin,' he had declared, 'and in future I shall play cards at the Assembly Rooms.'

'Go there, then,' roared Rhys, and swore at him, seeing his pigeon fly away, and funds running low. 'Shuffle the pasteboards with the tabby-cats and dowagers. Bound and determined to turn parson yourself, are you? Having a genuine one for an uncle and a defrocked monk for another not enough for you?'

Marcus ignored the insults, said sturdily, 'No need to shout at me, Rhys. I shan't change my mind. Uncle Francis was right about you, dammit.'

There was nothing Rhys Howell could do. The damage was already partly done. To be proven a cheat at cards or dice would brand him pariah for life, and he had no mind for that. Best to let it go, accuse the young fool of being light in the attic, trying to excuse his own bad luck and less skill by attacking another's honesty and reputation.

Of course, there was always Mrs Bel Merrick to fall back on, for others were declining to play in any game in which he was taking part. Lulsgate was slowly growing too hot to hold him, but he did not wish to leave yet. He felt safe in such a backwater, thought that his enemies from London and Paris might find it hard to track him down and harm him there.

Bel was sitting in her drawing-room when the doorknocker rattled and a man's voice was heard. Mrs Broughton, reading yet another romance, *The Curse of the Comparini* this time, looked up hopefully, and said, 'Lord Francis?'

Bel shook her head; it was a week since Francis had nearly had his way with her in the shrubbery, and they had met only in public, and both of them had been glacially proper, so much so that Almeria had sighed at the sight. Oh, dear, yet another chance for Francis to make a happy marriage seemed to be disappearing. What could have happened? Ever since she had asked Bel to show him around her shrubbery an arctic frost seemed to have descended on both of them.

She had always thought shrubberies were places where romantic interludes took place. Obviously Bel's had had no such effect on her and Francis. It was not that they were not speaking at all, but they were going on as though they were both ninety.

To Mrs Broughton's dismay, Bel was right, it was Captain Howell who was announced, and she did not like him—not the person to pursue dear Bel at all. She had seen the captain's eye on her mistress, and had interpreted his interest wrongly.

Not completely so, for, having an eye for a pretty woman, Rhys Howell not only wanted a good share of Bel Merrick's fortune, he also had an eye to her body. Now, if she possessed half Marina's possibilities. . .why, they would both be in clover.

'Your servant, ladies.' And he gave them his best bow, which did not mollify Mrs Broughton. She would rather have read *The Curse of the Comparini* than entertain the captain.

Bel rang for the tea-board; it was not long since they had dined, and she assumed that the captain had dined, too. They made unexceptional small talk, and Mrs Broughton looked longingly at the clock.

Her salvation came early, and Howell's intention to rid them of her presence was so boredly naked that Bel feared that even Mrs Broughton might notice how thin his excuse was. 'I have further private news for you,' he said bluntly, raising his eyebrows at the unwanted companion, so that Bel was compelled, flushing slightly, to indicate that she should leave.

Fortunately, for all her vague ways Mrs Broughton was discretion itself, never gossiped, but she must be beginning to ask herself what unlikely bond existed between Bel Merrick and Rhys Howell, that he should be bringing Bel private messages!

'You grow bold,' said Bel severely. 'Even Mrs Broughton will notice your cavalier manner to me and wonder at it.'

'Oh, as to that,' said the captain carelessly and beginning to roam round the room, picking up ornaments and staring at them, inspecting the bookshelves as though he were a bailiff pricing goods for distraint, 'you have the remedy in your own hands, my dear. Either hand over the dibs in large quantities, or join forces with me to our mutual advantage. I am surprised that you should wish to remain in this dull hole.'

Bel went on to the attack, that being the best form of defence.

'And I am surprised, sir, that you should wish to stay here, or should come here at all. The pickings must be small, compared to what you might hope to gain in London.'

'As clever as you are beautiful,' he remarked with a derisive bow. 'But you are a little off the mark. You are providing me with one reason — or rather, Marina's small fortune which you inherited, and your own person, more remarkable than I had dared to hope. I could make you Marina's best, you know. And also it suits me to be here at the moment.'

Bel knew nothing of the criminal underworld, but prolonged reading of the novels which Mrs Broughton loved had given her some insight into the nether side of life. 'London too hot for you?' she enquired politely.

He was across the room in one fell stride and had gathered her into his arms.

'Come, you bitch, are you lying to me as well as to the rest of the world? Are you still in touch with your London cullies, that you know such a thing?' And, pressing his lips roughly to hers, he forced a brutal kiss on her, so that Bel's senses reeled, not with the erotic passion which Francis's touch produced, but with the utmost revulsion.

If she had ever feared that any man's touch might stir her sexually, Rhys Howell had shown her in a moment that that fear had no basis.

As he forced her mouth open, she allowed him to do so, in order that she might bite hard on his invading tongue.

He reeled back with a curse, clapping his hand to his bleeding mouth.

'Damn you for the hellcat you are! I was right about you, I see. All that parade of virtue a mockery. I've a mind to proclaim what you are to the world from the steps of the Butter Cross.'

'And what a mistake that would be,' said Bel, heady with a feeling of sweet victory, even if it were to be temporary and unwise. 'For you would undoubtedly ruin me — at the expense of the possibility of gaining anything for yourself.'

The hard eyes which surveyed her were full of an unwilling admiration.

'By God, you're the shrewdest piece it's been my good fortune to meet. You remind me not to let passion rule reason. Now, madam, let us come to terms. If you wish to leave here with reputation intact, you must be seen to go with me willingly, for I have a mind to take you and your fortune both. My bed and my future assured at one go. With me to run you, there is no telling where we might end. No, do not turn away.' For Bel, sickened, had thrown out a hand, and walked to the fireplace, where, hands on the mantelpiece, she bent her head, staring at a hearth filled with flowers. 'No, I would not ruin you. Better, I would marry you. Thus I would gain everything — and you lose nothing. Refuse me, and you lose everything.'

What to do? Frantic, Bel stared blindly at the flowers. There must be something. She would not agree to this, she would not. If all else failed she would let him destroy her reputation rather than agree to such a bargain. But could she not, somehow, cheat him of both alternatives which he presented to her? The spirit, the courage with which she had so far triumphed over everything in her short life was strong in her still.

She would appear to agree with him. By what he said he did not intend to leave Lulsgate Spa yet, and it was to his long-term advantage to have her retain her reputation, if only that he might sell her more profitably in the end — for Bel had no doubt of his intentions. Ever since she had learned what Marianne had done, had read her letters, the letters of her lovers, examined her books, she had known of the harsher side of life usually concealed from young gentlewomen like herself. She had no illusions at all, none.

Yes, she would appear to give way—and then would scheme an escape—even if giving way meant that she would have to endure Rhys Howell's hateful company.

She swung around to face him. His handkerchief was at his mouth, the eyes on her were inimical, baleful. She drew a deep breath, summoned up all her arts. He had said that she was Marina's best. She would be Marina's best.

'Yes,' she said. 'Yes, I will do what you want; I have no alternative, it appears.'

His whole face changed, became darkly triumphant. He strode towards her, to assault her again, no doubt. Bel put her hands on his chest to push him away as he reached her.

'No,' she said. 'No. Most unwise. If you wish to take me away, my reputation intact, to be your wife, then you must court me in proper form, so that all will be deceived. No liberties, no hints or innuendoes. You are struck dumb by my virtue, sir. My apparent innocence is what you are after, is it not? Preserve that by your manner to me. Go slowly at first, and even after; a modest admiration will deceive all.'

He stepped back, and his face was full of an unwanted admiration for her. 'I was right,' he breathed. 'By God, we shall rule the world together, you and I. Between us there is nothing that we might not do. It was an unholy parsonage which spawned you and Marina, to be sure.' He made her a grinning, derisive bow. 'It shall be as you so wisely

advise. I don't want that damned canting swine of
an aristocrat after me over you, as he charged at me
to deprive me of his thick-headed nephew.'

He took her hand and kissed it with the greatest
solemnity, though winking as he straightened up.
'You will do me the honour, my dear Mrs Merrick,
of taking the air in my phaeton this late afternoon,
will you not? I have a mind to drive a little beyond
Morewood. One of the grooms from the inn will be
my tiger, to retain propriety's demands. You see
how well I know the manners of the world which I
intend we shall despoil.'

He released her hand, strolled to the door. 'Until
five of the clock, madam. Oh, I know that we shall
enjoy working together.'

He was gone. Bel sank into an armchair, her head
in her hands. She had gained herself a reprieve —
but for how long? And at what a cost. What would
Francis Carey think, when he saw her at such ins
with Captain Howell, but that she was exactly what
he thought her to be?

The faint hope that somehow she could convince
him of her purity and that they could begin their
relationship all over again on a better footing had
been destroyed forever this afternoon. And Lady
Almeria and Philip — what would they think of her,
to consort with such a creature as the captain was?
Would it not be better to have done, let him destroy
her, rather than have them all despise her — ?

She jumped to her feet. No! This way, she might
yet escape him. The other way, she was doomed
forever. Any hope that she might yet have Francis
in honour would be gone forever — and she knew

one thing, and one thing only. What she felt for Francis Carey was so strong, so powerful, that she would do anything to have him hers, to try to ensure that what she felt for him he would feel for her.

Meantime she must appear in public with Howell, and then this evening she was to sup at the Harleys'—and she could only imagine what would happen then. Best not to; best to take each moment as it came, and trust that the God who presided over all might yet spare Bel Merrick.

So, another splendid piece of gossip for everyone to chew over. Mrs Bel Merrick, that virtuous widow, pillar of the church, best friend of Lady Almeria Harley, a lady to her fingertips, was seen riding down Lulsgate Spa's main street in Captain Rhys Howell's flashy phaeton, with only a groom from the Peacock to act as chaperon!

And naturally, thought Bel despairingly, the first person whom they passed was Lord Francis, driving his curricle, who gave them both the coldest stare a man could, before cutting them stone-dead in full view of half of what Lulsgate Spa called society. By six that evening Mrs Venn had been told the delightful news and trumpeted at poor Henry how lucky he had been to escape the widow's toils, a view which Henry did not exactly share.

Bel walked into Almeria's drawing-room that evening, Mrs Broughton by her side, well aware of the furore she had caused, and defying Almeria to say anything.

She was dressed to perfection and beyond in lemon silk, the waist a little lower than had been fashionable at any time in the past fifteen years, seed-pearls sewn into the boat-shaped neck of her dress, Marianne's half-moon jewel in her hair, her fan a dream of a thing, lemon in colour with painted porcelain panels showing birds of paradise — it had been Marianne's, and in her state of anger and defiance of all the world Bel had deliberately carried it in as a kind of trophy.

Her red hair she had brushed into defiant curls; her usually ivory pallor was charmingly enhanced by a wild rose blush, for she would not be set down, she would not, and, ruined or not ruined, she would be Bel Merrick still.

Francis's eyes ran insultingly over her, his glance mocking, as much as to say, We have shown the world our true colours, have we not? But he said nothing; indeed, *everyone* determinedly said nothing, although Bel could feel that everyone was thinking everything.

What a strange world it was, that one indiscreet act could ruin one for life, she thought, but was as pleasant as ever, speaking to Marcus, whom Almeria had placed by her, and to Phillip, who was on her left at the head of the table, and with all the cool command of which she felt herself capable.

Marcus, indeed, conscious of having saved himself — he gave no credit to Francis — from Rhys Howell's clutches, said to her in a low voice, 'My dear Bel — you will allow me to call you Bel, Mrs Merrick; Almeria does, and it does so suit you — I would wish to have a private word with you before you leave us this evening — after supper, perhaps, when the tea-board comes round?'

Francis, who sat opposite, bodkin between Mrs
Robey and her daughter, frowned his disapproval at
what he saw as a tête-à-tête between Marcus and
Bel, which had the effect of making her begin to
flirt desperately with his nephew, just to show how
little she cared for all the lowering glares he was
throwing in her direction.

'Did you ever visit Astley's when you were in
London, Lord Tawstock?' she enquired sweetly,
fluttering her eyelashes at Marcus, who began to
think that, widow or not, travelling in Howell's
phaeton or not, the little widow might be worth
pursuing.

'Marcus,' he replied gallantly, 'do call me Marcus,
I beg of you,' and he said this loudly enough for
Francis to hear him and to grind his teeth as madam
brought her trollop's ways to the sanctity of the
vicarage supper table. Was she thinking of Marcus
as a possible protector? Were Howell and himself
not enough for her to try her claws on, without
attracting his ass of a nephew?

Marcus went on to recite the delights of Astley's
at some length to an apparently entranced Bel, who
could not resist laying a pretty hand on his arm, and
fluting at him with much eye-rolling and grimacing,
'Oh, never say so, Lord Tawstock — I mean
Marcus,' when he told her of the pretty female
equestriennes who ended their act by standing on
one leg on the back of their prancing steeds. 'I
should feel quite faint at the sight. But you, I
suppose, would enjoy it. Female and hippic beauty
in one joyful caracole must always be a delight.'

Bel knew that she was behaving badly, and that

she was leading Marcus on in the most dreadful fashion, but the sight of that damned canting aristocrat, the unfrocked monk, as Howell had dubbed Francis, was responsible for her wickedness; it was not her fault at all, it was he who was provoking her, and he who, once the meal was over, would, she was sure, be pouring recriminations, and unwanted advice over her, while being himself ready to fall on her in the most disgraceful manner, ready to relieve her of her virtue in quick-march time.

Philip spoke to her too, quietly and kindly, which made her feel a little ashamed, and she tailored her response to him, being the sedate Bel Merrick she had always been until first Francis and then Captain Howell had arrived to deprive her of sense by pursuing her, each in his own inimitable way.

Not that her measured replies, and discussion of her helping to decorate the church for the following Sunday, brought her any credit with Francis; rather, indeed, his expression as he surveyed her grew more and more sardonic, so that when she turned to speak to Marcus again she was wilder than ever.

Fortunately for Bel, when the meal ended it was Marcus who escorted her out, almost pushing Francis over when his uncle made a dead set at Bel, taking Bel into a corner of the room, to say confidentially, 'I know you will not take this amiss, Bel, I only speak for your own good, but I understand that you went driving with Captain Howell this afternoon. Ladies are not aware of such things, I know,' he added sagely, as though he had suddenly acquired the wisdom of Solomon, 'but the man has a wicked reputation and you should avoid him by all means in your power, not encourage him. You do not mind my saying this,' he went on anxiously, 'but a lady alone. . .'

'No, not at all,' said Bel, amused that Marcus, in Rhys Howell's toils until a few days ago, should now constitute himself a protector of the innocent. It was, she thought, almost flattering that Marcus should see her as such an innocent.

'I am always——' she began rapidly, laying her hand on Marcus's arm again, for she saw that Francis had stopped hovering and was advancing on them, a determined expression on his face, ready, she assumed, to hand her yet another sermon to digest, and she thought that she and Marcus might hold him off.

No such thing, for, interrupting her, he said through his teeth, in his most high-handed way, 'My dear nephew, you have monopolised Mrs Merrick all through dinner; now you must let someone else have a turn with her. Good manners require no less.'

'Suppose, Lord Francis,' retorted Bel sweetly, 'I told you that I preferred to continue my discourse with Marcus, rather than move on to another?'

'Then,' said Francis glacially, 'I should be compelled to conclude that the lack of wisdom which impelled you to share a carriage with such a blackguard as Captain Howell was still working in you this evening, madam.'

'Steady on, Uncle,' protested Marcus. 'No way to treat a lady, and Bel has a right to stay talking to me, if she wishes to do so.'

'Do you wish me to read you a lesson on good

manners, too?' asked Francis, aware that he was behaving as badly as Marcus and Bel, but unable to prevent himself. 'Go and help Almeria hand out the teacups — that should cool you off, and provide you with an occupation which, if not as exciting as whispering nothings to Mrs Merrick, is at least useful.'

This pedantic speech, delivered in Francis's best manner of captain reproving a misbehaving midshipman, had Marcus retreating and muttering, and Bel wanting to giggle, the manner and the matter being so at odds with one another.

Francis, seeing her mouth twitch, said dangerously, 'And what is amusing you, madam? The spectacle of yet one more of your victims caught in your toils? What a mermaid you are, to be sure. Have you tired of respectability, that you should allow Rhys Howell to ferry you about? Where was all that noble virtue you used with me the other afternoon? Left behind on the couch where you entertained him, I suppose.'

This was delivered in low tones and through his teeth, after such a fashion that, no one being near to them, no one could have any idea what he was saying to her.

The most appalling and delightful rage ran through Bel. How dared he, how dared he say such things to her? And then he said, again through his teeth, 'I warned you about Howell, madam, I told you that I knew him to be a villain of the first water, but what notice did you take of me? Recklessly, wantonly, you put yourself in the way of danger. . .'

'Pray stop,' said Bel, also in low tones, reduced

to whispering for fear that if she raised her voice it would be to tell him, and the room, exactly what she thought of Lord Francis Carey, unaware that love, desire, a care for her safety and plain green-eyed jealousy were all at work in her tormentor.

Francis opened his mouth again, and what would come out this time? thought Bel despairingly. She must stop this, she must, for her sake, and Almeria's and kind Philip's — she could see his thoughtful eye on them and was suddenly persuaded that he was understanding more than he ought.

Invention struck. She dropped her fan, gave a loud wail, clutched at her bosom — was that the right place to clutch? she wondered — said faintly, 'Oh, dear heavens, what is coming over me? Oh, I feel so faint; the heat —— ' and, speaking thus, her voice dying away, she allowed her knees to sag, and began to fall forward, head hanging, into Francis's arms. He, face disbelieving, caught her as, eyes rolling into her head, she willed herself to turn pale, by holding her breath, which had the effect of her turning purple, an even more awful sight, while Francis, enraged, certain that madam was at her tricks and doing this to confound him, was perforce compelled to carry her to a sofa and deposit her reverently on it, with Almeria fetching smelling salts, which did cause Bel to turn pale, and various gentlemen, Marcus the loudest, then to offer contradictory forms of assistance.

Marcus caught his uncle by the arm and hissed at him, 'And what were you saying to poor Bel, to overset her so?' for he had been watching them like a hawk, and was sure that Francis had been bullying her; he knew that look of his uncle's very well, having had to endure it so many times himself.

'I, you damned young pup?' returned Francis. 'I have said nothing to cause this. I'd take a bet there's nothing wrong with her but a desire to attract attention.'

For one moment Francis thought that his tongue had run away with him to the degree that Marcus was about to strike him, but Marcus restrained himself with difficulty, contenting himself with saying, 'What the devil do you mean by that?'

To which Francis replied wearily, 'Oh, never mind,' turning to look at Bel, who was now propped up against some cushions, offering the company a weak and watery smile before closing her eyes and moaning gently.

He had to hand it to her. What a devious bitch she was, to be sure. She had stopped him in his tracks — or anyone else who might try to reproach her — and had thoroughly disarmed everyone. He was not deceived by all this, and tomorrow he would let her know, and no mistake.

Bel opened one eye. She closed it again hastily when she saw Francis's disbelieving stare trained on her. 'I really do feel,' she announced bravely, 'a little better. I cannot think what came over me. It was all so sudden. One moment——' and she sighed as though words were too much for her '—I felt quite well, and then the next moment. . .' And she gave a delicate shudder as she spoke.

Privately she was again appalled at her own deviousness — and wondered, as before, where all this was coming from. It was Francis Carey's fault, she was sure. If only he would let her alone — or rather would *not* let her alone, but would treat her as he should, respectfully and lovingly — then she could go back to being well-behaved, innocent Bel Merrick again. As it was, she had to protect herself, and if throwing a fainting fit in Almeria's drawing-room was the only way to do it, then so be it.

'Let me assist you upstairs to my room,' said Almeria, who had no reason to doubt the truth of Bel's behaviour. 'And then Francis can take you home when you are feeling a little better. I shall send Mrs Broughton on to prepare a warm bed for you, and a restorative cordial. I have a splendid bottle of my own brewing which I shall give her — excellent with a little brandy before retiring — it always ensures a good night's sleep.'

Privately, and irreverently, Bel thought that a good draught of brandy might accomplish that for her without the cordial, but said nothing, only sighed gently, and when Almeria called on Francis to carry her upstairs she smiled up at him so limpidly that he almost began to laugh himself. Just let him get madam alone, and she would find out his opinion of mermaids who behaved as she did, he thought, as he laid her lovingly on the bed — he could not help but be loving, only wished that he could stay to. . .to. . .and he hurriedly left her to Almeria's ministrations before he forgot himself completely.

CHAPTER FOURTEEN

'You are better today, then?' Almeria asked Bel anxiously the next morning. Bel was lying on the sofa looking prettily *distraite* — she thought that she had better keep up the farce of being a little unwell. Not only Francis, but Captain Howell, could be kept at bay by it.

Mrs Broughton had been reading *The Curse of the Comparini* to her when Lady Almeria had arrived, and Bel replied to her question by saying in a low voice, 'Oh, I am a little recovered. Rest will assist me. . .I think,' and she lowered her long dark lashes over her eyes in what she hoped was an interesting fashion.

'I bring messages from us all,' went on Almeria, a concerned expression on her face. 'Marcus was particularly disturbed by your malaise — and Philip and Francis, too, it goes without saying. I am sure you are in good hands,' she ended, looking at Mrs Broughton.

'Oh, yes,' said that lady vaguely. 'I am breaking the habit of a lifetime by reading dear Bel a novel in the morning to comfort her.' And she waved a hand at *The Curse*, which was lying open on her knee.

This distracted Almeria, who picked it up, said eagerly, 'Oh, the Comparini — too exciting, dear Bel, for an invalid, I would have thought. That scene where the cowardly and dastardly Paolo Neroni blackmails poor Sophia Ermani. . .words fail me—such a brute. I thank God we live in dear quiet Lulsgate Spa where such dreadful events do not occur.'

Bel thought that, though she and Almeria might laugh together at the goings-on in Gothic novels, Almeria also enjoyed them on a different level. . . and what would she think if she knew of the pother Bel was in? It was not so different from Sophia's. Oh, if only there was someone in whom she could confide!

She thought that if Philip Harley had not been her friend's wife and Francis's brother-in-law she might have gone to him for advice, but, as it was. . .no such thing.

Later that afternoon, putting on a big bonnet, and venturing out when no one was about, she went to her little class, not so much to teach, but to ask the advice of Mr Birch.

Unworldly he might seem, but Bel thought there was an iron core to him, seldom shown, revealed a little when he had recently queried Francis's intentions towards her, in the most discreet fashion, of course.

After she had dismissed her class, taken indoors, for the weather was growing chilly, Mr Birch brought her a cup of tea and a slice of the cake which she had brought with her.

'What is it, my dear?' he asked her mildly. 'I cannot help but see that you are troubled in spirit. May I assist you in any way?'

Well, that showed percipience, Bel thought wryly,

since no one else about her seemed to have noticed *that*.

'I have a problem,' she said simply. 'But it is not one which I can properly confide to anyone.' She paused, and said, 'Is it ever proper, or truly Christian, to deceive people, even for the best of motives?' For this was one of the questions which occupied her thoughts more and more; it was a series of deceits, undertaken mostly with the best of motives, which had landed her in her current predicament.

Worse, she was beginning to feel more and more uncomfortable about the false face she presented to Almeria and her Lulsgate friends, the face of a widow, not the young untried girl she really was.

'As a Christian and a minister,' said Mr Birch gently, 'my answer must be, of course, no, as you are well aware. But, as a man of the world, living in the real world, the answer cannot be so clear-cut. Suffering human beings may feel it necessary to engage in them. I have to say that if they do so they must be prepared to take the consequences which must inevitably follow.'

'Yes,' said Bel, in a hollow tone, heart sinking. 'And suppose, only suppose, that one's heart is fixed on someone who may have the wrong view of one — ' for this was, she felt, as far as she could go ' — what then, Mr Birch, what then? Should one abandon one's feelings, or try to overcome the error?'

Mr Birch, as Bel suspected, was no fool. 'If,' he said, 'your object of affection were someone like the gentleman who has called for you lately, I would think it unwise to try to trick him. Perfect candour would answer better. From his looks and conversation he is upright to a fault, if a minister may properly say such a thing.'

Bel's answering, 'Yes, I suppose so,' was hollow again. 'Then one should never do a wrong, however slight, hoping that good might come from it?' she asked feverishly, feeling that her conversation was becoming more and more obscure, but, paradoxically, feeling also that Mr Birch somehow knew exactly of what she was speaking.

'Truth is always the best,' he answered, 'although sometimes it may be inconvenient to tell it. Only you, my dear, and no one else, save only God, can help yourself. I may advise you to be perfectly candid, but if, in your opinion, being so would be destructive to yourself, then in the real world one might have to think again. On the other hand, you may find that truth and only truth can save you. Put your trust in God, and he will tell you what to do.'

Bel took his old hand and pressed it. 'Oh, you are kind,' she said fervently, 'and wise. For many in your condition would simply have given me a stern answer without understanding how difficult my situation might be. You will forgive me if I do not tell you exactly what it is, but. . .' She hesitated.

Mr Birch looked at her agonised face. 'My dear,' he said, 'we have been friends for nearly two years, you and I, and I know you to be that rare thing, a good woman. But you are a woman on your own. I understand that you have no near relations, no family on whom to fall back, who might advise you, and, that being so, your conduct has been admirable. But you are very young, and the young may be foolish, impulsive. It is for you to try to remedy that by letting your head as well as your heart advise you, and God is there for you to ask for succour.'

Bel withdrew her hand and drank her tea. Having spoken to him, her heart felt lighter, even if he had only told her what she already knew.

'Thank you,' she said, voice low, for him to answer,

'My dear Mrs Merrick, you know that here you may always find refuge, should you need it. The children and I owe you at least that. You bring sunshine into our lives every week of the year.'

Well, that was that, she thought, walking home, and even as she breathed relief she heard carriage wheels and knew that Francis had been waiting for her to leave Mr Birch's cottage, and that the hour of reckoning for last night's naughtiness was on her.

Francis stopped the curricle, leaned down and said roughly, 'Come, you cannot refuse my offer of a lift. Almeria said that you were too overset to do anything today, but I was sure that you would not neglect your children. What a strange mixture you are, to be sure.' His face was rueful, and she knew that he was as tormented as herself, but for quite different reasons.

'No more so than another,' she said quietly, only to be met by his disbelieving face.

'And what does the old man make of you, madam? I should dearly love to know. And the trick you played on me and the company last night—what would he have made of that?'

Bel thought of the conversation which she had

had with Mr Birch, decided to tell Francis the truth — or at least a little of it. 'I could think of no other way of quietening you,' she said. 'Another moment and you would have ruined the pair of us.'

His eyebrows rose haughtily. 'Ruined me, madam? I can see how I could have ruined you, but how should I have ruined myself?'

'To let the company know of what you think is the truth of me would be also to admit that you had known of that truth for some time, and had said nothing, had allowed the woman you think of as a Cyprian not only to continue as Almeria's friend, but as the friend of her little children, polluting a pure home,' Bel said, wondering why this had not occurred to her before. 'What would Almeria think of your conduct then?'

Francis, mouth tightening, stared at the passing scenery, then, 'Not only a witch, madam, but were females allowed to be diplomats you would make a masterly one. Your mind is as sharp as it is devious. You admit, then, that you were shamming last night?'

'For a good reason,' said Bel wearily, 'although I do not think that Mr Birch would agree with what I did, were I to tell him of it.'

Francis was silent again, then finally he said in a stifled voice, 'Since I met you again in Lulsgate I think that I have run mad. I think only of you, want to talk only with you, be with you, want only you in my bed, wish that you were. . .honest, that we could have met in some other way. *That* is my ruin, madam, and you have worked it.'

How strange, thought Bel; last night I blamed

Francis for destroying my usual good conduct, and today he is blaming me for doing the same thing to him, and his thoughts are my thoughts: he wishes, as I do, that we had met under a different star.

'And now I must say again what I have said before,' he went on. 'That you should have nothing to do with Captain Howell. Most unwisely you choose to receive him, drive out with him, and I suppose that I shall be hearing next that he is taking you to the grandest Assembly of the year—the September Ball.'

Bel was silent, for that lunchtime a note had been delivered to her from Rhys Howell, stating that he expected her to attend the September Ball with him as a proof of her good faith.

Francis read her silence aright. 'No!' he exclaimed violently. 'Do not say that I have hit the nail on the head! You *are* going with him. Why, Bel, why? You, with your excellent judgement, must know that the man is a blackguard—will ruin you. . .' He fell silent, suddenly conscious of the absurdity of what he was saying.

'Now, how can that be,' wondered Bel, 'when according to you I am ruined already? What a mass of contradictions you are, Francis.'

'No contradictions at all,' he almost groaned. 'I cannot bear to think of you in his arms, or, indeed, in any man's. There. I have said it. You have wrung it from me. I shall not be answerable for the consequences if you go with him. I know what he is, I see the way in which he looks at you. He wishes to run you, to be your pander, to sell you to the highest bidder, that is plain to me, as plain as day, and do not ask me how I know, for I cannot tell you. Do you wish to be run by him, Bel? Do you wish to out-Marina Marina? Are you not content to stay virtuous in Lulsgate Spa? Does that. . .life. . .still attract you, call you back?'

She could not tell him that his intuitive guess about Rhys Howell's intentions towards her was correct. It trembled on her lips; she almost told him of Captain Howell's blackmailing of her — but could she trust Francis, either?

Had their relationship been different, been what she knew it ought to have been, then and only then could she have asked him for help. As it was. . . She hesitated and was lost; the moment passed. She saw his grim face. No, she must solve this problem herself. She could not beg for help from a man who thought her a trollop; pride alone prevented that.

They had reached her home. He helped her down, said, hoarsely, 'Remember, Bel, if you go to the ball with Howell I shall act. What I shall do, God help me, I don't know. But I saved Marcus from him, and I do not intend to do otherwise with you.' He saluted her with his whip, and was gone, Cassius at the back clinging on for dear life, favouring her with a wink as he flew by, which had her laughing despite her very real misery.

Oh, damn all men, good and bad, thought Bel as she entered her home. How much better if this world were peopled only by women, and the odd notions of men did not obtain, and babies did appear under the gooseberry bush — and all of them female!

* * *

Just to make life more exasperating than ever, Mrs
Broughton met her with a long face. The postman
had been and brought her a letter from her sister.
She was ill, and Mrs Broughton was needed to help
her, for her sister's husband was an invalid, the
housekeeper had deserted them, all was at sixes and
sevens, and only Mrs Broughton's presence would
help.

'Dear Bel, you will allow me leave to go, I trust.
I would not ask if the case were not dire. I shall
return as quickly as may be. And you do have dear
Lottie.'

Bel refrained from pointing out that dear Lottie
was growing old, was nearly at pensionable age, if
not beyond it, but she had no mind to do other than
accede to Mrs Broughton's wishes, even though she
used that lady as a bulwark against the man she
loved and the man she hated.

'Of course you must go,' she said, 'and of course
I shall manage. Stay as long as is necessary, my
dear. Lottie will help you to pack. You wish to go
on tomorrow's stage?'

'Indeed, as soon as I may. You will be careful
when I am gone, dear Bel. You are usually the soul
of discretion, though I cannot say that I fully
approve of this new friendship of yours with Captain
Howell. I do not feel that he is quite the thing. Lord
Francis, however. . .' And she trailed up the stairs,
murmuring benedictions on Bel, Lord Francis and
Lady Almeria—already seeing me as Lady Francis,
I suppose, thought Bel ruefully. Oh, dear, what a
tangled web we weave, when first we practise to

deceive. I never thought much of that verse in the
past. . .but now. . .

Bel was thinking of this again while waiting for
Captain Howell to call for her to take her to the
Grand Assembly. She had not seen Francis in
private again; she did not know that he was almost
afraid to be alone with her, and when they met in
public they were icy cold to one another — anything
less and there was the danger that they might be in
each other's arms, and for their own reasons neither
wanted that until the difference between them was
resolved.

'Oh, dear,' mourned Almeria to her, 'I am so
disappointed that you and Francis have not taken to
one another; at first I thought. . .' And then, mind-
ful of Philip's strictures, she said apologetically, 'I
do not mean to meddle, but you seemed so suited
to one another.'

She wished that she could ask what had gone
wrong, but sitting with Francis at breakfast that
morning she had thought that one of the things
which he and Bel had in common was an indomi-
table will, allied to a pride which was so strong that
it could almost be felt.

Perhaps *that* was what was wrong, thought
Almeria; they are too much alike, so strong, so
independent. For she had begun to see beneath the
surface gloss of Bel's gentleness to the steel core it
covered.

The doorknocker went in the middle of Bel's
musings over this conversation and Lottie came in.

'That nasty piece is here to take you to the dance,'

she said bluntly. 'I cannot imagine why you encourage such a low creature.'

And what to say to that? I have no alternative but to do as he wishes, so do not pester me with reproaches? Instead Bel said gently, 'He asked me before anyone else did, and it was difficult for me to refuse him without offence.'

'You have never found much difficulty in holding off those you do not care for before,' returned Lottie with incontrovertible and inconvenient truth.

'No matter,' said Bel, drawing on her long lace gloves, and seeing that the small circlet of silk flowers in her hair was in place — she was as fresh and lovely as she ever was, even though all this was put on for her to be escorted by a man she despised. For Francis was there, and she wished to be absolutely *à point*, even though he was not to know that she had dressed for him, and thought it was all for Rhys Howell.

Bel had long since lost the wish to provoke Francis Carey — except, of course, when he deliberately set out to provoke her.

'Oh, you are magnificent tonight, my dear,' sighed the captain gallantly over her hand, admiring the delicate blue silk of her dress, the creamy gauze which covered it, the new way in which she had made Lottie dress her hair — that unhappy servant trailing along behind them on the short walk to the Assembly Rooms, to sit with the other servants in an ante-room until the dance was over, seeing that there was no Mrs Broughton to protect her mistress.

They were early. The party from the vicarage had not yet arrived. Some of Rhys Howell's disreputable court were leaning against the wall, yawning, such small beer of excitement as Lulsgate could provide already boring them. Several more hangers-on had arrived during the week, although one hard-faced gentleman whom Bel had seen disputing with the captain in Lulsgate's main street was not there; nor, she discovered, did he later favour the dance with his presence.

Slowly, the room filled up. The Venns arrived, and Henry, on seeing Rhys Howell leave Bel to join one of his boon companions for a moment, and then go to the supper-table for a cool drink for them both, took the opportunity to come over to her to say, 'Is this wise, my dear? Your escort, I mean. My mother. . .'

Bel was tired of being hectored by everybody from Francis Carey downwards, all of whom seemed to know her own business better than she did herself.

'Your mother never approves of anything I do, as you well know, my dear Mr Venn. Now if she were to approve, you might trouble me about the matter. Otherwise, I will take her censure as read.'

Henry turned a dull red. 'She and I only mean you well,' he said stiffly, 'whereas I doubt whether the same can be said for Captain Howell. You choose your companions badly.'

The worst of it was, thought Bel, that so far as Rhys Howell went he was in the right. But all this was handed down from on high, and she also knew quite well that if Henry knew the truth about her — and Marianne — he would throw her over without a thought.

'I will take note of what you say,' she replied, attempting to be a little conciliatory, 'but it is for me to make my own decisions, as you, Mr Venn, make yours. I do not choose to lecture you on what you are to do.'

'But then I am not a young woman who needs advice lest she be led astray, women being so prone to that if not guarded with loving care,' was his swift response.

Fortunately, before Bel could say something unforgivable, Rhys Howell returned, a glass of lemonade for her, and a cold stare for Henry.

'Happy to see you are guarding Mrs Merrick for me,' he said. 'Now that I am back I thank you, and you may return to your mama.'

Henry turned red again, bowed stiffly and walked away to speak to the said mama, who turned her baleful and disapproving gaze on Bel.

I shall be ruined before Captain Howell gains his ends, she thought, and then had not time to think more, for the vicarage party arrived, Almeria and Philip leading, Francis and Marcus behind, Francis throwing every other man in the hall into the shade, and consequently had every female eye, married and unmarried, young and old, on him.

He was quite unmoved. Took it as his due, doubtless, thought Bel exasperatedly, and was far more exasperated when Captain Howell, who, seeing Francis's eye, even more baleful than Mrs Venn's, upon them, said loudly, 'Come, my dear Bel. Stand up with me, I beg. It is the waltz next, and none but your humble servant shall dance it with you.'

Bel tried to hang back, began to mutter some feeble negative, only he turned *his* baleful stare on her, saying, 'Remember what I have promised you, my dear, if you fail to co-operate with me.'

There was nothing she could do. Resigned, if inwardly mutinous, Bel stood up with him, and as the small group of musicians began to play she and the captain were the first on the floor, every eye upon them, as he had intended.

Bel was quite aware that if she allowed the captain to monopolise her it was as good as announcing that she and he were an engaged pair — or that she, Bel, was on the loose side of good behaviour. Lulsgate Spa was as narrow-minded as most small provincial towns, and breaches of etiquette were severely frowned upon.

She could almost feel Francis's eyes boring into her back, and was relieved when Mr Courtney, the Master of Ceremonies, waved his hand and the music stopped. Fortunately, she and the captain were not near the small group from the vicarage, and she was walked back to her seat by him, feeling that she was treading on eggshells or grenades, at the very least.

The captain began small talk, in the middle of which she saw Marcus Carey crossing the floor towards her, a purposeful look on his face.

He reached her, bowed, and said, 'You will allow me to reserve a dance with you, my dear Bel. I am sure that your card is not yet full.'

Bel's card, given to her as she entered the hall, was hanging from her wrist; she detached it and began to examine it, only for the captain to take it, saying, 'Mrs Merrick's card is reserved for me tonight, Tawstock.'

'No,' Bel protested without thinking, 'not so. I shall be happy to stand up with you in the quadrille, Marcus.'

'Marcus, is it?' said the captain nastily, snatching the card from Bel's hand and beginning to write his name beside every space. 'Well, you may stand up with this popinjay for the next dance, but the rest will be mine.'

'You are a very oaf, Howell, and how I endured you for so long I shall never know,' said Marcus indignantly. 'I shall speak to the MC. I understand that such monopolies are not allowed at Lulsgate Spa's Assembly Rooms. Things are done in proper form here. You have no right to take Bel's card from her.'

Bel, who was by now on her feet herself, furious with the captain, who she suddenly realised intended to compromise her hopelessly, so that she would be compelled to receive his protection, decent society being sure to cast her out once it saw her apparent relationship with him, said, 'Dear Marcus, I will stand up with you, and as for the card, rest assured that I shall dance with whom I please.'

'Not so,' said the captain again with a grin, 'and dancing with raw boys without manners or money is not what I intend for you at all.'

To Bel's horror, she saw Marcus begin to square up to the captain in protest at the manner which he was using to her, but before he could do anything a new actor arrived on the scene.

It was Francis Carey. His baleful stare took in the three of them.

'You are in danger of becoming the talk of the ballroom,' he said coldly. 'Are you at your tricks again, Howell? I understand that Lord Tawstock came over to ask Mrs Merrick to dance with him. The rules of the Assembly say that it is her choice with whom she dances. What is your wish, Mrs Merrick?' And his hard eyes were on her, pitiless, challenging her, she was sure, to state her position.

'I have already said that I will dance with Lord Tawstock,' Bel replied, as cold as he. 'You will hand me back my programme, Captain Howell. No one but myself shall fill it in.'

It was a declaration of war, and Bel knew it. She also knew that, faced with Francis Carey, Rhys Howell might not go so far as he had done with Marcus, and she read him aright.

For all his bravado the captain had no wish to fight with a man who reputation was as great as Francis's. Francis had, he knew, killed the man who had wantonly shot down one of his young officers in a duel not of the young man's making, and his bravery as a naval officer had been recognised on more than one occasion.

The captain had come to the Assembly Rooms with the half-formed idea of ruining Bel Merrick on the spot by his behaviour to and with her — but not at the risk of being killed himself. He would wait to finish her off when the mealy-mouthed aristocrat seeking to protect her was not about.

But Francis's expression was so grim that Bel feared for a moment that worse might befall, except that the MC, Mr Courtney, whose duty it was to see that such scenes did not occur, now joined them.

'Gentlemen,' he said, severely, 'may I remind you that before you were allowed to share in the pleasures organised here you signed a set of rules which demanded certain standards of behaviour and agreed to adhere to them? It is my duty to see that you do so. You will observe them, will you not?'

Mr Courtney was, in many ways, a silly, pompous man; nevertheless in a town like Lulsgate Spa the wishes of the MC were law. Those not agreeing to be bound by them were banned from the official festivities of the place, were banished from the very society which they had come to enjoy.

All the gentlemen, including Rhys Howell, bowed together to signify their submission to the MC's wishes. Marcus took Bel's hand to lead her on to the floor as the music began.

Like all reformed rakes and gamesters, Marcus wished to reform others. 'Dear Bel,' he said, 'you must know what a blackguard Rhys Howell is, as I now do, and I cannot understand why you should give him such encouragement.'

His voice was so sorrowful that Bel did not know how to answer him, and was reduced to saying, rather cryptically, 'I fear that he asks me for more than I wish to give, and it is hard to refuse him.'

Marcus mistook her meaning a little. 'Oh, you have no man to protect you,' he said. 'Why do you not ask my Uncle Frank to look out for you? I am sure that he would be only too pleased to do so,' and when Bel shook her head he said ingenuously, 'Oh, he is such a good fellow, I am sure that he would not mind. Look how he cared for me, and I am sure that I did not deserve it, whereas you. . .' And he paused, his artless face aglow with new-found goodwill.

Bel could see Francis watching her as she danced. He was almost the only man in the room not on the floor, and she could almost feel what he was thinking of her, and she was sure that it was not favourable. But at least he and Marcus, by their intervention, had saved her, for she was certain that the captain was frightened of Francis, and Marcus had given Francis the opportunity to intervene without it appearing that he was doing it for himself.

Marcus said nothing more after that, concentrating on the dance, until, the dance over, he said to her, 'Join us, Bel, dear; you surely do not wish to remain with a man who treats you in such a fashion.'

Bel hesitated; then, looking across at the captain, who was now talking angrily to one of his cronies, she knew that, whatever else, he would not ruin her tonight. He was too frightened of Francis and what he might do to him. He had backed down over Marcus the night that Francis had taken him away, and tonight he had let her go without making any real threats.

If she joined the Harleys' party she was sure that he would make no attempt to haul her back this evening, but would do so on another day.

Well, that other day was not with her yet, and—who knew?—by then she might have thought of something to thwart him in his designs on her. What that might be she could not foresee, but meantime Marcus was offering her salvation.

'Thank you,' she said. 'You know, I really do not care for him at all, Marcus, but he asked me to come here tonight before anyone else did, and in politeness it was difficult to refuse.' Which was, she thought, as good an excuse as any, and was the one which she had offered to Lottie.

Marcus nodded, satisfied. He knew how strict were the rules of etiquette which governed women's conduct, and that lone women like Bel were at particular risk. They were, by now, with Philip and Almeria, who both rose, Almeria saying, 'Oh, I am so happy to see that you no longer wish to remain with that man. Come and tell me what you think of *The Curse of the Comparini*. Did Mrs Broughton find time to finish it before she left? It is a pity she had to go. Captain Howell could not have been so particular with you had she been present.'

Bel nodded agreement to all this, before Almeria carefully seated her beside Francis, who was as glacial as ever. When Philip and Almeria had taken the floor, and Marcus had engaged Miss Robey, he said to her coldly, 'You put yourself in a false position, Mrs Merrick, accompanying such a creature as Howell is. Young Marcus did well to lead the column of relief for you.'

'Oh,' said Bel. 'The pair of you manoeuvred that, then?'

Francis nodded. 'I admit I was the instigator, once I saw that you had come with him as you had said that you would. But Marcus needed little prodding. He is thoroughly converted to good behaviour at the moment, is disillusioned with all such as Howell — and how long that will last is another matter. But you—what has got into you, unless it is a hankering for your old ways?'

'My old ways!' said Bel vigorously. 'I have no old ways—as one day you will realise.'

'And you will promise to avoid Howell from now on and save. . .Almeria. . .and myself from worry in the future.'

Bel went white. 'I cannot promise you that,' she said faintly, knowing that the captain would begin his campaign to persuade her to throw in her lot with him, once Francis was not about.

'I cannot understand you,' he said passionately. 'Until he arrived you were discretion itself, in your public life at least. Now you worry all those who care for you by your odd conduct.'

'And do you care for me?' queried Bel, eyes agleam, for oh, how wonderful it would be if he did, if he could abandon the false belief he had of her—which to be fair to him was one which she, and none other, had created. Oh, how she regretted the hasty words at Stanhope Street with which she had deceived him—and the trick which she had played upon him.

Francis wanted to cry, I more than 'care for you', I adore you, but I cannot tell you so. I want to protect you, as well as love you, and now I know that my love for you is more than lust I am beside myself.

Controlling himself almost visibly, he said instead, 'I do not care to see anyone exploited by such a cur as Howell,' and she had to be content with that, and with his invitation to her to dance the next waltz with him, to which she agreed with alacrity.

Oh, bliss for Bel to be in his arms, to be so near to him, and yet purgatory that she could be no nearer — and Francis? He, too, felt as Bel did. The intoxication of the music, the passionate feelings both were experiencing were, unknown to them, written on their faces; all the signs of their profound and mutual love gave them away to the watchers.

By God, the monk's in love with her — and she with him, thought Rhys Howell savagely, having taken a little more port than he ought in an effort to forget that he had once again given way to Francis Carey, while Philip and Almeria — and a hundred others — came to the same conclusion.

How lovely she is, thought Francis distractedly, and how brave, even in her wilfulness. The red hair, the green eyes, the damask cheek, the. . . I grow maudlin. While for Bel the athletic body, the strong face, straight mouth and hard grey eyes of the man whom she had come to love were more pleasing to her than the softer features of the other men who surrounded her. And each thought with longing of the other: male and female both *beaux-idéals* of beauty and strength.

The dance over, Francis led her back, thinking hard, at the last, of anything but the woman he so inconveniently loved, lest his arousal betray him to all the world. A period away from her and a cold drink might restore him, he thought wildly, and so he said to Almeria, who had been watching them, 'A drink, perhaps, Almy, and you, too, Bel?' and,

the two women assenting, he and Philip strolled off
to the supper-room together.

Neither Bel, Almeria nor Marcus, who stayed
behind with them, to talk lightly of Queen Caroline,
the weather, and various inconsiderable topics, ever
knew exactly what passed in the supper-room, which
stood at some distance from the ballroom itself.

The supper-room was laid out with tables containing food more substantial than, if not so fashionable
as, the light fare found at similar places in London.
As in London, long sideboards containing drink
stood at the side of the room, and Francis and Philip
made for these.

Rhys Howell, his pack of toadies about him, had
abandoned the dance-floor and was drinking fairly
steadily, even though he was, as yet, still relatively
sober. His eyes were ugly as he surveyed the
brothers-in-law choosing their partners' drinks after
drinking themselves — Philip sticking to lemonade,
Francis taking a glass of port.

'Enjoying the pretty widow, are you, Carey?' he
said jeeringly; he could not restrain himself at the
sight of the man he disliked, but was content to
address Francis's back — though not for long.

Francis swung round. 'I told you before not to
call me Carey, Howell,' he said coldly, 'and I will
also thank you not to speak of any lady before the
scum whom you call friends.' He felt Philip's hand
on his arm and threw it off. The anger mixed with
jealousy which he always experienced when he
thought of Bel having anything to do with this piece
of filth was strong in him. He was sure that Howell

wished to be Bel's pimp, and the desire to kill him with his bare hands was almost overwhelming.

Howell went purple. Even he could hardly swallow such an insult.

'Damn you. . .Carey. I'll call you out for that.'

'As I told you before,' returned Francis, 'I'll not fight you, ever. A horsewhip, now that would be a different matter. Shall I send for one?' If this was Drury Lane heroics, he thought savagely, then he was enjoying them. He felt Philip's restraining hand on his arm again, and threw it off again.

'By God,' swore Howell, 'if you think to continue insulting me with impunity, you are vastly mistaken,' and, made bold by the drink he had taken, he threw himself on his tormentor, to be met with Francis's iron fingers on his throat.

'Francis, think what you are doing!' Philip was trying to pull his brother-in-law off his victim, who was slowly turning purple; men were shouting, and, fortunately for Howell, the MC himself came bustling in, mewing fearfully,

'Gentlemen, gentlemen, remember where you are. There are ladies near by. Shame on you, sir,' he addressed Francis, and, strangely, the MC's fluttering tones restored him to sanity.

Francis let go of Howell, who fell to his knees, clutching his throat and croaking, 'By heaven, Carey, another minute and you'd have killed me.'

'Pity I didn't, for the sake of all the men you've cheated and the women you've seduced,' retorted Francis, cold again, and when Mr Courtney said, tremulously, looking at the pair of them,

'I shall have to ask you to leave, both of you, and

you must seek my permission before you are admitted again,' Francis replied in a more normal voice,

'I regret, sir, that what I did was done here. I cannot regret the doing. All the same, I beg your pardon, and I shall leave at once.'

He swung towards his brother-in-law. 'You were right to try to stop me, Philip, and you will give my apologies to Almy and Bel, but whenever I see that man——' and he indicated Howell, who was being led away by his cohorts '——reason seems to leave me.'

Philip nodded. In all the years he had known Francis, he had found him stern but always perfectly in control of himself, and the savage who had nearly strangled Howell was unknown to him. His belief that there was more than met the eye between Francis, Bel Merrick and Rhys Howell was further strengthened.

As if he knew what Philip was thinking, Francis said ruefully as Philip walked him to the back door, 'Pray forgive me but it is most unlike me to behave as I did. The devil seems to be in me these days.'

Philip thought, but did not say, that since Bel Merrick had come into Francis's life his whole world seemed to have turned upside-down, but it was Francis's problem, not his, and Francis would have to solve it.

Meantime he must return to Almeria, Marcus and Bel, and try to gloss over what had happened in the supper-room, and over the fact that Bel Merrick was the main cause of it—for of that one thing Philip was quite sure.

CHAPTER FIFTEEN

BEL, however, was soon made aware that whatever
had happened in the supper-room between Francis
and Rhys Howell must in some way have concerned
herself.

She had suspected it ever since Philip Harley, in
his quiet fashion, had told them that the MC had
asked Francis and Captain Howell to leave. She
remembered what Francis had said—that if she
persisted in attending the September Ball with Rhys
Howell he would take action. The stares and curious
glances which she received all evening, the triumphant expression on Mrs Venn's face, and Henry's
mild, forbearing one, almost as though he were
saying, I told you so, at a distance, carried their own
message.

She was determinedly gay, but the gaiety had
something febrile in it. She was almost sure, now,
that Philip Harley, alone of all the people she knew
in Lulsgate, thought that there was something a
little strange, subtly out of place, in her relationship
with Francis, and it was that which troubled him, as
much as her apparent friendship with Rhys Howell.

Suppertime arrived, but she could not eat or
drink, and suddenly everything seemed intolerable,
even Almeria's kindness and protection, for, while
the Harleys approved of her, Lulsgate would always
accept her.

She rose, saying to Almeria, 'You will forgive me if I leave you early. I have a headache coming on, and an early night will suit me.' She had stayed long enough, she knew, to remove suspicion that the fracas in the supper-room had driven her away early, and Almeria, looking at Bel's suddenly white face, had not the heart to persuade her to stay longer.

'Of course,' she said, then, 'Bel, dear, do not worry over what passed tonight. Francis has been. . .impulsive, I know, but I am sure that whatever he did was done to protect you. Most unlike him to act as he did, but I believe that that, and only that, lay behind his conduct.'

Bel saw Philip Harley, almost unconsciously, nod agreement. She fought an impulse to cry, knowing that what Almeria said was true—despite his suspicions of her, the mixture of desire and hostility which were the staple of Francis's dealings with her, he genuinely wanted to save her from Rhys Howell. She almost wished that she had confided in him.

'Thank you, Almeria,' she said through stiff lips. 'Now you will excuse me, I trust. I will go and fetch Lottie. It is time that she went home; she is growing too old for late-night sessions such as these.'

'And that is what I like about Bel Merrick,' remarked Philip as they watched her go, bowing to those who bade her goodnight, 'she has a true consideration for all those about her. I suppose,' he added slowly, 'that that might account for her taking up with such an unlikely person as Rhys Howell. . .' But he did not believe what he said.

* * *

Bel found Lottie, looking weary as she had expected, but also surprised at Bel's relatively early departure from an event which was the height of Lulsgate's small season.

'I thought that you were going home with him, or with the Harleys, Miss Bel,' was all she said when it became apparent that she was Bel's sole escort.

'No.' Bel was brief. 'I am tired, and do not wish to stay longer. You may accompany me home. After all, the journey is not far, and Lulsgate streets are safe at night.'

Once home, bone-weariness took over. She felt as though she had run the sort of race she had done as a youthful hoyden before ladylike considerations took over to make her the model of a parson's good and proper daughter.

When Lottie would have followed her into her bedroom to ready her for the night, she shook her head. 'No, we are both tired, you more than myself. You may go to bed at once. I will look after myself.'

She thought that Lottie was growing old, and would have to be pensioned off, found a little home, but she was the last link with her old life and she did not wish to lose her. She watched the old woman struggle upstairs to her bedroom on the second floor. The temporary loss of Mrs Broughton had never seemed more annoying, for it had thrown more responsibilities on to her old servant.

Sighing, she pushed open her bedroom door, the candle she held throwing strange shadows about the room, her own, monstrously distorted, moving with her. She placed the candle on the dressing-table, undid her pearl necklace — only to see a movement in the shadows reflected in her mirror.

Startled, Bel swung around, a scream on her lips as she saw that a male figure was seated in the armchair by her bed, a scream she stifled when she saw that it was Francis, his face white and drawn, his whole mien one of barely suppressed pain.

'You!' she exclaimed. 'How came you here? And, more to the point, what are you doing here?'

He answered her second question, not her first, standing up as he did so, all his usual formality of manner quite gone.

'I came through the connection between your garden and Almy's. I noticed the other day that one of the glass doors in your drawing-room had a faulty lock. It was the work of a moment to force it and to enter. I have done no permanent damage. In any case, for your own safety the lock needed replacing.'

There was nothing apologetic about him. Nothing to suggest that the last thing he ought to have done was to break and enter a house, force his way into a lady's bedroom.

Shocked though she was, Bel could not help saying sharply, before she asked him to leave at once, before she called for the constable to remove him, 'You took a great risk. Suppose Lottie had come in with me — she usually does? What would you have done then?'

'Then I should have hidden in the curtains, or in the closet yonder, until she left.' He gave a humourless smile. 'You see, where you are concerned, Mrs Bel Merrick, I am full of wicked invention, and I have no conscience or honour left at all. You have deprived me of it.'

'Oh, I see,' said Bel, fascination replacing fear. 'It is all my fault. I might have expected that. I have provoked you to this dishonourable conduct, unworthy of a man of your reputation, character and station in life.'

Why was she bandying words with him? she wondered. She must order him to leave, although how she could compel him to go if he chose not to she could not think. To scream, to call for Lottie, or Ben, the boy who did the odd-jobs for her — a handyman rather than a footman — would destroy the last shreds of her reputation in Lulsgate Spa, to say nothing of the humiliations which such an act would heap on Francis himself. A supposedly honourable man who had arrived, uninvited, in a lady's bedroom, presumably to force her. . .or so the world would think. She did not really believe that that was why he had come.

'Yes, you have provoked me,' was his reply to that, 'by encouraging that damned swine Howell. God forgive me, I nearly killed him tonight, after seeing you with him. You must know only too well what a blackguard he is, that he can only mean you harm——'

'And what harm do *you* mean me?' flashed Bel. 'It is you who are in my bedroom, uninvited, at nigh on midnight, not Rhys Howell — who, of course, I know to be a villain, and one who means me harm. And now I ask again that you leave me, at once.'

'Not before you have heard me out,' he replied hoarsely, his face full of an almost physical pain. 'It has been murder, pure murder, for me to watch you tonight — aye, and all the recent days when I have seen you with *him*. Do you not know how you affect me, madam? Oh, Bel, I burn for you, feel how I burn,' and he grasped her hand, held it against his forehead for a moment, and it was true, he was on fire.

Bel wrenched her own hand back, for through it the fire had passed from him to her, and she was suddenly shaking, consumed by the same flames. Her breath had shortened at his touch, and the sight of him, here in her most secret place, the room where she had dreamed of him so often, was rousing her to the same pitch of excitement which Francis was suffering — or enjoying. . .perhaps the two sensations were the same, pleasure so exquisite that it was almost pain.

Francis saw her state, saw everything about her as though she had become transparent, open to him, felt her desire for him in the same measure that he felt his for her.

'Oh, you feel as I do!' he cried exultantly. 'Oh, Bel, you must not torment me longer. The more you hold me off, the more you inflame me, particularly when I know that you are deceiving me when you deny me. I vowed two years ago that I would enjoy you without paying you anything, that as a punishment for cheating me you would lie with me willingly, would beg me to do so, as I am now begging you. I told myself that I hated you for being a cheating whore, but I was wrong. I cannot pretend any more. I wish to be in your arms so strongly that I will gladly pay any price you name to be there.'

He loved her with all the passion of a passionate nature long denied, but he could not say so. He could not confess that he loved a Cyprian, and the sister of a Cyprian so notorious that two years after her death her name was still remembered — that was beyond him. Besides, he feared that she might laugh at him if he made any such confession; she had mocked him so often for much less than that.

Bel swallowed at his words, especially at the one word 'price'. He *still* thought her a whore after all these weeks together. How could he, oh, how could he? Her unconsidered acts of two years ago had ruined the future for both of them. Suppose she had said then, I am Marina St George's innocent sister, and can prove it — then they would not be standing here, dying of love for one another, and unable to do anything about it without each violating his or her most inward self.

For if Francis felt that he was betraying himself by loving a whore — for Bel now had no doubts that he loved her — she too would betray herself, destroy her own virtue, by consenting to lie with him in other than honourable marriage, because now she knew that she loved him beyond life, beyond reputation.

Love's cross-currents flung them now together, now apart — except that tonight, alone at last, hidden from the prying world, Bel knew that nothing could prevent her from giving him what he wanted so desperately to take — and she as desperately to offer.

He would not, she knew, keep her, take her as his mistress. She knew that his dead wife stood between him and a lesser permanent union. He would have her for one night, she thought—to assuage what? Was he strong enough to love her and leave her—was she strong enough to accept him as a lover, without marriage, risking social disgrace, and perhaps pregnancy—which was possible from even one night's loving?

And if she gave way to herself, as well as to him, what price would she demand of him—and of herself?

Francis had grasped her hand again, and again she pulled it away. She said coldly, denying the passion within her, 'Why do you ask me, Francis?' and her voice was almost cruel. 'We are here alone. You may take what you wish, with or without my consent. Many would not hesitate to take a whore without her consent. Why do *you* hesitate, Francis, thinking so little of me as you do?'

'Oh, God, not that, no, never that,' he said violently, putting his hands over his eyes. 'Not rape, Bel, never rape. Only with your consent, ever. You must accept me willingly, or not at all. If not for love, then for money, and you may name your price.'

She could not take him in the name of love—for she thought that he might not believe her if she told him that she loved him, and that would be to dishonour love. Knowing that, she also knew that in the end she would take him for the lesser reason. For, against all logic, all common sense, she was as determined to have him as he her, and if that meant the surrender of her chastity, then so be it—but he must pay in another coin first.

'Then beg me, Francis,' she said fiercely. 'Would you care for me to give you brandy, as you gave it to me at Almeria's table, that first night? Beg me, Francis, beg me on your knees for me to take you to my bed, if you wish to lie with me, for whore though I *might* be,' and she stressed the might, 'though any may offer me payment, I and only I choose who may visit my bed—and I am not yet sure that I wish to choose you.'

Francis fell on his knees before her, put his head in her lap, before looking up at her to see her face almost saintly in the halo created by the candlelight behind her.

'Oh, Bel, be merciful. Would you have me walk through the fire as well as burn?'

As I would walk through fire for you, and as I burn for you, was her unspoken reply. Yes, I would have you do that, so that we might be equal.

Instead, she answered him gently, 'No, not for mercy, Francis, but for payment. Whores have no pity, look only for payment. Your payment is—that you should beg again.'

Bel thought for a moment that she had gone too far. He lifted his head, stared at her, rose; pride had returned. He saw her white face, disembodied in the mirror, saw with astonishment that she was suffering as he did, for she was beside herself, lost in her own torment—and feeling his.

He was not to know, even though some strong message, unspoken, passed between them, informing him of the depths of her feelings, that, untried, chaste though she was, she would have taken him in love and was now, as she thought, prepared to take him in despite, seeing that there was no other way in which she could accept him.

Francis had no means of knowing this. Love's cross-currents were now so strong that both were drowning in them.

'I ask you, Mrs Bel Merrick, for I have no other name for you, to take me, Francis Carey, as I am, as your lover, for whatever reason, for love, for pity or for money, so long as we may enjoy together what I now see that we both so palpably want. Beyond reason, beyond honour, what I feel for you — and I have no name to give it — is so strong that you alone can give me something which I never thought to feel again.'

He fell silent, and Bel knew that, mistaking what she was, it was as near to a declaration of undying love as he could make to her. She thought of his dead wife and child, of her dead sister, and all doubts, all hesitations and resentments, were burned away.

'Yes,' she said simply. 'Yes, Francis, you need say no more. No payment of any kind is needed. Now it is my turn to beg you to come to me, to assuage *my* longing, *my* desire, for I, too, am beyond reason and honour and need no payment for what I so dearly wish.'

Francis's eyes, wide already from his body's arousal, widened still further, for he had thought that she was about to inflict the final humiliation on him — either refusal, or an acceptance so insulting that their loving would be bitter.

'*You* beg *me*?'

'Yes, Francis,' she said quietly, her voice so full

of love for him that he ached at the sound, her face as soft as an angel's in a painting. 'That was what you wanted, was it not? For me to beg you? Shall I beg you again? Love for love, Francis, not hate for hate. No payment needed on either side. We are to meet as willing equals.'

Bel saw that she had cut the Gordian knot, broken down all the barriers which had arisen between them. She had, at one stroke, freed them from the hateful past, for now his eyes were glowing, triumphant, but loving, too.

'Equals, Bel? You mean that?'

'Equals, Francis. As though we meet for the first time, no taint of our mutual past upon us, free to enjoy one another without bitterness, revenge or the desire to hurt.'

'Then I kneel to you willingly,' he said, and proud Francis Carey went down before her, and this time when he took her hand he let him keep it. He kissed it, and said, looking up at her, 'Oh, you are generous, my heart, and now let me see all of you; not only that which you show the world, but the treasures which you normally hide — except from your lovers, of whom I am humbly one.'

Bel shivered under his ardent gaze, internally quaked at the thought of stripping herself before him. But, after all that she had said she could not refuse him, even though her modesty shrank before the act.

She stood up, he still kneeling, pulling her dress over her head, removed her underclothing, her stockings, until she stood naked before him. His gaze on her had never wavered. His eyes were wider than ever, and as her last garment fell away, and she instinctively dropped her hands to cover herself—there—he was there before her, had clasped her round the knees and was kissing her where the red-gold fleece hid her most secret parts.

'Oh,' he said fervently, looking up at her perfect, unspoiled body, a very chaste Diana as she was, although he was not yet to know that, 'you are even more lovely than I had dared to hope. Bel, you are *belle* indeed,' and he rose, saying, 'And now you may prepare me for the sacred rite we are about to undertake, for there shall be nothing between us, nothing, all subterfuge stripped away.'

Again Bel could not deny him, and it was she who undid his cravat, peeled off his coat, undid the buttons of his shirt, and then, when he bore her to the bed, between them they reduced him to the same state as herself, so that now she saw all of him, and as they came together nothing, no, nothing lay between them, symbolic of the fashion in which they had mentally stripped themselves before beginning the physical act of loving and finally offering to one another two perfect bodies.

The fierceness of her passion surprised Bel, who had thought herself a calm and reasoned soul. But she could not have enough of him, as he wished to have all of her; mouth, hands, legs, eyes and voice, all played their part, and as he loved and caressed her breasts and her mouth, so she too rejoiced to stroke his hard body, kissing and caressing his torso, the muscles which stood on his arms and shoulders, ran her hands up his inward thighs—as he had done to her—so that as she cried out for surcease, so did he, and finally his passion, so long restrained, could be held in check no more and he entered her.

To find, too late, that she was the virgin she had always said she was. But there was nothing he could do; the very shock of the forced entry brought Francis relief, a relief so strong and fierce that Bel, too, shared in it, immediate though it was, for the strength of their passion and their preliminary loving, and the frustrations of the previous weeks, would brook no delay for either of them.

Time and space disappeared. The sense of separateness disappeared, too, as they achieved the truest union of all, not given to many to experience. Francis was too far gone in sensation to register his shock at finding his lightskirt, his ladybird, his bit of muslin, his courtesan a virgin, although when, shuddering and gasping, the first transports were over, Bel, who regretted nothing, found him still shaking, but this time in grief, not in love.

'Oh, God forgive me, Bel, for you never can, for what I thought, said and did to you. I have wronged you for months in thought, and now in deed. I have seduced an innocent girl. I am Rhys Howell's worst.'

Bel clasped him to her. 'Oh, Frank,' she said, the pet name coming naturally to her lips, 'my darling Frank, there is nothing to forgive. I misled you first, and tonight I freely invited you to love me, as we both wished, and there is nothing you say which can change that.'

He lifted his ravaged face from the pillow in which he had buried it. 'Oh, you are an angel, my darling, to speak so, but for weeks I have miscalled you, taunted you, and now. . .I have ruined you. Now you must marry me.'

'Marry you!' Bel sat up. 'Oh, I cannot do that. You cannot marry me. It would not be fitting. I bring you a dishonoured name. I have told so many lies, not only to you, but to all the world. You must marry someone truly innocent. Captain Howell. . .' she began, then hesitated, finally said resolutely, 'Captain Howell has been trying to blackmail me, about Marianne and my supposed past; that is why I was compelled to endure his advances. You cannot wish to marry someone who may have other such creatures arrive in the future to soil your good name.'

'My good name?' said Francis bitterly. 'And what is that, pray? I have, in effect, seduced you, bullied you until you gave way to me. If you marry me, then I will protect you from any who might try to harm you—or me. Oh, my love, you should have come to me for protection from him—but how could you, speaking to you and treating you as I did?'

He does not say that he loves me, thought Bel— but then he turned towards her, kissed her, and said hoarsely, 'Oh, I worship you, Bel, worship you, so gallant as you are. Why did you pretend to be the same as your sister, *why*?'

'Because,' said Bel, inwardly joyful at the declaration which he had just made, 'I was so angry when you treated me as a courtesan that I pretended to be one—and then cheated you, something which I have regretted ever since, for after that you could never believe me innocent. But I had no idea that I should ever meet you again, or that you had affected me so strongly, so quickly—as you did. You see, I am shameless where you are concerned.'

'Then,' said Francis, kissing her on the cheek, 'with you feeling as you do, I fail to see why you refuse to marry me.'

'You could. . .keep me,' said Bel gently, to have him say, violently,

'No, indeed. It is bad enough that I have ruined you, without proclaiming it to all the world; besides, it is not a thing I am prepared to do. I despise the immorality I see all around me, and now you may laugh at me for saying that, in view of my behaviour to you. I fail to see why you cannot accept my honourable proposal when you have accepted my dishonourable one—against all your beliefs, I am sure.'

'Because I love you,' Bel said, 'and because I accepted your dishonourable one, then the other is forbidden to me, and besides, although I come from a good family and my father was a parson, think of what my sister was, and what you are. You cannot marry such as myself.' And she leaned forward and kissed him on the cheek.

They were both now sitting up, and he took her face in his hands and said, 'It is not your sister whom I hope to marry, but you. Let me try to persuade you otherwise,' and he kissed her on the lips, gently at first, and then with renewed and rising passion, so that, all his good intentions forgotten, he turned her beneath him again, and they resumed where they had so recently left off. Only this time he treated her with such loving and patient care that in her transports she almost wept beneath him.

And when, sated, they lay in one another's arms, and he would again have asked her to marry him, Bel put her fingers on his mouth and said, 'Go to sleep, Francis, let us have tonight.'

He nodded his head, but replied, 'But I must leave soon, I must not ruin you completely,' and they fell asleep, sitting up, propped against the pillows, arms round one another, as though to be parted physically was death itself.

Bel slept as she had not done for weeks, and Francis too, so deeply that dawn came and went, and the door opened, for Lottie had knocked, and Bel had not answered, nor did she wake until her old servant, worried, entered the room ——

To see Francis still there, sleeping, his head now on Bel's breast, and Bel's gaze, steady, unashamed, meeting hers, left hand to her lips commanding silence, for she knew, instinctively, that Francis was at peace as he, too, had not been for years.

The old woman, who had seen even more of the world than Bel suspected, nodded her head and left, but the closing door broke Francis's slumbers. He sat up, looked at Bel, saw the daylight through the curtains, and said, 'My God, Bel, whatever is the time? I said that I would not ruin you, but I am like to do so,' and he sprang out of the bed, alternately pulling on his clothing and demanding that she marry him.

Bel rose from the bed, pulled on her dressing-gown and began to help him, buttoning his shirt, tying his cravat, assisting him into his tight, fashionable coat, shaking her head, finally saying, 'Then give me leave to think on the matter, Francis,' for him to begin to kiss her passionately.

'Yes, my darling, for that answer is better than last night's refusal, but not enough!' And then, 'But I must be away, before I am seen.'

Together they stole downstairs — it was now eight-thirty on a fine morning — and Bel let him out through the glass doors in the drawing-room, for him to escape, not by the way to Almeria's garden, but through a small gate to a side-alley, so that he might steal back unseen — after claiming yet another kiss.

Then Bel went back indoors, to meet Lottie's reproving stare. 'I might have known,' said the old woman resignedly. 'You are not your sister, but you are loving enough. Could he not wait for you, then, or were you only too ready to make him your lover without so much as a wedding-ring, or a betrothal?'

'He has asked me to marry him,' began Bel, 'but —'

'But?' said Lottie. 'What but is there? The man is besotted. Has been since he met you as was plain for all to see — who had eyes, that is, and were not full of their own consequence. To be Lady Francis — what "but" can there be? Your wits are addled, Bel Passmore, for I will not call you by a name that is not yours. Does he know that yet?'

'No,' said Bel, 'and I do not think that he cares. I have promised to think on the matter.'

'Think for one minute and then say yes before he changes his mind,' said her servant acidly, for Bel to walk by her, clutching to her the memory of the night, and with the intention of considering carefully what she ought to do. Impulsiveness had brought her to this day; would careful thought do better for her?

Francis made his way to the vicarage as warily as he could. No one was about, and he knew that neither Almeria nor Philip would rise early after last night's junketing. With luck he could slip in — he possessed a door-key — and be up the stairs before anyone stirred.

Good fortune was not with him. Little Frank had been ill in the night, and though he took all the care in the world Francis had no more luck than to start up the stairs just as Philip and Almeria arrived on the landing, early risers after being awake most of the night caring for the little boy.

They both stared at the sight of him, still in last night's clothes for the ball, dishevelled, not at all his usual orderly self, walking in after a night spent — where? To try to explain would make matters worse. Neither his half-sister nor his brother-in-law said anything. Francis smiled ruefully, and continued on his way. It was only too patent that he had spent the night away from the vicarage. He shrugged his shoulders. Well, that could not be helped; after all, he was more than of age.

Only to meet Marcus's accusing stare as he, too, arrived to see his uncle coming in after a night's debauch. Marcus's smile was knowing, almost derisory, and the only consolation was that not one of the three of them could have any idea in whose bed he had actually spent the night.

'Celebrating?' said Marcus, thinking he had

caught his high-minded uncle on his way home after a bout with one of Lulsgate Spa's rather seedy Cyprians. Never say the old fellow has turned human at last! was his inward thought.

Francis cursed his ill luck, said, 'Good morning,' as cheerfully as though he were not rumpled, unshaven, and full of a goodwill brought on by a thoroughly satisfactory night's loving—of which he could say nothing to anyone. Neither Marcus's broad grin, nor Almeria and Philip's faint expression of shock, had the power to move him. He was suddenly sure that his heart's desire would be granted, that Bel would agree to marry him, and his lonely years would be over.

Bel did not have long to debate over Francis's proposal, or over her own surrender of her virginity. She had expected to feel some faint regret, but could only feel pleasure. Francis's loving had been so kind and careful, as well as passionate—exactly what she might have expected it to be.

But could she really accept him? Eating breakfast, dressing for the day, a sense of well-being lapping round her, she was coming to feel that perhaps she could—but that she must not hurry her decision.

Just before luncheon, however, Lottie came in, her face one big O, bursting with news. 'Oh, Miss Bel, you would never guess what has happened!'

'No,' said Bel, smiling, 'I refuse to guess, for I am sure that you are determined to tell me.'

'It's that Captain Howell. He was found shot dead in his room at the White Peacock not an hour ago. They had to break his door down when he failed to

rise this morning, and his man could not make him
hear. Such a thing to happen! And him taking you
to the ball, last night! I can't say that I'm sorry to
hear the news, I disliked the man greatly, but I hope
no one thinks Lord Francis had anything to do with
it, after his quarrel with Captain Howell last night.'

'Goodness!' said Bel. 'That's the most unlikely
thing I ever heard,' only for Lottie to look at her,
and say,

'Well, at least, Miss Bel, *we* know that Lord
Francis couldn't have murdered Captain
Howell. . .' And she almost winked at her mistress.

Bel was not surprised that Captain Howell had
been murdered. Given the way in which he had
behaved towards her, and what Francis had hinted
about his career in London and Paris, it was perhaps
to be expected that someone should see fit to
dispose of him.

One more thing which I do not need to worry
about, thought Bel. I don't like to be relieved that a
man, even a man like Rhys Howell, was murdered,
but his death has saved me from further difficulties—and perhaps may change my intentions about
marrying Francis.

She suddenly had a desperate, aching desire to
see him, to be with him, and her resolve not to
marry him was shaken. Oh, to love someone was so
all-consuming, how could she bear to wait to see
him again? Thank God, she thought, that I am to
dine at the vicarage tonight, when we may meet at
last in friendship, even if we are not able to acknowledge our love openly.

Her smile was so purely happy that Lottie, looking at her, thought wisely, No need to worry about Miss Bel. He's an honourable man, for all that he got her into bed before he asked her to marry him, but he'll do the right thing by her, I'm sure, and whatever she says I'm sure that she'll accept him.

She sighed sentimentally. She knew that she should have been shocked, but the sight of Bel with Francis in her arms had warmed her, not shocked her, for Lottie's view of life, like that of many servants, was earthier than that of the gentry whom they served. I know Miss Bel, she thought; she'll make a good wife, and a good mother, not like Miss Marianne — she always wanted things easy. . .not surprising that she went wrong in London.

Which was Marianne's epitaph and Bel's eulogy.

CHAPTER SIXTEEN

Captain Howell provided Lulsgate Spa with as much scandalised and excited gossip in death as in life. From the moment he was discovered on the floor, a pistol thrown down by him, which had been held close to his body when it fired, presumably to muffle its noise of the shot, speculation roared about who had done the deed. Opinion was divided between whether the murderer ought to be hanged — or rewarded, the innkeeper's belief inclining to the latter since it turned out that Captain Howell had left nothing behind him with which to pay his huge bill.

Inevitably the discord between Lord Francis Carey and the dead man, ending in the fracas the night before the murder, was also discussed in gleeful tones. Among those worried by the news was Almeria, remembering that Francis had spent the night away from the vicarage — of course he could not have murdered Captain Howell, could he? But where had he been, what had he been doing?

Speculation even invaded the vicarage itself at the dinner which Bel attended. There had been talk of sending for the Bow Street Runners, but Mr Thomas Fancourt, a local landlord, who was one of Lulsgate Spa's magistrates, said that he had been informed by Sir Charles Walton, the chief of them, that that would probably not be necessary—he knew no details, but Sir Charles had been on his high ropes, had said that the identity of the murderer would cause great excitement, and he would not move against him until he was sure of his case.

Mrs Venn informed the table, 'The sooner that such a creature is apprehended the better; we are none of us safe in our beds.'

Ever inwardly inflamed by Mrs Venn, Bel wanted to retort, On the contrary, we are all safer now that he is dead, and he has probably been killed by someone whom he has bammed, this last delightful piece of slang having come from her latest novel from the subscription library, partly set in London's underworld, *The Bells of St Giles*.

Almeria had sat her by Francis, and his speech and manner to her at dinner were so loving that Bel almost feared that they would cause comment; but no such thing—everyone was too busy dissecting the dead captain. For once she saw little of Francis after the dinner, the men congregating together to discuss the day's news; and the women, too, in their own excited huddle, wondered at it, and said how little surprised they were, the dead man having become universally disliked, although a few had favoured him at first.

Over the tea-board, Francis took the opportunity to pass her cup to her and sit beside her, saying in a low voice, 'You have thought of what I said? You have reached a decision?' and the hard grey eyes were suddenly so soft and full of hope that Bel hardly knew him. She could see Philip and Almeria watching them, presumably also hopeful, and she felt compelled to say,

'Not yet, Francis, not yet. I have had no time to think.'

'No time?' he said tenderly. 'You have had since morning. An eternity. If all time passes as slowly as this while I wait for you to make up your mind, I shall have a white beard down to my knees by the week's end.'

Bel choked back a laugh, said, severely, 'You are as naughty in your admiration as you were when you despised me.'

'No,' he said, suddenly deadly sincere in his manner. 'I never despised you, however hard I tried — that was the trouble. Oh, I cannot see why you hesitate; we are two halves come together, and my life will be incomplete without you. Ever since my dear Cassie died I have lived without love — and now I see what a half-life it was, and how hard it has made me. Marry me, Bel, and save me.'

Almost she said yes on the spot, but Mrs Venn came up, spiteful eyes on them. She did not want Henry to have Bel, nor did she want Francis Carey to succeed with her either.

'So,' she said to Bel, 'you have lost your admirer, Mrs Merrick. Not that I can say I cared for your taste, but then Lulsgate Spa probably contains few who can please you, you being so discriminating in all things.' The last was said in such a manner that it indicated Mrs Venn believed that Bel was nothing of the kind.

Bel was fearful of what Francis's reactions might be, but he merely bowed — he had risen on Mrs

Venn's approach — and said lightly, 'I believe that Mrs Merrick has always a good reason for even her lightest decisions, and one must remember that, whatever else, Captain Rhys Howell once held the King's Commission.'

That Mrs Venn was annoyed at Francis's refusal to be ruffled went without saying; she tossed her head and moved on, Francis remarking mildly when she was out of earshot, 'I am so near to happiness today that even such arrows as Mrs Venn cares to loose at us cannot touch me. Have we reached harbour, Bel? Say that we have, I beg of you,' and even though she shook her head at him her eyes were giving him another message — and it was the one he wanted. Paradise seemed near.

Those around them thought so, too. Almeria kissed Philip when Francis had retired for the night, said joyfully, 'I do believe, my dear, that my good little Bel is going to make Francis a happy man. You could not but notice his manner to her, and hers to him. And you must not say that I interfered to arrange it, for I followed your instructions, and left them to solve their problems together.'

'Better so,' said Philip gently, 'and I agree that Bel will do Francis the world of good. He was in danger of becoming a lost soul, and I feared for him a little.'

'So, we go to bed happy,' said Almeria gaily, kissing him again, 'and the thought that Francis will have someone, as I have you, and will no longer be lonely, is a comforting one.'

* * *

Bel thought of Francis's proposal the next day when she sat reading a letter from Mrs Broughton, who said that although her return was delayed it would not be many days before she was with dear Bel again. Bel put the letter down, and thought that if she accepted Francis he would almost certainly help her to find a place for Mrs Broughton somewhere in his vast establishment. Almeria had told her of his wealth, and the great house in the north which his mother had left him.

Which means, she told herself joyfully, that I have made up my mind to accept him, for he is right, we are two halves, and must come together. I am foolish to let what Marina was come between us. After all, we came from a good family, and in normal circumstances there would be no bar to our marriage. We love each other, our minds meet as well, and that is all that matters in the end. Oh, I can hardly wait to tell him.

A comic thought struck her: and Cassius will be so pleased that we have stopped wrangling, so there is a good thing! She must remember to share that joke with Francis. She knew that he would appreciate it, and now they would share their jokes, not hurl them at one another — as she hoped they would share everything else.

While she had been reading there had been noise in the street, and now she heard the sound of running footsteps, and the door flew open.

It was Lottie, her face white. 'Oh, Miss Bel. Such terrible news. Sir Charles is at the vicarage, with the constables. Betty from the kitchens has told me that the pistol found by Captain Howell's body was Lord

Francis's. He says it was stolen from him in Paris, but they knew that he was out all night, will not say where he was, and they are threatening to arrest him for murder, for all the world knows how much at outs he was with the captain, and that he had attacked and threatened him only the evening before. Betty says that were he not who he is they would have had him in the lock-up by now!'

Bel rose to her feet, mouth trembling. 'Francis, murder Captain Howell! Are they all run mad? Besides, he can have done no such thing. He was with me all night, as you know. Oh. . .!' And the implications of *that* struck her immediately, and she knew, though no one else did, why Francis would offer no explanation of where he had spent the night.

It was her honour, her reputation which he was protecting, at the expense of his freedom — possibly of his life.

White to the lips, her whole body shaking, she said hoarsely, 'You must be mistaken, Lottie. Sir Charles cannot believe that Lord Francis would do such a thing.'

'And so he apparently said, Miss Bel, but the evidence is so strong. . . Why? What are you about to do?' For Bel had picked up her shawl, thrown it around her shoulders and was making for the glass doors and the back path to the vicarage.

'Do?' said Bel energetically. 'Why, go there at once, and tell them the truth — that he was with me.'

'No,' said Lottie, barring her way. 'Oh, no, Miss Bel. Think; your reputation will be gone in an instant. You will be no better than poor Miss Marianne. You will have to leave Lulsgate.'

'I cannot allow them to try Francis, possibly hang him, for something which I can prove he did not do,' said Bel, her heart sinking into her pretty little kid slippers at the thought of what telling the truth might do to her.

But Mr Birch had told her that there might come a time when she ought to tell the truth, and now she had no choice — that time had come.

Ironically, what Francis had thought of her would shortly come true. She would be a pariah, a light woman, not fit for society. She would almost certainly have to leave Lulsgate, forfeit her friendships here, and her good name. . .but what was that against what might be done to Francis if she kept silent?

She could not allow him to do this, she could not, and, pushing by Lottie, she ran towards the vicarage, praying that she was not too late.

Francis, at bay in the vicarage drawing-room, Philip and Almeria with him, was at his haughtiest.

He had laughed contemptuously at what he called the so-called evidence, said that the pistol with his arms and initials on it was one of a pair stolen from him in Paris, and he could prove it, that he was certain that Howell had been killed by someone he had cheated, almost certainly from outside Lulsgate. And no, he could not deny that he had not been in his bed at the vicarage the night that the captain was murdered, but would not, on any account, say where he *had* been.

'You leave me no alternative but to arrest you, Lord Francis,' said the harassed Sir Charles. 'You threatened him more than once, before many witnesses, the last time on the night before the murder when you had to be pulled off him before you killed him. Your pistol is found by his body, and you refuse to say where you were — hardly the action of an innocent man.' He refrained from adding that were he anyone but *Lord* Francis he would not be debating the matter at such length before taking a man with such a wealth of evidence against him to the lock-up.

'Francis,' said Philip gently, 'is there nothing you can tell Sir Charles of your whereabouts on the fatal night? Nothing at all?' He was suddenly sure where Francis had been that night, but, in the face of Francis's own silence, he too could say nothing, could offer no hint.

'Only,' said Francis, and his voice was stone, 'that I was troubled in my mind, and spent the night walking and thinking.'

'All night?' said Sir Charles, with Philip's expression echoing his words. 'You must see that that beggars belief.'

They had reached this impasse when there was the sound of an altercation outside, the door was unceremoniously thrown open, and Bel almost threw herself into the room.

Francis took one agonised look at her and knew why she had arrived, what she was about to do. The haughtily indifferent languor which had infuriated Sir Charles and his brother-in-law flew away in an instant.

'No, Bel,' he said, walking towards her and

seizing her hands. 'No, you have no business here. You know nothing of the matter,' and then he saw her implacable face, felt her trembling at what she was about to say, and said loudly, 'No, I forbid it, you understand? I positively forbid it. You are not to speak.'

He swung on the startled spectators, his face anguished. 'Tell her to leave. She has no place here,' and he tried to push her to the door. Neither Philip nor Almeria had ever seen him so moved before. Stern, implacable Francis Carey had disappeared.

Bel freed herself from his clutching hands. 'No, Francis, I cannot allow this. You must not lie yourself to the gallows by refusing to speak.'

She turned to Sir Charles, who knew her a little and was staring at her wild manner and informal dress with astonishment. Not in such a fashion was Mrs Bel Merrick wont to be seen abroad in Lulsgate Spa.

'Do I collect, sir, that the gravamen of the case against Lord Francis is that he cannot prove, or will not say, where he was on Thursday night when Captain Howell was murdered?'

Sir Charles nodded. 'Yes, madam, but I fail to see —— '

'You will see this, sir,' said Bel steadily. She was aware, for all the world suddenly seemed hard and clear, that Francis had sunk into a chair, his head in his hands, compelled to realise that nothing he could say or do would stop his gallant love from ruining herself for him. 'Lord Francis could not possibly have killed Captain Howell, for he spent the entire night with me. I arrived home with him a little time after eleven of the clock, and we were together until gone eight the next morning. He is refusing to speak in order to save me, but I cannot allow him to do so at the expense of his freedom and his life. I must tell the truth.'

The world, from being so sharp, became dull and blurred. She heard Almeria's indrawn breath, saw Philip's kind and understanding face, and Sir Charles's almost disdainful one as she finished speaking.

Francis lifted his head, said hoarsely, 'Not so, I say. It is good of her to do this, but she is lying to save me,' and Sir Charles, seeing how matters must stand between them, began to say,

'Just so ——' only for Bel to interrupt him, shaking her head and looking steadily at Francis.

'It is useless, Francis,' she said gently, 'for you must know that my maid Lottie came to my. . . room while you were still sleeping in the early morning, and I was awake and she. . .saw you there. And so she will testify. I appreciate the sacrifice you have been making in order to save my reputation, but it is your life which might be at stake, and I cannot allow you to save me at such an expense.'

She saw Philip's approving nod, heard Almeria give a half-sob, but nothing mattered to Bel except that Francis must be saved. The passion which had ruled since Lottie had told her of Sir Charles arriving to arrest Francis, and his refusal to say where he had been, was beginning to fade. There was a ringing in her ears, and she was fearful that she would disgrace herself by fainting. And this time the faint would be a true one. . .

Philip, indeed, looking at Sir Charles, moved forward and took her hand; he could see that she was *in extremis*.

'Look at me, my dear Bel,' he said gently, an expression of infinite pity on his face which had her fighting against tears. 'You are telling the truth, are you not? You are not simply trying to save Francis by sacrificing yourself?'

Bel looked at him, beyond him to where Francis had turned his back to them all, and was, she knew by his whole stance, fighting for his composure.

'Yes,' she said, and her voice was suddenly strong. 'I have told you so many lies, dear Philip, as you will shortly discover, but I am not lying to you over this, I swear it.'

Philip looked over the top of her head at Sir Charles, said, 'I am sure that Mrs Merrick is speaking the truth. Everything which she has said bears the stamp of veracity, and, that being so, it would be most unwise to arrest my brother-in-law before her servant has been questioned. Best to make enquiries about the theft of the pistol as well. You really have no case against him now.'

He released Bel's hand, but not before, with a look of infinite compassion on his face, he had kissed it. Almeria was looking from Bel to Francis, and the glance which she gave her half-brother was a fierce one, all the usual affection which she felt for him quite banished.

Sir Charles bowed to them all, gestured to the two constables to leave with him, not before saying stiffly to Francis, 'You will forgive me the accusation I made, but your refusal to answer me, or to divulge your whereabouts, made it inevitable that I did so. Mrs Merrick's evidence, given that her servant supports it, leaves you innocent of all accusations relating to Captain Howell's death. I shall make enquiries about the theft of your pistols. I am inclined to the belief that if they were, as you say, stolen in Paris, then someone from that city may have come here to murder him. I understand, and not only from yourself, that his reputation was a bad one.'

And so it later proved. Captain Howell's death was a nine-day wonder, ended only when it appeared that he had been engaged in criminal activities in both Paris and London, and his associates, whom he had cheated, had found means to dispose of him — Francis's pistol, bearing his initials and arms, being a useful red herring.

The door closed behind them. Bel, around whom Almeria had placed a protective arm, had begun to shiver. Francis swung towards her, his face ravaged.

'Oh, my darling Bel!' he exclaimed. 'You should not have done what you did — the accusation against me could never have stood, I am sure — but oh, how I honour you for it.' And he fell on to his knees before her, clutching her hand as he did so, ignoring Philip and Almeria who stared at him in wonder.

Proud and stern Francis Carey, almost fighting tears, was saying to the woman he loved and who had destroyed herself for him, 'You cannot refuse to marry me now, Bel; it is the least that I can offer you. . .if I thought that I loved you before, think what I feel for you now.'

Bel snatched her hand away, and turned impetuously from him to face Philip and Almeria. 'No! You cannot marry a ruined woman, and one of such a bad reputation. I must tell you all the truth, I must.'

She was thinking of what Mr Birch had said as she poured this out. 'I have told you so many lies. I am not even Mrs Merrick — there is no Mr Merrick. I am Bel Passmore, a respectable clergyman's daughter, but I am also the younger sister of Marina St George, the noted courtesan, as Francis knows, and until two days ago I was virtuous, but am no longer. Francis cannot marry such a woman, a woman whom Rhys Howell felt free to blackmail. No, do not argue with me, Francis; you know that what I say is true, and that is why I refused to marry you two days ago, and do so now.' And before any of them could stop her she ran from the room.

Francis rose, started to follow her, but was stopped by Philip, his face stern. 'No,' he said. 'leave her alone, Francis. You seduced her, did you not? And that you wished to marry her afterwards does not mitigate what you did.' And Almeria's eyes were as accusing as her husband's.

Francis turned towards them again, his face a mask of torment, tears in his eyes, quite changed from what he had been.

'I love her to distraction,' he said hoarsely. 'I first met her two years ago, shortly after her sister died. I never thought to meet her again, and then here she was in Lulsgate. I thought at first that she was unworthy, but it is I who am that, not my dear Bel. You are both right to despise me. And now you must let me go to her, for I shall not rest until she consents to become my wife. I have mourned my dear Cassie too long; it is time to let her go — in any case she would hate what I have done to Bel as much as you do. I cannot spare her scandal, but with my name she may face the world down.'

'Oh, you do love her, Francis,' said Almeria wonderingly. 'Why did you seduce her, then? All you needed to do was offer her honourable marriage.'

Francis could make no reply to that without giving away the tangle of his relationship with Bel. He saw Philip raise warning brows at his wife, and then, like Bel, he ran through the door, out into the garden to take the path to Bel's glass doors. To find her, to ask her to forgive him — and become his wife.

Almeria turned to Philip, bewildered. 'I do not understand him at all,' she complained. 'If he loved her, and wished to marry her, why did he do what he did? He had no need——' And then, as Philip looked at her steadily, she said, 'Oh, you always thought that there was something odd about them, did you not? And you would not wish me to pry, I understand. . .or rather I don't.'

'There are some things about others,' Philip said, 'which it is best for us not to ask about, or even to know. I said once before that Francis and Bel must solve their own problems, and despite all that has passed this morning I think that they are about to do so. And now we must think of other things — and try to stop Lulsgate from tearing them both to pieces, for this morning's doings will be all about Lulsgate in the hour.'

But Francis discovered that Bel was not at home, only found Lottie there, who had just confirmed Bel's story to Sir Charles, for if Miss Bel had sacrificed her good name to save Francis then she could do no less than tell the truth.

'Where is she?' they both said together, Francis recovering himself first. 'She has not come here?'

'No,' said Lottie, staring, 'I thought that she was still with you.'

'Oh, God,' said Francis frantically, 'where has she gone, if she has not come back here?'

'And why should I tell you anything,' said the old woman fiercely, 'seeing that you have ruined her with your wickedness? Such a good girl, my dear Miss Bel, not at all like that silly Miss Marianne. Shame on you if you thought Miss Bel was no better.'

'You cannot despise me more than I despise myself,' said Francis humbly. 'Have you no idea where she may have gone?'

Lottie shook her head, and Francis ran back to the vicarage, his head on fire, to enquire frantically, 'Oh, Almy, my dear, do not look at me like that. I have no idea where she has gone, and I must find her, I must.'

'Before every tabby-cat in Lulsgate rips her to bits when today's news leaks out, as it will,' said Almeria. 'I hardly know you, Francis. Such a good girl as my dear Bel was. How could you treat her so?' And then was silent, remembering what Philip had counselled.

'But none of this helps me to find her,' said Francis grimly, and he looked so distressed that Philip, who had come in while they were talking, pushed him gently into a chair, pouring him a glass of wine from the bottle which he had brought in with him, then handing the glass to his brother-in-law who pushed it away.

'No,' said Philip gently, 'drink it. You look as though you are about to drop dead any minute. Think, Francis, think. You know her as well as anyone. Where in Lulsgate Spa could she have found refuge?'

Francis drank the wine, shuddering. Something in Philip's words struck him, and he stared at him. Even Almeria was beginning to show a little pity for him in his distracted state.

'Not in Lulsgate Spa,' he said slowly, 'but in Morewood.'

'Morewood!' they both said together, then Almeria,

'Why Morewood?'

'Because,' said Francis, 'and I see that you do not know this, she helped the Methodist minister, Mr Birch, to run a small dame school for poor children at Morewood twice a week. She extended her love and compassion to them — as she did to me.'

'On Wednesdays and Fridays!' said Almeria. 'Which explains why she was always unavailable on those days.'

'Exactly,' said Francis, colour returning to his cheeks. 'Morewood, I am sure of it. To the old man there. I know that he thinks a great deal of her, and she respects him. I will go there at once. Not in the curricle. To take that would be to emphasise the difference which once existed between us.' And before Philip and Almeria could stop him he ran out of the room again.

Almeria turned to Philip, shocked. 'I would never have believed it,' she said slowly. 'He adores her, that is plain. And if so, why did he ruin her? For that is what he did. I shall never understand him, ever. So upright he was, and now this.'

'He is human,' replied her husband, 'and he has been so severe with himself for so long—and now he must try to find his salvation—for that is what Bel is, I suspect. And, as I said before, he must do it himself.'

Francis followed Bel, who, as he suspected, had gone to Mr Birch at Morewood for succour. Like her, he ran through the streets unheeding, surprised spectators turning to follow his progress, as they had followed Bel's.

Bel, indeed, had had only one idea in her head, and that was to get away from everyone, and find absolution with Mr Birch. Why this was so she did not know. Only, at the moment when she had told the truth about the night which Francis had spent with her, she had had a kind of revelation—that it was important to tell the truth about everything; there must be no more lies, however good the reasons she might once have had for telling them.

She must go to see Mr Birch, to tell him what she had done, and only then could she allow herself to think about Francis and his needs — for she knew that she could not abandon him, only that before she could speak to him again she must clear her conscience, and she could only do that when she had spoken to the old man. Philip Harley would not have done at all, for it was not Philip to whom she had earlier hinted of her dilemma, but Mr Birch.

Mr Birch was in his garden when Bel arrived, panting, her eyes wild, nothing of the refined young lady left. She threw open the garden gate and ran to him, half sobbing, 'Oh, Mr Birch, dear Mr Birch, pray let me speak to you.'

He put an arm around her, led her gently into the house, sat her down in his big Windsor chair, and brought her a glass of water to still her shaking and sobbing.

'Now what is it, my dear? How can I help you?'

'I have told the truth,' she wailed, 'and I feel worse than ever. Not only am I ruined, but I have told the whole world of it, and more beside.' And she broke into the sobs which she had held back for so long. 'And it is all my fault. Oh, dear Mr Birch, I did a wrong thing two years ago; I told a great lie — or rather implied it — to the gentleman who has come here for me several times, and though I love him dearly I cannot marry him.'

'He rejects you, then,' said Mr Birch gently. 'I told you I thought that he was not a man to play with.'

'Oh, no,' said Bel, showing him a tear-stained face. 'He wishes to marry me, but I feel so unworthy.'

Mr Birch looked puzzled. 'But you said that you

were ruined. You mean that there is another suitor, of whom you have not told me?'

'Oh, it is all so difficult,' wailed Bel again. 'I allowed him to ruin me because I loved him so, and he thought that I was not virtuous, but then he found out that I *was* virtuous after all, and now he wishes to marry me. But it would not be fair to him. Oh, I have done my duty, and even that does not answer.'

This muddled explanation served to enlighten Mr Birch a little. He handed poor Bel a man's large handkerchief and said, 'And if you truly care for him, my dear, and he wishes to marry you, and you are — or were — virtuous then I do not see your problem. But always remember that virtue and telling the truth are their own rewards — although sometimes God sees fit to give us more.'

He had hardly finished speaking when there was a hammering on his front door. Bel heard the housekeeper answer it, and then Francis's agitated voice echoed through the house.

Bel rose to her feet, turned towards the door, and said to Mr Birch, 'It's Francis.' Her lip trembled. 'Should I see him?'

'It is your life and your decision, under God, of course,' said the old man gently.

'Yes,' said Bel, and as Francis came through the door he saw them together, Bel's hand in Mr Birch's, a look of peace on her face such as he had never seen before.

And what did Bel see? She saw that Francis had in some strange way found his peace, too. The mixture of desire and pain which had driven him ever since he had first met her had disappeared.

He bowed to Mr Birch, and said, 'You will allow me to speak to Mrs Merrick, I trust.'

'Miss Anne Isabella Passmore,' said Bel. 'I must not deceive either of you, or the world, any more. I am the daughter of the Reverend Mr Caius Passmore, sometime rector of Brangton in Lincolnshire, who was cousin to Sir Titus Passmore of Dallow in Cheshire. It is little enough to claim, but I must tell you at last who I really am.'

'Miss Passmore, then,' said Francis gravely. 'I have something which I wish to say to her privately, sir. We have had too much discussion in public today.'

'If Miss Passmore wishes it,' said Mr Birch, 'then it shall be so. It is your wish, Miss Passmore?'

'Yes,' said Bel, suddenly and unwontedly shy. 'If Lord Francis wishes it.'

'Then I will leave you,' said the old man, and, as he reached the door, 'May the Lord be with you both.'

Francis bowed again. His punctiliousness and care for the old man pleased Bel more than she could say. All his pride and hauteur seemed to have leaked out of him. She thought that they might return, but that he would never again be entirely as he was.

And now he bowed to Bel. 'I am pleased to make your acquaintance, Miss Passmore,' he said, as though they had never met before. 'I have something to say to you, to which I hope you will give your most earnest consideration. You will allow?'

Bel bowed her head, signed for him to continue. She felt barely able to speak.

'Yes,' she achieved, 'pray do,' as though, she thought, they had not so recently been together, as close as a man and woman might be.

'Miss Passmore, I have known you long enough now to be aware that above all things I would wish you to be my wife. You are the woman I have always wanted to meet: kind, brave and generous. You have borne my recent intolerable behaviour after a fashion so admirable that it gains my utmost respect. More, I know that I love you as I have never loved any other woman.

'What I felt for my dear Cassie was quite different, if no less true. Today you honoured me by offering up your reputation in order to save me obloquy, pain and possible death. If you can bring yourself to accept my suit you will make me the happiest man in Britain, as I hope to make you the happiest woman. I cannot say fairer than that.' And he took her hand and kissed it, bowing his head, then lifting it to show her his eyes, brimming with love. 'Please, my dear Miss Passmore, marry me, as soon as possible.'

Bel could not speak. Her throat had filled. What he had said to her was said so humbly, so differently from all his previous offers to her, either honourable or dishonourable.

She lifted his hand to her lips, kissed it, and said, 'If you can bring yourself to offer for me, Francis, knowing my true circumstances, then, loving you as I do, I cannot refuse such a noble offer. Yes, I will accept you.'

Francis broke on that. The perfect courteous calm which he had shown to her ever since he had entered the room was suddenly gone; he took her in his arms and began to kiss her, kiss away the tears which ran down her face — tears of joy, not of sorrow.

'And you will not regret this,' said Bel, pulling back a little, 'knowing of me, and mine, what you do?'

'I would regret not asking you,' he said. 'And if you can bring yourself to forgive me, then some time, perhaps, I can forgive myself.'

Bel put her hand on his lips. 'The fault lay in both of us,' she said, 'and we have a lifetime to repair it. And now, sir, we must be decorous. It is Mr Birch's home we grace, and it is time that we informed him that we intend to behave honourably in future.'

'Indeed,' he said, putting an arm around her, and kissing the top of her head. 'We must behave ourselves now, until we marry. I shall go to London for a special licence, and Philip shall marry us if you think you can face the world here. If not, we can be married at my home in the north.'

'I think,' said Bel steadily, 'that it would be only fair to Philip and Almeria, whom we have both deceived, to be married here as quietly as possible.'

As she spoke, there was a knock at the door and then Mr Birch came in, carrying tea-things for three on a small tray.

He looked at them shrewdly, and said, 'I thought that you might like to celebrate with me. You *are* about to celebrate, are you not?'

Francis and Bel stared at him, astonished. He

gave a dry chuckle. 'Come,' he said, 'I have lived in the world these many years, and I know the faces which men and women assume. You are a man and a woman of sense; I could not but think that you would behave sensibly in the end, and so it proves.'

He handed the cups around, and said, 'I toast the pair of you, and I firmly believe that you will soon be Lord and Lady Francis, and happy together.'

Francis Carey had never expected to become betrothed to the woman whom he so passionately loved in a Methodist minister's shabby parlour, nor that the minister's prophecy would come as true as it did when he forecast a happy life for him with the Cyprian's sister.

NOTES FOR THE READER

MARIANNE PASSMORE's death from a 'fulminating stomach' was, in modern terms, from a burst appendix. Appendicitis in the early nineteenth century usually resulted in death.

In the early nineteenth century, the notorious courtesan Harriette Wilson blackmailed her famous lovers just as Marianne did in the novel. She was also in league with dubious adventurers of good family, come down in the world, very similar to Rhys Howell.

Lulsgate Spa is an imaginary town: it does not exist in Leicestershire or any other country. Its environment, social life and characteristics are based on many of the spas which were popular in the eighteenth and nineteenth centuries. The MCs in such towns were very powerful people who controlled social life in them, keeping it respectable.

Morewood also is imaginary, although again there were many small and depressed villages like it in the Midland counties, both during and after the Napoleonic wars. Beacon Hill, however, does exist, and may still be visited.

LEGACY *of* LOVE

Coming next month

DEBT OF HONOUR
Gail Mallin

Cumbria 1793

Sophie Fleming knew that she had an indulgent guardian in her Uncle Thomas, after all, at 20 and an heiress, she might have been expected to be married long since. It was flattering to receive the attentions of Sir Pelham Stanton, but Sophie wasn't quite sure what she thought of him. She definitely knew what she thought of Kirk Thorburn! He was rude and abrupt and completely lacking in manners! He was also the most exciting man she had ever seen, and clearly there was very bad feeling between Kirk and Pelham. Caught in the middle, not aware of how long standing the feud was, how could Sophie know which man to believe?

DEVIL-MAY-DARE
Mary Nichols

Regency

Jack Bellingham knew something peculiar was going on, and it seemed that Lydia Wenthorpe was at the centre of the intrigue. He had enough to do trying to trace the owners of a cache of jewels he had found when fighting in the French wars, but when it seemed that Lydia also might be after the jewels, Jack was determined to find out exactly what she was up to!

Lydia, in fear of being discovered, found herself torn between wanting Jack near her, yet as far away as she could send him. There seemed no answer to her dilemma. . .

LEGACY of LOVE

Coming next month

STARDUST AND WHIRLWINDS
Pamela Litton

Texas 1873

In the dusty town of Santa Angela, the only law was the gun, and Amelia Cummings' no-good husband had died by it, leaving her with a debt-ridden mercantile business. Gunslinger Ross Tanner seemed anxious for her to leave, but she wasn't ready to give up just yet.

To Ross, Amelia appeared to be made of stronger stuff than her husband. Still, the frontier was no place for a lady, and she needed someone to protect her from the dangerous men the harsh land seemed to breed. Someone besides himself. Because as far as the widow Cummings was concerned, he was the most dangerous of all.

AUTUMN ROSE
Louisa Rawlings

France 1672

Years spent cloistered in Normandy had done little to temper the spirited Amalie de Saint-Hillaire. While travelling to her father's château, she had flirted shamelessly with handsome Jean-Marc Beaunoir, never dreaming the rogue was on his way to the very same destination.

What had begun as a playful seduction had turned into something far more serious than Jean-Marc had intended. The young architect marvelled as Amalie blossomed with each forbidden caress, but the past had taught him that love could not bridge the barriers of class. Had destiny made them prisoners of a love that could never be?

MILLS & BOON

Experience the thrill of *Legacy of Love* with 4 romances absolutely free!

Experience the trials and the tribulations, the joys and the passions of bygone days with 4 gripping historical romances - absolutely FREE! Follow the path of true love and bring the past alive. Then, if you wish, look forward to receiving a regular supply of 4 *Legacy of Love* romances, delivered to your door! Turn the page for details of how to claim more FREE gifts.

An irresistible offer for you

We'd love you to become a regular *Legacy of Love* reader. And we will send you 4 books, a cuddly teddy bear and a mystery gift absolutely FREE.

You can then look forward to receiving 4 brand new *Legacy of Love* romances every month for just £2.50 each. Delivered to your door, along with our regular Newsletter featuring authors, competitions, special offers and lots more. Postage and packing is FREE!

This offer comes with no strings attached. You may cancel or suspend your subscription at any time and still keep your FREE books and gifts. It's so easy. Send no money now but simply complete the coupon below and return it today to:-

Mills & Boon Reader Service, FREEPOST, PO Box 236, Croydon, Surrey CR9 9EL.

— — — — — — — `NO STAMP REQUIRED` — — — — ✂

YES! Please rush me 4 FREE *Legacy of Love* romances and 2 FREE gifts! Please also reserve me a Reader Service subscription. If I decide to subscribe, I can look forward to receiving 4 brand new *Legacy of Love* romances for just £10.00 every month - postage and packing FREE. If I choose not to subscribe, I shall write to you within 10 days and still keep the FREE books and gifts. I may cancel or suspend my subscription at any time simply by writing to you. I am over 18 years of age.

Please write in BLOCK CAPITALS.

Ms/Mrs/Miss/Mr _____ EP60M

Address _____

_____

_____ Postcode _____

Signature _____